BANE
OF THE
HUNTER

BOOK TWO
OF
ANIMALIANS HALL
A HUNDRED HALLS NOVEL

THOMAS K. CARPENTER

Bane of the Hunter
Book Two of Animalians Hall

A Hundred Halls Novel

by Thomas K. Carpenter

Published by Black Moon Books

Cover design by Ravven
www.ravven.com

Discover other titles by this author on:
www.thomaskcarpenter.com

ISBN-10: 9798578080142

Other Hundred Halls Novels

For Stacy

BANE
OF THE
HUNTER

Chapter One

Pax stared out the second-floor window in the Lovelace building at driving rain with her hand deep in the intestines of a speckled locanath. The lizard-like creature had white-dotted amber scales that turned crimson near the tail, and a firm underbelly that was currently split down the middle, the tough skin stretched wide like a kite. To some people, her situation would be a horror show, but to Pax, this was exactly where she wanted to be, even if events weren't always perfect.

"Nothing like a rainy day in Portland," said Esmerelda, nodding towards the streaked window as she lifted the bloody fist-sized heart from the corpse. "Which is, like, every day, but that can't be what's got you sighing more than a preteen after her favorite celebrity mage."

Pax bit her lower lip. "It's Kali. She's been gone for a few days. Not that it's totally unlike her, but since I'm leaving tomorrow..."

Esmerelda gave her a warm smile as she plopped the bloody organ onto the scale, splattering blood on her light blue leather apron.

"I bet she'll be waiting for you when you get back home, curled up on your bed waiting to cuddle. Given, you know, what she is, I doubt she would let you leave without her," said Esmerelda, shifting her mouth to the side.

After revealing the truth about Kali to her friends, she'd done the same with Esmerelda when she'd returned to the zoo that summer. She'd always suspected that Kali was different, but how different was something of a shock, even for an Animalians alumnus. They usually kept the dangerous predators behind glass, not invited them into their beds for belly scratches.

"You're probably right," said Pax. She almost sighed, but bared her teeth in a feral grin instead. Esmerelda, despite the difference in their ages, had been her best friend since she was a preteen. But as much as she leaned on the older Animalians alum, she wanted to learn how to navigate her unusual challenge on her own.

Esmerelda tapped on the intestines, raising her eyebrow. "Found the venom sac yet?"

"Almost, I think," said Pax, scrunching up her face as she dug deeper into the squishy, warm tubes.

Her rubber gloves went up to her armpits, but she was getting dangerously close to reaching that limit. The locanath was nearly seven feet long, an enormous specimen for the supernatural creature, which meant there was a lot of inner cavity to search.

"It should be right above the coprodeum, or not far from the cloaca," said Esmerelda.

The protective rubber gloves made searching difficult, especially since everything felt like a wet bag of mulch.

"Still nothing," said Pax. "How'd it die?"

Esmerelda sighed. "Don't know. She was eating fine,

nothing unusual on her checkups except for a little weight gain. Our biggest worry was that she was our only speckled locanath. They're usually found in groups. But I can't imagine she died of loneliness."

The inner cavity confused Pax until she pulled her hand out—complete with sucking sound—then shoved it back in further up. Almost as soon as she dug around with her fingers she came upon a firm sac.

The look on her face brought Esmerelda around next to her, shoving her hands in parallel until she found the same spot. Together they wedged the viscera to the side, revealing an amniotic sac with a tiny, but dead, speckled locanath inside.

"What the...? I thought you said this was the only locanath in the zoo?" asked Pax.

Eyes widening by the second, Esmerelda shook her head, which made her ponytail dance.

"This explains a lot," she said as she wiggled her hands back out of the cavity, complete with a giggle-inducing sucking sound. "Though I never would have guessed it."

"Virgin birth? You're not going to claim divine intervention or something," said Pax, laughing as she stepped away from the table.

"Parthenogenesis," said Esmerelda suddenly. "Which, technically, is a virgin birth. Some critters can have a regular birth, but when they can't find a mate, they clone themselves. There are some sharks, Komodo dragons, a few other species that can manage the trick. She probably had a complication which did her in. Poor thing."

"Wow, that's crazy. I've never heard of that," said Pax.

"Nature comes up with all sorts of crazy ways to stay alive," said Esmerelda, shaking her head. "If you think this is weird, you should see this amphibian called *Themyscira* that steals DNA from other amphibians, not even their own kind. Frogs, lizards, whatever it can get its hands on so it can use their survival tools for their offspring."

Pax was about to shove her hands back into the dead locanath when she noticed the time.

"Shit. I need to get home. I told my parents I'd be cooking tonight," she said.

Esmerelda nodded towards the sink. "Sure thing. But I'm surprised they agreed. Things getting better?"

"They're not getting worse," said Pax, thinking about the uneasy truce that had been her first summer back. "Which in itself is a win."

"Small miracles," said Esmerelda as she dug her arms back into the bloody cavity in search of the venom sac while Pax washed off in the sink, being careful not to get the blood on her in case the sac had ruptured. "I'd give you a hug, but, you know. Good luck this year in Hunters. I still can't believe you joined those crazies."

"Patron Adele seemed to think that I'll fit in," said Pax, lifting a single shoulder before grabbing her pack. "Sorry about rushing off. Maybe I'll see you again during the school year? Though preferably without Logan, next time."

"Try not to die, Pax!"

§

The afternoon rain had turned the air into a sauna, leaving Pax blotting off her forehead with a blue towel as she hurried back to the little Victorian house that had been her home. A silver fox, or at least a creature that looked a lot like a silver fox, lay stretched out on the porch, near the top of the wooden steps, her pink tongue hanging out slightly.

"Hey Kali," said Pax as the thump-thump of a bushy tail brought a grin to her lips.

It was hard to imagine that Kali was as dangerous as the

literature about her kind indicated. *Mutatio imhotep parasitus*. Supposedly, they psychically attached themselves to a host and then drained them as they grew. Pax was beginning to wonder if that was a myth, or at least she hoped it was.

"Had a good, long hunt, huh?" she asked as she dug her fingers into Kali's belly for a good scratching. The foxlike creature made pleased whines as her tail danced and wriggled.

Pax paused, tilting her head as her hand slowed its belly work. "You look...longer?"

Kali rolled back onto her haunches. A pine sensation entered Pax's mind, which was the equivalent to a "yes, but" or "yes, and." There was something more to it, almost like a picture, but maybe that was a function of their long time together. Pax would play the question game with Kali, but there wasn't time.

"It's a good thing you're back," said Pax. "I'm making dinner for my parents. You still up for trying that thing with them?"

Kali nodded.

"Good," said Pax. "Hide in the living room while I cook. I can hear them in the kitchen."

She entered her house, being careful not to let the door slam and upset her dad, who reacted unfavorably to loud noises.

"Hello, Mom and Dad, I'm home," she said, hanging up her backpack inside the entryway.

Pax liked to announce her presence to give them a chance to get used to the idea that she was in their space. She tried to think of them as PTSD survivors. The crag worm bite had made them insufferable, but maybe she could use Kali to fix them, or at the very least, to be not so awful.

Her mother, Sandra, sat at the kitchen table, working knitting needles. Her gray hair fell down around her ears, unbound from its ponytail.

"You're still fixing dinner, right? Or did you forget?" asked Sandra.

The question brought a snort of derision from her father, Edwin, but that was as far as it went and he returned to his crossword puzzle, which was a win in Pax's book.

"I left work early to make sure I could cook," said Pax tentatively. "Thank you again for letting me take a turn. I wanted to do something special for you before I went back to school tomorrow."

A pair of wrinkled foreheads signaled their confused remembrance. Pax told them about her return date just about every day, but they acted surprised each time.

"Well," said her mother. "At least someone's willing to take you off our hands."

Ignoring the comment was second nature, and she wondered if that was wise, to internalize their pain, pushing aside her own, but wasn't that what people with trauma did? It wasn't like she'd turned to drugs or cutting herself, just an obsession with the animal kingdom—supernatural or otherwise—and a companion who may or may not steal her life energy at a later, unspecified date.

Pax got right to work, pulling the breakfast steaks out of the refrigerator, along with bacon, onions, peppers, tomatoes, spicy mustard, and a packet of spices she'd prepared. Rouladen was a favorite of her parents, but it usually was prepared by Baba, who was back in Sweden. It was a dish she'd learned when she took a year of school in Munich.

Not having Baba around was a blessing and a curse. Her grandmother had always been first to defend her from her parents, even if Pax had only wanted to fade into the background and head back to the shed where she worked with her animal friends. She missed Baba and their side-huddles in the garden. The lessons about horticulture had been of little interest to Pax, but it was enough to hear her grandmother talk.

While Pax waited for the rouladen to cook on the gas stove, she leaned against the counter after checking to confirm that Kali had managed to slink beneath the living room table. She was there, lying on her belly.

"That's a nice scarf you're making," said Pax, keeping her voice as neutral as possible.

"Just nice? Not that you would know since you never bothered learning to knit," said Sandra, heavy on the exasperation.

The truth was that Pax had tried numerous times to get her mom to teach her knitting, but it always ended up with her running from the room with cheeks stained with tears.

Pax stole a glance at Kali before saying, "I like the way the aquamarine blends with the royal blue."

The insult that throttled up her mother's throat dissipated when her eyebrows wrinkled. Her mouth hung open for a long time before she finally closed it as if she'd accidentally swallowed a bug.

Pax shot Kali a thumbs-up, receiving the sensation of warm cherry pie in response. The initial salvo had gone splendidly, with Kali dampening her mother's emotional response by flooding her with good feelings. That it'd worked told Pax that fixing her parents was possible, even if it were only temporary.

"Mom," she said softly to get her mother's attention. "Do you think you'd ever visit me at school? The city and the hall especially are quite amazing."

Her father shook his paper as if he were warding away bad spirits. "We're not city people. You should know that. Nothing but pickpockets and criminals there. I can't imagine how much worse it would be adding magic to the mix."

"It's not too bad," said Pax, forgetting that Kali was only dampening her mother's mood, cringing as the paper crumpled in his fists, ripping at the center, and his forehead pulsed crimson.

"You dare back talk me like that?" he asked as he rose from the table.

Pax bit her lower lip and lowered her gaze as if deflecting the anger of an unruly unicorn. She stole a glance towards Kali, nodding to her father in hopes she could reduce the temperature of the room.

"I'm sorry," she said. "I should have been more polite."

"You're damn right you should have," he said, circling around the table towards her, which only made her stomach drop to her knees as dinner was quickly spiraling out of control. The venom of the crag worm had turned her father into a madman. She hated seeing him in its thrall, hands squeezed to fists at his side, looking almost as if he were having a waking seizure.

When he grabbed her shoulder, Pax reacted instinctively. "*Stoi!*"

The dislocation of air shattered a glass near the sink and knocked her father back into the table, which spilled wine into her mother's lap.

Pax expected rage and prepared to defend herself further, but her father's eyes rounded with fear instead. He backed away, holding his hands up, looking like he might be sick, while her mother threw her wine-soaked knitting onto the table.

"You ruined it. You ruin everything. Go back to school. Stop making our lives so miserable," she said, storming out of the room after her father, who'd grabbed his car keys on the way out the door.

Moments after the screen banged closed, her father's sedan rumbled to life and screeched out of the driveway, leaving Pax in the ruined kitchen alone.

When the timer went off, announcing the rouladen was ready, Pax burst into deranged laughter and slid down the front of the cabinet until she was hunched on the ground with her arms around her knees, all her plans in ruin.

Kali came slinking up with her head down and her bushy tail low, giving a low whine.

"Not your fault, little one," said Pax with a sigh as she dug her fingers into Kali's comforting fur. "I went too fast." She shook her head. "Not that it matters. You can't keep their madness at bay all the time. It worked, but it's not a solution. I should just leave well enough alone. Maybe some trauma is too deep to fix."

Her phone buzzed a moment later. The message was from her parents, informing her that they would be sleeping at a hotel until she had left to return to the Hundred Halls.

Pax turned off the buzzer, pulled out a couple of plates, and ladled dinner onto them. Though she knew she'd cooked it perfectly, the rouladen was tasteless and Pax could barely finish her meal, staring out the window instead.

"At least you like it," said Pax as Kali lapped up the meat gravy, leaving brown droplets on her fur. "I hope things go better than this at my second year in Animalians."

Chapter Two

By the afternoon of the next day, Pax strolled onto the grounds of Animalians, Kali at her side rather than riding on her shoulders since the little fox had gained weight during the summer. Kali was still pouting about having to trot alongside, because it meant she wasn't at the same height as everyone else.

"You're just fluffier now," said Pax, smirking.

A wild whoop came from across the grounds as Janelle came running up, arms wide, a considerable feat with her two-inch black heels. Pax crashed into her arms and the two friends hugged for a long time while Kali watched them patiently.

"Missed you, Pax. Texting just ain't the same thing," said Janelle as she crouched down with the little fox, nuzzling forehead to forehead.

"Miss you too, big time. Nervous as a paper lion in a fire bug's cage about coming back to Hunters, but at least I get to go through it with my friends. Speaking of which, where's our third wheel? Him being on trail most of the summer made it hard to keep up," said Pax.

"Haven't seen him yet," said Janelle, poking her in the side with a long fingernail. "Still mad at him, or...?"

"Busy with school," said Pax, looking down her nose with a grin.

They hooked arms together and strolled towards the Arena, which was the housing for the Hunters. Professor Cassius King stood outside the building in a brown oilskin duster and a river hat with a snakeskin band.

"Welcome back, lassies. I hope you're excited for your first year in Hunters," said Professor Cassius with his hands spread wide. "You too, little one." He winked at Kali, who was looking up at the professor with her head tilted.

"As excited as a dragon in Fort Knox," said Janelle, reaching out and tugging on the professor's jacket. "Isn't this a little on the nose considering where you're from? You'd look quite handsome in a pinstripe jacket."

The professor's whole body shook as he laughed, while Pax blushed for her friend. Eventually Cassius opened the flap of his oilskin, revealing bandages covering a healthy section of his right shoulder.

"Oh, I'm sorry, Professor," said Janelle, biting her lower lip. "Are you okay?"

"Feisty as an ostrich on fire," said Professor Cassius, tapping on his shoulder. "An acid-spitting canatholopy got me last week. Currently regrowing some skin. No worries," he added when Janelle grimaced. "The good news is there were some tattoos I wasn't happy with that I get to have redone after the skin heals." He tilted his head. "Speakin' of fashion, those are some nice cone heels, but might not be so practical inside."

Janelle slipped a shoe from her foot and held it like a dagger with the heel pointed down. "I can't, you know, stab an eye out with these as a weapon?"

The professor let out a huge guffaw, slapping his hip repeatedly until he grimaced and held his injured shoulder.

"Oi, Janelle, we're gonna get along great this year." He hitched his thumb towards the door. "Yer mate was looking for the both of ya. Might want to get in there before he goes cross-eyed."

"See ya, Professor," said Pax and Janelle at the same time as they went into the Hunter house for the first time.

Beyond the thick black door, Pax had the impression she'd stepped into a rainforest dome at the Portland Zoo by the cool humidity. Through the entryway, verdant leafy plants dominated the view.

"Weird," said Pax, receiving a nod from Janelle.

From the outside the Arena was five stories tall in an octagon shape, which gave the building its name. Given the task of the Hunters, Pax had always had the impression the interior would be a nod to the battle between mage and prey, but the natural confines suggested a symbiotic relationship rather than adversarial.

The central chamber went all the way up, filled with leafy green plants that felt prehistoric and an enormous unknown tree that nearly reached the ceiling. A purple-and-yellow flower the size of a beanbag tickled her nose with a pleasing scent.

"I think I understand his shoe comment now," said Janelle, craning her head at the sights.

A joyful whoop from their right alerted them in time to see Liam swinging down from an upper floor balcony on a chunky vine, landing in a crouch.

"Is this place great, or what?" he asked, a grin practically splitting his face in half.

"It's pretty amazing," said Pax as she leaned her head back. "Though I'm still trying to wrap my head around it,

Tarzan."

"Just wait until you see the rooms," said Liam. "The idea is to get us used to living in the wild. I mean, it's not at all like being on trail, but it gives the impression."

"I get it, Nature Boy," said Janelle. "But if I have to sleep in a tent all year, I'm gonna knife someone with my shoe."

Liam wrinkled his forehead, but shook it off as he looked to Pax with his sparkling green eyes.

"Hey," he said, a summer's worth of built-up feelings contained within that word.

Janelle snorted softly. "I'm gonna go check this place out. Come on, Kali."

Liam tugged on the hem of his untucked khaki shirt, glancing askance.

"Liam," Pax said as sternly as she could. "Let's not complicate things again."

He tried to hide his wince, but it was too late. While she entertained raw carnal thoughts about him in private moments, there was no way she could trust him after he'd nearly gotten them killed with his lies. Fool me once, and all.

Liam sucked in a big breath and nodded with his eyes closed. "Yeah, I figured as much."

"Is that why you were avoiding my texts this summer?" she asked, hooking her arm in his to stroll around the room.

"I really was deep in trail...but, I will admit it was easier than not spilling my feelings for you over the phone, which probably would have been super tacky," he said.

Pax squeezed his arm. "Let's live with pent-up unresolved desires." She gestured randomly. "So how do I get to my room? Do I need to shimmy up a vine? I don't see any charros here to scrape."

He chuckled. "There are stairs back through these hallways which circle around the outer walls, but they're not near as fun."

On the next floor where the second years would be living, they found Janelle talking to two upperclassmen. The first was a compact girl with gorgeous eye makeup who looked like she could squat a hippo with ease, while the second was a handsome dark-haired guy that made her heart skip. Pax was so enthralled with his pop star good looks, she nearly missed Liam stiffening up.

"Hey Jae-Yong, Maxine," said Liam. "This is my friend, Pax."

Jae-Yong shot her a playful wink. "Nice to meet you."

Maxine put a hand on her hip. "Get your flirting out of the way, kids, you're not going to have time for it once we get started. Hell, you're not going to feel like flirting after the first day of training."

The way she turned towards the four of them, rather than just Pax and her friends, brought a question to her lips.

"You're not an upperclassman?"

Jae-Yong scratched his forehead. "Not exactly."

Maxine crossed her arms. "JY *should* be a year below me, but he supposedly got stung by a spotted wyvern in some far-realm, spent two years in Golden Willow in a coma."

He held up his hands. "I don't remember much of anything. Only woke up eight months ago. Been in rehab since."

"Two years ago," said Janelle breathlessly. "That would have been under the last head of Hunters?"

Both Maxine and Jae-Yong dipped their heads reverently.

"Ernest Valentine," said Maxine, lips squeezed tight. "He died along with the other two students on that mission."

Before anyone looked at Jae-Yong, he held his hands up. "I don't remember anything. Wish I could."

"Shit, sorry for asking," said Janelle, putting a hand on his arm.

He pumped his shoulders. "You would have found out eventually."

"There'll be enough time for heavy shit later," said Maxine, giving Kali a strange look. "For now, get comfy in your rooms. Tomorrow we start training, bright and early. Bring good footwear."

"But these are tactical heels," said Janelle sweetly, holding her hand under her chin.

After the others left, Liam showed Pax and Janelle to their room, which could have been confused for an enclosure at the Portland Zoo. After an entryway, there was a high step up to a floor covered in green moss, where two hammocks hung from stocky trees that circled the room.

"What in the actual Merlin is this?" asked Janelle.

"Take your shoes off and climb onto the floor. It's divine," said Liam.

Leaving her backpack and shoes on the lower level, Pax pulled herself up. The spongy moss cushioned her knees and hands, so she rolled onto her back.

"I think I might sleep here," said Pax in a spread eagle.

"This *is* nice," said Janelle, testing the hammock before climbing into the cocoon.

"Okay," said Pax. "All boys out of the room. I need to unpack."

"No boys here," said Liam with a wink. "But I shall retire to my room, nevertheless. JY promised to take me into the city. You two are welcome to come along with us."

"Go on ahead," said Pax. "I'm tired from my flight, and I want to check out the rest of the building."

"I have a thing with a book," said Janelle, nodding towards the stack of tomes on the entryway table that had been left for them. "Working with Keepers too might be the death of me this year."

After Liam left, Pax sat sideways on her hammock, swinging softly by kicking her feet.

"What do you think, or hope, our second year is going to be like?" she asked, inhaling deeply.

While the natural room seemed a little weird at first, the greenery provided an unexpected fresh comfort that was the antithesis to the normal sterile dormitory rooms.

"Hope? I *hope* it's uneventful and productive," said Janelle as she pulled stacks of clothes from her luggage, setting them neatly on the shelves in the entryway. "But I *think* it'll be a chaotic mess, full of learning, heartbreak, muscle aches, and at least one significant tragedy."

Pax wrinkled her forehead. "Why would you think that?"

Janelle raised her eyebrows. "Because you're my roommate, Pax."

"Oh, yeah, good point," said Pax as she slipped into the embrace of the hammock. "Good point."

Chapter Three

The nervous energy was only suffered by half the group beneath the enormous ballyban tree because it was a mix of second and third years. The older students chattered amongst themselves with an easy confidence, while Pax and the other second years shifted from foot to foot.

"Where are we going? A run through the city? Into the Undercity?" asked Pax as she squeezed her arms across her chest.

Jae-Yong shifted his mouth to the side. "I don't want to spoil the fun, but let's say that it's neither."

"I feel like I'm being set up," said Janelle as the corners of her eyes creased. "Everyone has water carriers and little bags and thingamabobs on their hiking gear, while I'm wearing an aquamarine running outfit. Now, I look as stylish as fuck, and this color matches my eyes, but I don't get the feeling this is a light jog."

Pax checked her own thrift store outfit, which was slightly too big for her. She flicked Liam with her fingernail.

"You're nearly dressed like them. You could have told us," she said.

He shrugged. "This is how I always dress when I'm headed out."

The chatter faded away as Professor Cassius, in khakis and a heavy-duty backpack, along with the fifth year Maxine, looking equally ready for a long march, appeared near the base of the tree.

"G'day, class. You all should know Ms. Maxine Nolan, who will be my assistant in charge of the second years. You take her instructions like you would mine, or you're bloody likely to end up six feet under," said Professor Cassius without his normal jovial banter.

He surveyed the group with his hands on his hips. "Any questions, or shall we get started?" His gaze fell upon Pax. "Ms. Nygard. Where's your little friend?"

Pax stiffened. "Is Kali supposed to join us?"

"Aye," he said with a nod. "You'll wanna use any advantage you can get in our line of work."

Before Pax could even turn, Kali came bounding through the foliage to land at her side, bringing smiles from the rest of the hall. She was a big hit with the rest of her classmates, though only her friends and the professor knew what she was. Everyone else thought she was a thoratic fox.

Pax crouched down and ran her hand along Kali's silky black fur. "You ready to work?"

Kali made a squeaky noise as she lolled her tongue.

"Alright," said Professor Cassius. "Form up, we're going through the ballyban. It'll be a little disorienting, but don't worry, it's as safe as dental work on a crocodile."

He chuckled to himself as he placed his hand on the big crack on the side of the base of the trunk. To Pax's delight, it split, revealing a chamber inside.

The older students went first, stepping into the tree then disappearing from view. Pax assumed that there was a stairwell heading beneath the building, maybe to a secret tunnel or private train. She wasn't expecting a smooth, glossy black stone the size of a person inside the trunk.

Professor Cassius gestured towards the stone. "Place your hand on it, and give a little juice of faez, then hold onto your britches." He glanced down. "Oh, and you might want to hold Kali for the ride."

The fox jumped into her arms, quivering slightly with nervousness.

"I'm sure it's fine, Kali."

Pax placed her hand against the cool stone. As soon as the faez trickled from her mind, the world rotated beneath her. For a brief, awful second, she couldn't breathe, and worried she'd been sent off course, but then she landed, crashing to her knees as Kali leapt away into the grass.

She had to squint, which didn't make sense, as the sky was sunless. There was a greenish cast to everything, but she couldn't see a source of light. Max helped her to her feet.

"Don't want Janelle crashing on top of you," said Max. "There you go. If you have to spit, do it behind the tree."

On wobbly legs, Pax stepped away, rotating to take in the view. A matching—twin?—ballyban tree commanded the center of an idyllic clearing, encircled by long-limbed willows draped in an eerily pale material that looked like a grandmother's shawl. She could smell water nearby.

Professor Cassius was the last to come through the portal. He took off his river hat, knocked it on his leg, and shoved it into a pouch. He craned his neck speculatively in multiple directions, a sour expression on his lips.

"Max?"

His question brought a shake of Maxine's head.

Pax whispered to Janelle, "Whatdya think is going on?"

"Dunno, but they look like something's wrong," replied Janelle. "Even the third years."

"Yeah, my thought too," said Pax.

"Right," said Professor Cassius as he turned to the class. "Might have a bit of a delay. I'm gonna range ahead. No one leaves the area. This place can be dangerous for the uninformed."

He jogged across the grass towards a gap in the willows, disappearing as soon as he passed through.

"What is this place?" Liam asked Jae-Yong.

"Caer Corsydd," he replied, never taking his eyes off the surrounding trees.

"That sounds Fae," said Janelle.

"The Fae realms are hard to reach these days," said Maxine, who'd overheard their conversation. "Only the Maetrie have made themselves available to the city, but that's a shit bargain in my opinion. They're mostly gangsters and criminals. This place, on the other hand, is a replacement home for a certain class of fae."

Maxine continued to speak, but Pax was suddenly aware that Kali was no longer by her side. Pax circled the tree, looking for her furry companion, only to see her tail sticking from beneath the willows.

Kali, come back, she thought towards her.

When the fox didn't move, Pax went over, and even though it was only thirty feet between the back of the ballyban to the willows, the gulf was intimidating.

"Kali," said Pax through gritted teeth. "Quit screwing around."

The black-and-silver tail disappeared beneath the willow. Pax hesitated before pushing through the draping limbs, the fluffy bog-cotton softly caressing her arm.

"Kali."

A trickle of worry went down her spine, leaving her whole body on high alert.

"Kali."

The ground on the other side of the willow slid into water. It was clear enough to see to the bottom, which was covered in an orange grass that waved in an unseen current. The wetlands were dotted with willows connected by thin slivers of land, which appeared meticulously kept, much like the clearing around the ballyban.

Kali had pushed through the knee-high heather, sniffing at a pale fish the size of a book with luminous eyes like a moth right beneath the surface of the water. Downy feathers rather than scales covered the watery creature that seemed to be enticing Kali to push her black nose through the surface.

"Kali, away from there. We have to go back. We're not supposed to wander."

Across the bog, Pax had a sense of movement like a great clump of vines and foliage had shifted towards her, but when she looked up, she couldn't find it.

"Kali." Pax crouched down to tug on her tail. "We have to go. Now. We're not supposed to be here."

"So you admit you are trespassing," said a stern, melodic voice.

Pax popped up, spinning around and stiffening in one motion, nearly toppling into the water.

A man stood behind her, keen of eye, dark-feathered cloak on his shoulders, wearing a dour, but hungry expression, as if she were a treat that had wandered onto his plate. His skin was a rich, intoxicating sepia that she wanted to reach out and caress.

"My apologies," said Pax, finding it hard to meet his tectonic gaze. "My companion wandered off and I was retrieving her."

The man—she was certain he wasn't a human, but could not place his origin—leaned his head to the side a sliver, his too-full lips a contradiction of his demeanor. When his gaze fell upon Kali a darkness swirled in his eyes.

An explosion of power was only contained when a hurried Professor Cassius pushed through the willows, his worried expression turning to dread.

"Lord Asphodel," said the professor. "My student has wandered away. Let me take her back so we can begin."

A sly smile ticked at the corner of Asphodel's lips. "She does not have permission to be outside of the portal clearing. Therefore, she is in violation of our agreement. It always amazes me that your students cannot follow simple directions. In addition, her companion is a foul beast that has no place in Caer Corsydd. Since when did the Hall of Bwystfil suckle its natural predator at its breast?"

Professor Cassius swallowed as he dipped his forehead. "You have me at a disadvantage. I assure you that Kali is not a danger, or Patron Adele would not have let her stay within the hall."

Asphodel snorted derisively. "That beast may not be a problem now, but I can see she is changing. The scent is on her. Soon you will not be able to control her."

The accusation seemed at odds with the foxlike creature, who sat passively on her haunches looking up at the imposing figure as if she were waiting to be fed.

"She is my companion, sir," said Pax earnestly. "She will not harm me, nor anyone else."

"Says the whelp who has barely taken breath in her own world, let alone another," said Asphodel with chin raised in judgement.

Professor Cassius' jaw pulsed. "What do you want? I

bloody well know that you don't like me, but leave my student out of it."

"No," said Pax. "It's my fault. Kali and I wandered away. We should pay the price, whatever the punishment."

The professor scrunched his face at her, while Asphodel licked his lips.

"Such bravery, such foolishness, but are they not one in the same, the coin flip landing on the fate of survival." Before Cassius could open his mouth, Lord Asphodel shot his hand towards her. "I accept your contrition, for a favor later, nothing terrible, but a punishment just the same." He let his lips part, showing white teeth. "You and your students may stay in Caer Corsydd for their training under the normal conditions."

Lord Asphodel swept back through the willows, leaving Pax and Kali with the professor. His shoulders sank.

"You don't know what you've agreed to do," said Professor Cassius.

"No, but it was mine and Kali's mistake," said Pax, checking with her companion, who lay on the bog grass, head covered with her paws. "But...it would help if I knew who he was."

"Caer Corsydd. Fortress of the Bog. This is the home of the Gwyllion. They are the outcasts of Fae. In return for help in other regards, Lord Asphodel lets us train here," said a subdued Professor Cassius.

"You and him have a history?" asked Pax tentatively.

Gray clouds moved through Professor Cassius' gaze, and he pushed back through the willows, leading her and Pax back to the group.

"A little bit of excitement for our first morning," said Professor Cassius as he stood in front of the group. "Now it's time to work. We're going to be taking a nice leisurely thirty-mile jog as a warm-up. Maxine is handing out today's elixirs, which are a derivative of direllion blood. Second years get a full dose, thirds a half. Be warned, they taste awful and come with a kick, but you must keep them down, or you'll have to return to the Arena."

Pax received her vial with trepidation. The oily blue-green liquid warmed her fingers as she held the glass. The older students had already thrown their elixirs back as if they were shots, grimacing and retching their tongues out.

"All together on three?" asked Liam.

Pax popped the lid off the vial, her eyes watering immediately from the fumes.

"One. Two. Three."

The liquid burned as it shot down her throat. She clamped her hand over her mouth to keep from spitting it back up. It tasted like rancid pickle juice and burned like ghost peppers. She swallowed back bile as she danced on her feet, willing the overwhelming sensation of heat to subside. She'd been hot before, but it felt like every cell in her body had turned up its thermometer.

"I think my eyes are sweating," said Janelle, waving her hand before her face.

Jae-Yong bent at the waist. "Oh Merlin, I forgot how awful this was."

Liam had closed his eyes and was shaking his head. "I don't know if I can do this every day. This is horrific."

"Oh, don't worry," said Jae-Yong, who'd turned a pale shade of green. "They get worse. But it's better than the alternative."

Professor Cassius clapped his hands once to get everyone's attention. "Good, no spits. Now it's time to run, which will help with the heat you're experiencing. Max will take the lead, while I'll bring up the rear."

Jackson, one of the other second-year hunters, raised his hand. "Why did we drink that?"

"We need to condition your bodies to extremes, strengthen it for the trials of hunting, protect it from the toxic substances you will encounter," said the professor. "Enough questions, we need to move before some of you overheat."

Maxine led the line of hunters through the willows, knocking the bog-cotton into the air to swirl like summer snow as they ran across the thin path, beset on both sides by sedge grasses and cattails.

The quickened pace left Pax worried at first, but the faster she ran, the cooler she felt. The pumping of limbs and the cool boggy air washed away the heat rolling from her skin. For the first part of the run, she could see nothing but Janelle's aquamarine shirt, the blur of sedge grass only the frame for her vision.

As the heat subsided, her peripheral vision expanded, allowing her to get a better sense of the place. In the distance, small huts made of mud bricks and grasses stuck up from the moor. Sometimes shapes moved in the shadows of those hovels, but always too far away to get more than a wrinkly impression. Birds of all shapes and colors winged across the eternally blue-gray sky, the largest of which were jet-black ravens, which watched them from the rare leafless trees that occasionally dotted the moor. Pax had never heard of Gwyllion, but it looked like the hillbilly version of Fae.

After a few hours of running, they passed a great mound at the center of a lake. Shallow boats glided across the surface, propelled by long poles in the hands of humanoids with long-beaked faces that she realized were masks when a boat passed near the path. Pax was reminded of plague doctors, and recalled Lord Asphodel's raven-feathered cloak.

Towards the end of the day—a construct of her mind since there'd been no visible sun to mark time—when her energy flagged, the line of students came to a stop and Pax found herself back at the ballyban tree in the center of the willow clearing.

Kali immediately plopped to the cool grass, tongue hanging out as her belly heaved.

The lack of forward motion left Pax unsteady on her feet as the first twinges of soreness reverberated through her body.

"After a difficult start, that was a good first run," said Professor Cassius, who looked like he hadn't been running at all, while even the third-year students grimaced. "Max will hand out a restorative which will help you recover, and be warned, you will have a voracious appetite. Do not worry, you will need to recover the calories."

Janelle made a face at the vial when Maxine handed it to her. "If this tastes as bad as the first, I'm out."

Jae-Yong popped the lid off. "They're usually much better. Usually."

Pax threw her vial back before she could get second thoughts, surprised by the burst of strawberry on her tongue.

After the restoratives, Maxine led them through the portal back into the Arena.

"Go eat," she said. "But try to make it back to your room before you fall asleep. I'm not responsible for what the upperclassmen will do to you if they find you in the cafeteria passed out. Tomorrow, same time, back here. Have fun."

During the run, Pax hadn't been hungry or thirsty, but back in the Hunters' home, her appetite hit her like a tsunami. The group of them hit the eating area like a swarm of locust, but it'd been made ready for them with tables full of breads, cooked meats, sauces, desserts, fruits, and other delights.

Pax barely remembered shoving edibles past her lips, but when her stomach felt grotesquely extended, she remarked, "I feel like Hansel made fat for the witch."

With heavy-laden eyes, Liam ripped a piece of succulent

greasy turkey meat from a bone, and juice splattered across his chin. "I'd take a bite of myself if you cooked me."

Janelle had pulled her running shoes off and massaged her feet as she groaned.

"I have blisters on blisters," she said.

"There'll be tubes of ointment in your rooms," said Jae-Yong. "Make sure you smear it on before you fall asleep. They'll help toughen up your feet."

After gorging herself on a dozen plates of food, Pax zombie-walked back to her room, and after applying the ointment, collapsed on the mossy floor, rather than expend one more ounce of effort to crawl into her hammock.

As death-like slumber claimed her waking mind, Lord Asphodel's favor swirled through her thoughts, a promise of future troubles. Pax forced her eyes open momentarily to gaze upon her companion, curled in the crook of her arm, already snoring softly. Her last thought before oblivion was that Lord Asphodel had been waiting for her like a trap.

Chapter Four

On the tenth day of training, only the second years entered Caer Corsydd. Without the third years, their class of six students seemed painfully small, especially since Kali had been given the day off too. They drank no elixirs, and rather than the usual fifty-plus-mile run, Professor Cassius led them down a different path contained by purple moor grass at a leisurely pace.

"While I'm glad not to be running today, since even my hair and fingernails are sore, I feel like whatever he's cooking up for us is going to be worse," said Janelle as she massaged her forehead.

"Stop smirking and tell us," said Pax, catching Jae-Yong grinning.

"Don't bother," said Liam. "I've tried to get it out of him, but he promised the professor not to spoil the training."

Jae-Yong held his hands up. "It was a condition on me coming back, for which I'm eternally grateful."

"You're lucky this is Animalians. I hear the other halls

aren't so forgiving," said Janelle.

"They have to be, considering how dangerous our hall is," said Jae-Yong. "Otherwise there'd be nobody left."

"It's not that dangerous," said Pax. "Coterie mages turn themselves into swamp things when they enunciate the wrong word."

"Yeah, but you can choose not to do difficult and dangerous things," said Jae-Yong knowingly. "The very nature of our work is deadly, and you know, we're the low-faez kids, so it's not like we're packing extra firepower." He looked away, his lips pursed. "I'm sure if I'd been a little faster, had a little more power..."

Out of respect, no one from their little group had asked Jae-Yong about his accident yet, but since he was bringing it up, Pax started to form a question, only to catch sight of the clearing ahead, covered in old ruins. A third of the vine-choked stone walls had slumped into the bog, but a larger flat section had been covered in strange wooden contraptions that were either torture devices or malformed jungle gym equipment.

"Whoa, that looks like it could be fun," said Liam.

"He says before experiencing it," said Jae-Yong with his eyebrows raised.

Professor Cassius bounded up a short, angled crumbling wall like a mountain goat until he reached the peak.

"G'day, class. Now that you're a little fitter than you were a few weeks ago, we're going to work on your reflexes. The difference between living and dying as a hunter is often the tenth of a second, a blink of an eye." He lifted up his shirt, exposing burn marks on his right side. "This came from a pretty little lava-tongued haraguana who'd been lying under a thin layer of gravel like a trap spider. Had I been a hair slower, I wouldn't be speakin' to ya right now."

The professor gestured towards the contraptions in the courtyard of the old keep.

"After a concoction to help with your reflexes, you'll work your way through the trials, hone your movements until they become second nature."

"Will we always need potions to give us an advantage?" asked Janelle.

Professor Cassius tapped his temple. "This is the real advantage, using your brain, which is why you have to learn all those books on nomenclature, memorizing what there is to know about every dangerous critter in the known realms. Speed, power, magic. Those are great, but we're not performing magic in a sterile classroom where we can control everything. We're often operating in unfamiliar places without home-field advantage. Better to anticipate what might happen, rather than react. But. There will be times when those reflexes are the only thing between you and the grave. Advantage? No, the potions never give us an advantage. They give us a chance of survival when events go pear shaped. Which they always do eventually, no matter how well you prepare. It's a law of life and statistics. More variables mean more uncertainty."

The short lecture was followed by passing out vials with a chalky gray liquid. The greasy flavor stuck to Pax's tongue, but wasn't unpleasant like the others, and after a minute of full body tingles, the potion took hold, and the world dialed into focus as if she'd never truly seen it before.

She stepped to the first trial, a narrow beam that she had to cross while dodging spinning horizontal wooden bars. Pax found herself mesmerized by the whirling devices, until Maxine nudged her with her foot.

"Stop gawking and move forward," said the fifth year.

Pax moved tentatively onto the beam, carefully placing one foot after another as if she were walking above lava. The bars spun at various heights—head, waist, knees, ankles—and she would have to avoid them by jumping or ducking. They were spinning from both sides and both directions, which meant she couldn't focus on only one thing.

"Come on, Miss Nygard. Catch the rhythm of the whirlers and then go for it. You can't learn by standing still," said Maxine.

Maybe it was the drugs, but Pax sensed an animosity from the fifth year as she glared across the equipment. She pushed it away as she refocused on the task, waiting for the right moment, shifting forward while ducking under a bar only to have her ankles taken out from under her, tossing her off the beam to land on her back in the soft grass ten feet below.

A hand from Jae-Yong pulled her up on unsteady feet as her ankle smarted from the impact.

"Don't worry, no one makes it far on their first try," he said. "Or their fiftieth."

Standing so close to Jae-Yong made her face tingly. "Your eyes are so big."

"It's the potion," he said. "Helps us see better."

Her tongue playfully tickled her teeth as a rush of warmth ran through her. "Helps me see how handsome you are."

Jae-Yong blushed, bit his lip, and looked away.

"Sorry," said Pax, grimacing. "This potion is making me feel a little goofy."

"No worries," he said, winking. "I appreciate the compliment, but we'd better get back in line."

As they turned towards the next contraption, Pax caught Liam staring, his face drained of emotion. She could see what he was thinking and wanted to march over and tell him that not wanting to complicate things went for everyone, Jae-Yong included, despite how gorgeous he was.

"Boys and their emotions," Pax said to Janelle at the next

station.

"Huh?" asked Janelle, who'd been staring at her palm as if it were a television.

"Nothing," said Pax. "How'd you do?"

Janelle turned sideways, showing a blotch of dark purple marring the reddish-brown skin on her upper arm.

"There's no way anyone can get through that without getting hit." She rubbed the shaved hair on the side of her head. "Not that I care. This is some good stuff, whatever it is."

The next station involved a field of pendulums swinging in multiple directions without hitting each other. Pax made it past the first two before getting creamed by the third, leaving a welt on her thigh.

The rest of the morning was no different, except getting the nerve to attempt the trials, knowing what was coming, grew harder.

"Don't be shy. It'll only hurt for a moment," said Maxine as Pax hesitated at the whirling contraption.

"There's no way anyone can get through this," said Pax, exasperated. "This isn't practice, this is torture."

"You can't fix everything with your furry companion," said Maxine sternly. "Trust me. You can get through it, but not if you don't find the rhythm."

After getting pummeled by sticks for hours, the quip about Kali left Pax blind with anger. Rather than try to dodge the bars, she bared her teeth and ran across the beam like a linebacker...catching the first pole in the midsection, which spun her into the grass, landing face-first.

Spitting out grass and rubbing her tender gut, Pax rolled over on her rear in time to see Maxine climb onto the beam, bow gracefully to Pax, and then, after rocking on her heels for a brief second, enter the whirler.

At a dozen points, Pax thought Maxine was going to get

pummeled by a whirling bar, but she'd roll, summersault, or handspring past the speeding obstacle. Her bodybuilder physique did nothing to hinder her, as she remained as flexible as a gymnast.

When Maxine exited the beam, the class applauded the fifth year, who bowed again—directly at Pax, who hung her head.

"Don't worry, Miss Nygard," said Professor Cassius, who'd come up from behind. "She'd been waiting for someone to spout off like that all morning."

"Doesn't make me any less an asshole," said Pax, climbing to her feet, knocking the grass from her face.

"Oi. You'll get it in time, but not today." He raised his voice to their small class. "Alright, we've one more task before you're done for the day, and you can firmly place your nose back in your tomes."

The professor led them back through the tree, and upon exiting, Jae-Yong saluted them and headed towards his room.

"Good luck," he said with a pained expression that put a stone in Pax's gut.

"I really don't like the fact that he's not coming with us," said Janelle. "Whatever is about to happen seems like it's not going to be pleasant."

Professor Cassius led them to upper floors in the Menagerie, where the infirmary was located. Cassius addressed the five of them: Pax, Janelle, Liam, Jackson, and Bryanna.

"I'm afraid this next part will be quite unpleasant." He squeezed his lips white. "But there's no getting around it. Your bodies aren't hardy enough to withstand the trials ahead."

"More elixirs?" asked Bryanna, who had decided that today was the day that side-ponytails were back in fashion.

"Not today," said Professor Cassius. "Today we're giving you stronger bones."

Pax shared a glance with her classmates. It didn't sound as bad as he was making it out to be, but she guessed there was a hidden catch.

"Right," he said with a heavy sigh. "If there was another way, but there ain't, so let's get to it. Who wants to go first?"

Pax stepped forward. "I'm already in pain, so what's a little more."

Professor Cassius' grimace made her stomach tighten up as she entered the sterile examination room with Professor Ansel. An angled chair with leather ankle and wrist bindings waited at the center.

Professor Ansel wore round glasses and had a kind face. He motioned for her to stop before she climbed into the chair.

"I'm going to tell you what's going to happen so you can fully decide if you want to go through with it," he said.

Pax gently pushed his hand out of the way. "I'll pay the price, whatever it is. This is the path I've chosen."

The professor snorted softly as he helped her limbs into position, tightening the leather straps around her ankles and wrists. Soft padding had been placed on the interior of the leather bindings.

"When a bone breaks, it regrows stronger, for a time anyway," said Professor Ansel. "Today, I'm going to magically break the bones in your legs in a similar fashion to what we call a green stick fracture. Afterwards, with the help of a specific alchemical mixture, they will grow together, bonding until they'll become nearly as hard as steel."

Pax tugged on the wrist binding. "Let me guess. The procedure is extremely painful."

He nodded.

"What about my classmates?" she asked, nodding toward the door. "Won't it freak them out to hear me screaming?"

"The room is enchanted for silence," said Professor Ansel.

"You may scream as much or as little as you want, though I will need your attention during the procedure to ensure I do not cause other damage."

With a quivering sigh, Pax responded, "Wonderful. Let's get this over with, shall we?"

"Once I start, I can't stop, no matter how much you ask me to," he said.

"Just do it."

Professor Ansel pulled a black metal ring out of a cabinet. The hoop was flat with gold runes around the outside that glowed faintly even in the fluorescent light. With two hands, he maneuvered the ring over her foot while chanting in an unintelligible tongue.

A warmth started in her toes, almost pleasant, before growing to the level of a hot plate at a restaurant. Pax tugged her leg back, only to find the binding held tight. As the heat grew unbearable, she yanked her leg harder, trying to avoid the pain.

"Okay," panted Pax in shallow breaths. "This is worse than I thought."

The quick, apologetic glance from the professor told her that this was only the beginning.

As the professor moved the ring down her foot, the pain began anew in the next section. Reflexively she tugged at the bindings, feeling like a rat caught in a trap. She rocked in the chair, shaking her head, as sweat beaded on her forehead.

"Oh please, oh please," she mumbled deliriously. "I can't, I can't, it's so much."

When the ring slipped over her kneecap, she passed out for a few seconds—time only marked by the location of the pain—waking to a cold sweat, while the breaking of her thigh bone would have triggered vomit had she had anything in her stomach.

Then it was over.

Relief wasn't quite the word for what she felt afterwards. Her shattered bones throbbed with the beat of her heart.

But it was infinitely better than the ring.

Professor Ansel placed a cup against her lips and helped her drink the concoction, which tasted like cool mint as it trickled down her throat. The ache and lingering agony faded, followed by a slumber-induced heaviness.

"That felt good," said Pax drearily as she fought to keep her eyes open.

The professor fitted a containment boot around her leg, which immobilized it, and then a secondary door opened and Maxine appeared to help remove her from the chair. The thick fifth year easily lifted Pax onto her feet using the leverage of her shoulder.

Before Pax left the room, she asked, "How many more sessions?"

"Four or five, depending on your pain tolerance," said Professor Ansel. "The ribs and spine are particularly delicate, which makes that last part tricky."

"And my skull?" she asked, as Maxine held her up.

The professor frowned. "Protect your head."

Pax trudged in silence as Maxine took her through tunnels between the buildings.

"Don't want to freak out the first years?" asked Pax.

"Among other things," said Maxine.

"Do people ever give up? Not go through with it after the first?" asked Pax.

"Are you thinking of giving up?" asked Maxine.

Pax was delirious from the procedure and the potions, so she couldn't tell if it were a hopeful or empathetic question, given the events from earlier in the day.

"Never," said Pax. "I just don't want to lose any of my

friends."

"A fair point," said Maxine. "Most years have a couple. Some have none."

"Sorry about earlier today." Pax sniffed at herself. "And for sweating all over you right now. I'm gross."

"You can shower when you wake up," said Maxine tightly.

"What about the boot?"

Maxine pushed open a door with her foot. "You can take it off when you wake. The bone knits together quickly with the help of the potion. It helps you sleep too."

By the time Pax made it back to the room, her mind was blanked with fog. The hammock, of course, was out of the question, and she spent another night asleep on the moss.

Chapter Five

Pax met Professor Cassius for her first lesson about Kali beneath the ballyban tree, where they took the portal to Caer Corsydd. Her companion had been subdued all morning, but had come along willingly, despite the nature of the visit.

The professor kept his river hat on, despite the unchanging blue-gray skies of the otherworldly realm, while Kali rolled on her back in the grass before flipping back to her feet.

"How are your bones, Miss Nygard?" asked Professor Cassius.

"The soreness is mostly gone now," said Pax, rubbing the back of her neck. "Just glad to have that over."

He nodded, looking like he had something to say, before walking away, tugging his hat off and holding it before him. When he came back, a vein on his forehead pulsed.

Pax took a step back when he approached, while Kali scampered behind her.

"Miss Nygard. Pax. Tell me what Patron Adele told you about what we would be doing during these private lessons," said Professor Cassius.

She looked down at her companion, who lifted her head. "To learn how we can coexist with Kali."

The professor made a noise in the back of his throat. "Do you know that the vote to let you stay was quite close?"

"I'm sure, given the literature about Kali's kind, but I'm sure we can dispel those myths through our work together," said Pax, smiling hopefully in the face of the professor's apprehension.

Kali sent her a sensation of warmth.

"How do you think the vote went?" asked the professor.

Pax closed one eye as she imagined the positions of each head of house.

"I would guess that Professor Kako and you were a yes, probably Patron Adele as well," said Pax.

Professor Cassius knocked his hat on his leg. "Everyone but Professor Constantine and Patron Adele voted to remove you from the school."

"What? Kako said no? And I thought Vlad the Inhaler hated me?" asked Pax.

The professor snorted softly at the nickname. "Vladimir is the head of Tamers. He always believes that he can control any creature. I'm sure he would have relished the challenge if Adele had allowed him to mentor you."

"But I don't understand. If it was two to three, how are we still here?" asked Pax.

"Patron Adele's vote weighs more. Despite our counsel that you not be admitted, she overruled us." He searched her face. "I want you to be clear about what we're doing. I will do everything I can to help you both, but she chose me to mentor you because I was the largest voice of opposition."

"If you're a hunter, then everything is a prey," Pax said tightly.

He tilted his head as he removed his hat. "You're not wrong. But I assure you that I always do everything I can to protect the creatures we're dealing with, even if it brings personal danger. I have the scars to prove it."

"I'm sorry, Professor, that was rude of me," she said.

"No need to apologize. If we're going to work together I want there to be no illusions about our task, no misunderstandings." He crouched on his heels, facing Kali. "You especially. If you're true to Pax, truly not a danger, then I expect no obfuscations from you."

The foxlike creature tilted her head, which brought a chuckle to his lips.

"Obfuscation means to hide, to camouflage your intentions. Do you understand that?"

Kali approached the professor, placed her paw on his knee. He responded by scratching her neck, which she leaned into, arching her back.

He placed a single finger under her chin, lifted her head while he placed his face mere inches away. The picture reminded Pax of two boxers squaring off during pre-fight promotions. Pax resisted the urge to knock him over in her defense, but she knew that what he was doing was important, even if it brought heat to her face.

"I cannot tell if you are not a danger, or a master of disguising intention, but let me be clear that if you prove yourself false, then it will be my job to hunt you down," said Professor Cassius.

Kali dipped her head, which the professor took as an acknowledgement.

"Right. Enough of that unpleasantness. We have some training to do. On the upside of this, if this works out, you two will be a ripper of a partnership. So let's focus on that and not the other thing," said the professor as he shoved his hat back on his head. "Now let's take a short jog."

After the tension of their discussion it felt good to stretch her legs. It was the first time she'd run without training potions, and with her alchemically hardened bones. The concoctions they received tended to space her out for a time, so it was nice to be able to crane her neck and enjoy the surroundings.

While Caer Corsydd was mostly water, the connecting paths made it surprisingly easy to traverse. The mournfully desolate region sprouted pockets of color: vibrant coral pinks nestled in hollows, the bright blue scales of a serpent slithering through the sedge upon their approach, brilliant orange cup-shaped fungus hanging on the dead-but-not-dead trees that dotted the landscape.

Their passage took unfamiliar paths, heading away from the manicured lands of Lord Asphodel and into more treacherous terrain. The waters grew dingy, and the cattails bent ominously as larger critters sped away from their approach, until at last, they came upon a small rise in a heather-strewn field of soft, soggy soil.

Professor Cassius circled the area, examining plants and grasses, finally returning to Pax and Kali, who waited at the spot he'd indicated.

As Pax looked out at the emptiness—no sign of hovels, far from the portal—she realized that it all could have been a trick. That she'd been brought out alone so he could eliminate the threat that Kali presented. The thought was only a flash through her mind, but she tensed, eliciting a mirrored reaction in her companion.

Professor Cassius tugged off his hat, shoved it in a pocket on his pants.

"I see that look. No, I didn't take ya all the way out here to finish ya off. If I were to bloody well do the deed, I would have done it already and there'd be nothing you could do to stop me," said Professor Cassius. "Ya ken me?"

"Yeah," said Pax, nodding. "I understand."

"Good, 'cause I don't want to have to watch my back, thinkin' yer gonna put the knife in deep. Trust goes both ways." He put his hands on his sides. "Now tell me what you know about your companion, true Hunter style."

"Kali, yeah, she's a callidus, *mutatio imhotep parasitus* to be exact. Supposedly, her kind psychically attaches themselves to a host, drains them of life force while it grows, and eventually turns into a mage killer," said Pax.

"What kind of abilities does Kali have?" asked the professor.

"She can project images and emotions into others. She used to help me calm the injured critters I rescued so I could fix them, but she also uses that to convince mice and other prey not to run so she can kill them," said Pax.

Professor Cassius nodded as he paced across the uneven scrubland. "The mage Imhotep wrote about his companion hunting cobras in the palace when she was young, then later escaped slaves when she was as big as a tiger."

"Big as a tiger," exclaimed Pax as she looked down at Kali. "Is that why you're getting chunkier in the middle?"

"His writings suggest that there are phases to a callidus' growth, but not how many nor what abilities are associated with the creature," said the professor.

"You're saying she will develop other abilities? Not just the ones she has now?" asked Pax.

"Imhotep, and the few others that recorded their experiences, say little about their exact nature, but they're clear that the callidus surprised them in later stages with what they could do." He squinted into the distance at a flock of black birds that rose into the sky as if startled. "Do you know the name of Imhotep's callidus?"

"No."

"Bastet."

Pax snapped up straight. "Like the Egyptian goddess? Of cats?"

"The very one. It's odd that Kali is more foxlike. It suggests an ability to camouflage themselves. My theory is that she chose a fox since that was an outdoor creature much like those that you were rescuing. Do you remember when you found her?" he asked.

"No," said Pax, shaking her head. "Patron Adele asked me the same thing. I was always taking in new creatures, so I can't recall the exact meeting. She came at a rough time of my life. My parents and I had suffered a terrible trauma. There are a lot of things from that time that I can't remember, so it's not unusual."

"I believe you, Pax." He gestured towards the location the birds had taken flight as the corner of his lips tugged upward. "I think we'll find something interesting in that direction, but it might not be as easy to get there without getting wet."

The professor stalked ahead, his hand hovering above a huge bowie knife at his hip. The uneven, squishy ground felt like she was moving across a lumpy, sodden mattress. Water hissed out of the earth between the golden stalks of grass that did their best to stay rooted in the soil as her shoe pressed down. One of the aspects of her bone transformation that she was still getting used to was carrying an extra fifteen pounds.

The landscape angled downward into black mucky pits between clumps of sedge. The professor produced a metal staff from his slim backpack and used it to probe the ground before stepping on it. After a ten-minute traverse, Pax's shoes were soaked through from stepping into muddy water, often unexpectedly when the ground sunk beneath her weight.

Professor Cassius crouched behind a clump of cattails

near a lily-covered pond. Using his metal staff, he parted the thick stalks, revealing the tranquil scene before them.

"See that lump of plants out past the blue flower lilies?" he whispered in her ear. His breath smelled like coffee.

Pax searched the surface of the pond, using the lilies as a marker.

"Yeah, looks like old plant garbage," she said.

"I can't pronounce the Gwyllion version of it, but we call it a feymoor thrasher. It's a master of camouflage. Beneath that plant garbage, as you called it, is a pretty little beastie with powerful tentacles and a mouth full of efficient cutting teeth. If there were cows in this land, a thrasher could strip one as if it were corn on the cob on a summer day," said Professor Cassius. "They like to lurk in pools with caprarium grass in it. A lot of the critters around here eat the grass for its copper and iron minerals, which only make them a nice meal for our friend over there."

"You sound like you admire the thrasher," said Pax.

His face split with a grin. "Our world is a relatively safe place compared to the realms we can reach through the portals. If I had to survive out here, I'd come up with a pretty nasty set of abilities too."

"Right, so what are we doing out here? Are we going to serenade it? Bring it some treats?" she asked, rolling her eyes.

Professor Cassius clasped her shoulder. "You and Kali are going to creep onto that ridge near the thrasher. I want you to coax it from the water so we can get a good look at her."

"Coax it from the water?" she asked incredulously. "Like offer my arm as bait?"

Professor Cassius nodded towards Kali, who had been peeking through the cattails between them.

"You say she can project images into minds, or calm emotions, but I suspect that Kali can do more than that, and I'm certain you've noticed this as well," he said.

"I don't understand how this is going to help," she said.

"When you pitched the idea of staying in Animalians to Patron Adele, you spoke of understanding Kali's kind better so we might peacefully coexist. After all, we're the Society for the Understanding of Animals. We need to test those abilities, find out what they truly are beyond the superstitions and rumors in the ancient texts."

Pax peered back through the bent cattails at the lump in the water. "Couldn't we do it on something a little less murdery? Like a nice seagull, or maybe a ferret with a bow tie?"

He screwed up his lips. "Where's the Pax I know that rushes into dangerous situations without regard for herself?"

"Trying to break myself of that habit," said Pax with a sigh. "But I guess I'm not going to get much of a chance of that in Hunters."

With Kali at her side, she crept up the crumbling slope to the ridge that wound behind the pond. It was only a few feet above the surface of the water, which wouldn't give her any protection should the thrasher decide she was lunch, but she'd agreed to work with Cassius so she could stay in Hunters with Kali.

Once they were about fifteen feet away from the plant lump near the lilies, she checked back with the professor, who motioned to get closer.

"Come on, Kali," she whispered faintly. "Do your thing."

The foxlike creature looked up at her with expressive, confused yellow-brown eyes, and sat on her haunches.

Pax sighed.

While they'd worked together in her little infirmary, the task had always been clear. Even the time with Logan had been in her defense, the danger evident and not requiring her instruction, but this was different.

"Can you tell the thrasher to peek its head out of the water so we can see it? Just a little lookie-loo?" asked Pax.

Kali lay down on the grass, resting her face on her paws while looking back at Pax with arched eyebrows.

"Yeah, me too," said Pax, sitting on her butt and wrapping her arms around her knees. "It's just minding its own business, and here we are, wanting to bother it."

No one moved for a good long time. Pax looked out across the bog, watching the occasional bird wing across the eternal blue-gray sky. The rugged landscape, while treacherous and full of surprises, soothed the exhaustion from the first month of school. Previous visits to Caer Corsydd had been drugged forced marches, so it was pleasant to just *be*.

After checking back to the cattail blind to see Professor Cassius shaking his head, clearly exasperated, Pax asked, "Wanna go back?"

Pax confirmed the thrasher hadn't moved before returning across the short rise, while Kali padded ahead.

"I don't understand, Miss Nygard," said the professor with his hands on his hips. "You and Kali want to stay, so why didn't you try to affect the thrasher?"

"It was just hanging out, doing its thing," said Pax, spreading her arms. "We didn't want to bother it."

The professor rubbed his muscled jaw, before giving a curt nod.

"Fine, I suppose that's an acceptable answer given our hall," he said. "But that doesn't help us with the task at hand, which is understanding Kali better."

"I understand her just—"

Kali sent her a warning the moment before the cattails exploded. Professor Cassius reacted at the same time, reaching for his knife as a tentacle wrapped around his ankle and ripped him off his feet.

He grabbed the cattails to keep from getting pulled into the muddy water, where the feymoor thrasher had moved. Pax grabbed the dropped steel staff and jumped into the pond, which was deeper than she expected, going under briefly before finding her feet.

Professor Cassius held the cattails with one hand and his bowie knife with the other, slashing under the water at the tentacle wrapped around his ankle.

With the steel pole in two hands, Pax jabbed forward in the water towards the lump of plant mass. She connected solidly once, but it did nothing to loosen the grip of the tentacle.

"Kali, help us!"

Her companion watched passively from the dry spot behind the cattails.

"Kali!"

But she didn't move, so Pax waded deeper into the water where the thrasher and its mouth full of efficient teeth waited, jabbing her pole forward, hoping she was wrong about why Kali hadn't acted yet.

A tentacle bumped into her hip, and Pax stabbed downward with the staff frantically as fear flooded into her limbs. She saw nothing but splashing water where the professor had gone under.

When the lump of plant matter rose above the surface, revealing a round mouth of thousands of teeth, Pax lifted the staff to stab it, but before she could, it shrieked and sped away from their location, leaving behind swirling muddy water and discarded lilies.

Professor Cassius broke through the surface with his knife at the ready, searching every direction for the thrasher.

"It's gone," said Pax as she waded towards the land. "Kali sent it away somehow."

Both drenched, they moved all the way back to the previous field and collapsed on the boggy soil, while Kali cleaned her paws with her tongue as if nothing had happened.

Thousands of thoughts passed across the professor's face as he kept glancing at the foxlike creature. She knew what he was thinking, that Kali had somehow lured the thrasher to attack him, and the only thing that had made her send it away was putting herself in danger.

"Thank you, Kali," said Professor Cassius as he knocked the water out of his ear by banging on the side of his head. "I should have been more careful. I guess we learned something, but not in the way I would have liked."

"You're not mad?" asked Pax, forehead wrinkling.

He lifted one shoulder. "And why would I be? Any encounter you survive alive and with all your limbs is a good one. Now let's go back home and get cleaned up."

As they traversed the bog, Pax squeezed the water from her clothes and hair. In a short time, it almost seemed like Professor Cassius had put the whole near-death experience behind him, as he whistled softly.

When they returned to the Arena, Professor Cassius said, "While our little lesson went sideways, I did learn something, and that's that Kali only wants to use her abilities to protect her friends. I promise you, little one, that our next lesson won't be so dangerous."

"What will we do?" asked Pax.

The professor scrunched up his face as he pulled a piece of bog grass from his shirt. "I don't know yet. But I'm sure it'll be a ripper."

Chapter Six

On an early October day, they returned from Caer Corsydd through the portal tree after working on their reflexes. Pax had yet to make it even halfway across the whirler, and she had a black eye to prove it, but she could at least imagine it was possible as she massaged her shoulder while rotating it.

"What's the best way to get grass out of your teeth?" asked Liam, digging his finger into his mouth as he came to a complete stop.

Pax hadn't been paying attention, but the way he froze sent a spike of adrenaline through her. She snapped her head around—sweaty hair slapping against her cheek—to find a gorgeous woman with dark eyebrows and dirty blonde hair pulled back in a ponytail wearing black tactical gear with a tranq gun strapped to her leg.

"Pietra!"

Professor Cassius, who was last to come through the portal, jogged up to the woman, collapsing his enormous arms around her in a hug. Pietra, who was slightly taller, squeezed him back, lifting him off his feet in a bear hug.

"Cass. You handsome beast, you look good, much better than last time," she said in a rich South American accent that Pax couldn't place.

"Oh, shit," muttered Jae-Yong to the other second years. "Pietra's famous for taking down a razor-backed behemoth with only a snare wire."

"Last time I was in a bed hooked up to a dozen wires and tubes," said the professor, grinning like a schoolboy. He turned towards the class of second years with his arm around her. "This is Pietra Santos. We were in the same year together."

Everyone crowded around the professor and Pietra. With a smirk, Pax placed the back of her hand against Liam's chin and pressed upward to close his mouth. He widened his eyes in acknowledgement.

"What are you doing in town?" asked the professor.

"A little business. I wanted to stop by and take you out for a drink." Pietra raised an eyebrow and tapped a playful tongue on her teeth. "Maybe I could take the whole class out? I'm sure they'd love to hear some stories about you."

Before Professor Cassius could open his mouth, Janelle grabbed him by the arm. "If you don't say yes then we're going to have to make Vlad our favorite professor."

Professor Cassius placed a hand over his heart. "You wound me. But of course. Everyone get changed and meet us at the Bantu Queen. Drinks are on Pietra."

After showering and getting ready, Pax, Janelle, and Bryanna took the green line to the fifth ward. The Bantu Queen was not the upscale bar that Pax was expecting, with only a flat brick front and no sign.

"Is this the right place?" asked Pax with her hand on the door.

Janelle shook her smart phone as she scrunched up her

face. "This thing says it is, but it sure don't look like it."

Bryanna sniffed the air. "I can smell Jae-Yong's body spray. He must have put a gallon on. So this is the right place."

"Pietra is so gorgeous," said Janelle. "It'll be fun to see the boys fall all over themselves."

"Let's not be sexist," said Bryanna with a wink. "I plan on falling all over her myself."

Inside, the Bantu Queen was remarkably different than the staid exterior. The mahogany wood, soft lighting, and glassware hanging above the bar said high end, though the only customers in the place were Professor Cassius, Pietra, Max, and the three guys from their class.

"Hey, you made it," said Pietra, shooting a wink towards Pax. "I hear you're the Cass of your group."

"The Cass of my group?" asked Pax, with her fingertips on her breastbone.

The professor lifted a glass of frothy black liquid. "Reckless and prone to accident. Which is why I agreed to come back and teach. Figured it'd give me a longer lifespan."

"Drinks for the newcomers, Dane," said Pietra, motioning towards the one-armed man behind the bar with easy grace. He had dusty brown hair and kind, sad eyes.

"What is this place?" asked Janelle, craning her head in all directions. "We're the only ones here."

"This bar is exclusive to current students and alumni of Animalians, though it's mostly Hunters that come here. Dane is an alumni. He gave up the life after an amarok took his arm," said Professor Cassius.

Dane shoved a glass under a spigot, filling it with a bright green bubbly liquid.

"You're welcome anytime. I live upstairs, but don't worry if I'm not here. This place is always open," said Dane as he slid the drink to Pax.

The green apple and ginger flavor burst across her tongue. "That's delicious. Thank you. Why the Bantu Queen?"

When both Pietra and Cassius shared glances, Maxine shook her head.

"You remember the story Patron Adele told last year about the Lioness Queen of Zambia?" asked Maxine.

They nodded.

"She tells that to every class, but the part she doesn't tell is that was her twin sister," said Maxine.

"Oh, shit," said Jae-Yong. "She didn't, you know, hunt her down or anything?"

"No," said Professor Cassius.

"So that means she really is hundreds of years old," said Pax, trying to fathom living that long and what it would do to a person.

"Older," said Pietra with a lift of the shoulder, "but no one knows how old."

"That still doesn't explain the name of the bar," said Janelle.

Dane snorted softly. "Zambia didn't exist at the time of the story. Really, even Bantu isn't correct because that's the colonist name of the people from that region. But she uses Zambia because it's what people know now, and Patron Adele, for all her faults, always looks forward."

"Does she...ever come here?" asked Liam as he cradled his glass.

Dane blinked and shook his head as he shoved another glass under the tap. "Nope. Not even one time. I probably shouldn't have named the place after her twin, but I thought she might like it, to honor her, and represent the danger that we face in Animalians."

The moment of heaviness that fell ended when Maxine

blurted out, "Pietra. Are you in the city to hunt that creature in the seventh ward that attacked that homeless guy?"

Pietra pursed her lips to the side. "No, but I have heard of it. Invictus PD offered a reward, not a contract, stingy bastards, especially considering three people have died now."

"Three people?" asked Maxine incredulously. "Why haven't they offered a contract? Don't they care about the people they're supposed to protect?"

"Contracts like that come out of their salary pool, so they don't offer them. A reward is a low risk way to encourage professional and wannabe hunters," said Pietra.

"That's awful," said Maxine, who looked like she was going to be sick. Her head snapped up. "Why don't you go after it?"

"If they wanted to pay me, I would consider it," said Pietra with a half-shrug.

Professor Cassius tapped on the bar twice. "You're too high priced for them now since you've gone corporate."

"Hey, don't knock it until you try it," said Pietra. "The Phoenix Corp gives me functioning gear and a team to ensure the hunts are safe and successful. You might consider it when you return to the field."

"So what happened that put you in Golden Willow?" asked Janelle.

The professor took a drink from his glass, then wiped the foam off his lip, giving Pietra a sideways glance.

"It was his bane," she said, holding her hands up when he glared at her. "Sorry, Cass. I know you don't like to hear it, but it's true."

"What's a bane?" asked Pax.

Pietra leaned comfortably against the bar. "Every hunter has a bane. It's that one creature that they just can't quite capture, or kill, and every attempt turns to tragedy. It's like a jinx, but in animal form."

The Brazilian hunter glanced at Professor Cassius, who lifted his drink and said, "You started. You might as well finish. They'll hear these stories eventually."

"Let me show you all something," said Pietra, leading everyone into a back room with a strange black rock at the center. She placed her hand against the stone, which flashed briefly, then a dark-skinned figure appeared in the air above the black rock, slowly rotating.

"Whoa," said Jae-Yong. "Nice illusion."

"That's Marcus Atwell," said Pietra, gesturing at the handsome black man in khakis. "He graduated in the '70s. Killed by a grootslang in the Mongolian steppes that had been hunting the tribe folk. It was his third encounter with a grootslang, none of them successful."

After rotating for half a minute, Marcus Atwell disappeared, replaced by a short, intense looking pale woman with neck tattoos and a cropped haircut.

"Lindy Voltamere. Graduated in '05. Don't know what killed her. The creature was never found, nor was most of her body. She'd been on a foolish expedition to a realm called Harmony," said Pietra with a sigh. "Good kid. Bad choice."

For the next few minutes, Pietra waved her hand over the stone, summoning new dead Hunters, while everyone sipped from their drinks, expressions heavy.

Everyone glanced at Jae-Yong the moment the former head of Hunters, Ernest Valentine, appeared above the stone. The second year squeezed his eyes closed and marched out of the room. But a short time later, their somber attitudes snapped alert when a familiar face appeared above the stone.

"Cassius?" asked Pax, looking to the professor as he lifted his drink towards his illusionary visage above the stone, then chugged it.

"They thought I was dead," he said eventually. "What can

I say, I'm hard to kill. Now I get the unique honor of being the only Hunter in the stone that's alive."

Pietra dismissed the image and led them back to the bar, where Dane gave them another round of drinks.

"What is your bane, Professor?" asked Maxine, who clearly hadn't heard the stories either by the way her forehead knitted.

When he didn't answer, Pietra stepped in again. "Cassius' bane is a critter called a *draig y madfall*, or the dragon salamander, though it is not a dragon, nor does it breathe fire."

"For the record," said Cassius, leaning towards Pietra, "I do not believe in banes, but I won't stop you if you do."

Pietra raised an exquisite eyebrow at him. "I'm shocked, Cass. After the last encounter you ended up with your picture in the remembrance stone, and you still don't believe?"

The professor downed his glass and slid it over to Dane, who promptly shoved it under the spigot.

"I won't deny that particular species has caused me some difficulties," said Professor Cassius as he massaged his palm, flexing his thick muscles. "But I won't allow myself to believe that I cannot defeat it, bane or no. As Hunters, we control what we can control. Everything else is just statistics."

"You've been one of the most successful hunters in a generation, Cass. No other critter has remotely come as close to thwarting you, yet this one has multiple times," said Pietra.

Professor Cassius sighed heavily and glanced away, thoughts clouding his gaze. "There's something I still don't understand about the dragon salamander. That's why I've failed so far."

Pietra clasped him on the shoulder, gazing at him appreciatively. "It's your bane, Cass. Accept it, and stay the hell away from it in the future."

"What's your bane, Pietra?" asked Pax.

The gorgeous Hunter winked. "A guy who won't cheat on me when I'm away on long missions."

The professor jabbed his thumb. "She hasn't discovered hers yet, or we could also say that she's really good at her job."

"I don't take as many risks as you, Cass. It may not be as heroic, but I prefer to eliminate every source of hazard first," said Pietra.

"Sometimes you don't have that luxury when people's lives are on the line," said the professor darkly.

The two Hunters, suddenly remembering that they were surrounded by students, cracked artificial grins. Cassius lifted his new drink, half rolled his eyes.

"To living long and never having to kill another single living being," said Professor Cassius.

As everyone finished their drink, Pietra received a business call. She gave the professor a kiss on the cheek, hugs for everyone else, and promised to stop by when she was in town again.

The class stayed at the Bantu Queen, ordering another round, until Maxine reminded everyone that they had an eighty-mile run early the next day. The excitement of Pietra's visit and the talk of banes left everyone ready to return to the comfort of their rooms in the Arena. As they left, Pax took one last look into the bar, where the professor sat, cradling his glass between his hands, staring at the foam as if it held answers.

Chapter Seven

The week after Pietra's visit, the class tried to get the circumstances of Professor Cassius' failed missions against the dragon salamander out of him, but he waved them off, telling them that they didn't have time for the extra work.

When they persisted, Janelle argued that they'd only been discussing theoretical hunts during their lectures, rather than actual ones. It wasn't until Maxine took up their cause—which was a surprise since she seemed to enjoy inflicting agony on them—that he finally decided they could work on a real case. They'd study the killings in the seventh ward. He only agreed if all the second years promised not to rush off and investigate on their own without his supervision.

"What do we know about the creature in the seventh ward?" asked the professor as they sat around a table in the Bantu Queen.

"It's killed three people, that we know of," said Pax.

"The reward is up to fifteen thousand dollars," said Bryanna, wagging her eyebrows upward.

"Don't be a drongo, Bryanna," said Professor Cassius with a smirk. "Focus on the task, not the end result."

Janelle pulled a bright pink notebook from her backpack and opened it to a page marked with an orange tab.

"The first victim was a homeless man who'd been living beneath the Longfellow Street Bridge. That detail was added afterwards since he died in his hospital room later. The second was a college kid, who'd wandered away from his friends after a night at the bars. They found his remains next to the canal. The third was actually in the sixth ward, near the MOMA. A woman on a late-night jog never returned to home, and her husband called the cops. They found the remains in an alleyway."

"Where'd you get all this?" asked Liam.

"I'm doing a rotation at Golden Willow. Any death suspected of supernatural origins go to their morgue. I asked to see it," said Janelle sweetly.

"Nice work, Janelle," said the professor, offering her a fist bump across the table. "Anything else about the deaths?"

"Yeah. In all three cases, the creature went after the abdomen of its victims, and in two of them, ate the liver," said Janelle.

"Strange," said the professor, tapping on his chin.

"Gross is more like it," said Bryanna. "My grandparents eat liver and onions. Stinks like dead feet."

"What kind of wounds?" asked Pax.

"The first two had serrated marks, the third were individual parallel marks, suggesting talons or claws," said Janelle.

"So our pretty little beastie has serrated teeth like a shark and wicked claws like a bear," said the professor.

"It has to be big enough to take down a human, maybe fast, or good at camouflage," said Jae-Yong.

"The homeless guy was probably asleep, the college kid

drunk," countered Jackson.   "It might have just happened upon them while they were out."

"Doesn't explain the woman jogging," said Pax. "She definitely wasn't lying around."

"If there's a proper beastie on the loose in the seventh ward, where might it be living?" asked the professor with squinted eyes.

"There are some lovely brownstones along the canal," said Bryanna, batting her eyes. "But the rents are a bitch."

"Yeah, the canal," said Liam, snapping his fingers. "It could be living there."

"Except the bars and restaurants have boats gliding over them all the time. Someone would have seen a creature large enough to take down a human swimming in its waters," said Pax as she twirled a piece of her hair around a finger.

"There's always the sewers, like Pax's little adventure last year," said Jackson.

"It wasn't just me," said Pax, gesturing towards Janelle and Liam. "And Professor Cassius saved us. But yeah, why not the sewers?"

"It's a possibility," said the professor. "But until we go tromping around in muck water, let's explore our other options."

"The Undercity?" asked Jae-Yong.

"Too far beneath the city," said the professor. "Not that things don't come up from there occasionally, so it might have originated below, but once they do, they stay. It's not like our beastie is using it as a home base."

No one spoke for a while, staring at the table or out the window until the professor said, "Alright, let's table that one for later. What else can we theorize?"

"When did the attacks happen?" asked Liam.

"All three at night," said Janelle, tapping her pencil on her lower lip. "Maybe it has poor day vision?"

"That's what I was thinking," said Liam, nodding.

"Why, again, the liver?" asked Pax. "Are there any supernatural creatures that have a craving for livers?"

Jae-Yong raised his hand as if he were in class, then, making a face at his own gesture, said, "The aswang is a Filipino legend about a ghoul-like creature that eats livers. No known creature fits the myth, but maybe it just hasn't been found yet?"

Bryanna scrunched up her face, leaving everyone to groan in anticipation of a joke.

"I was going to suggest a kelpie. Don't they live in rivers and eat livers or something? That could be like the canals?" she asked.

"Kelpies are nice water-bound people who've gotten a bad rap," said Professor Cassius. "This wouldn't be a kelpie. I'm sure of that. But good idea. No stone should be left unturned." The professor smirked. "Other thoughts? Anything you're missing?"

No one spoke as they stared at the table or out the window. Pax watched Dane clean the bar with one arm and thought about the dangers of being a hunter. There were worse professions, but tracking down dangerous creatures had a high rate of fatalities, or in Dane's case, life-long disability.

Pax snapped her head around. "How do we even know it's a creature?"

The way the professor's lips spread wide told her she'd caught his thread.

"If you only have a hammer, then everything looks like a nail," said Professor Cassius. "While this, on the surface, looks like a creature, there's a chance it could be a sick person, or an otherworldly being. And if it is, then this isn't a job for our hall."

"When can we visit the site? Maybe we can learn something in the seventh ward," said Janelle.

"We will, after your next set of lessons," said the professor.

"Shouldn't we be looking right now? People *are* dying," said Pax.

"You'd likely get yourselves killed," said Professor Cassius sternly. "You don't know enough not to be a danger to yourself and everyone else. You all promised not to check out the place without my supervision, so I'm going to hold you to that. If I find out anyone's been doing any investigating, we'll be going on a good two-hundred-mile hike through the back country in Caer Corsydd."

When they all kept looking at him expectantly, he added with a sigh, "It's not like I'm not teachin' ya. Bloody hell. You're just kids, and I don't want to see ya hurt. But the good news is tomorrow we start learning magic that'll help you if you run into this or any other beastie, so I expect the lot of ya will be giving these lessons your full attention. Is that right?"

The class, Pax included, nodded enthusiastically. She knew that whatever the lesson, it would likely involve pain and suffering, but that prospect didn't seem as bad in light of the circumstances.

"Go on now, get back to the Arena," he said, waving both his hands at them in a shooing motion. "Get your studies done. We have a lot of work to do. Crikey." He shook his head as they were all leaving. "You kids are going to be the death of me."

Chapter Eight

The last few months of instruction had come with a certain amount of dread. The countless hours running through the bogs and the stomach cramp inducing potions they ingested daily—to say nothing of the whirling contraptions that left bruises over every inch of their bodies—had left them with a healthy mistrust of the daily lessons, but on this rainy day, they were spread out on the dirt floor of the Barn, patiently waiting for Professor Cassius with what could only be called brimming anticipation. Pax had skipped the whole way over to the Barn, the home of the Tamers' house, where they would be receiving their instruction.

Professor Cassius appeared in his tan khakis, bald head gleaming, while Maxine pulled a cart full of equipment behind her as easily as if it were made of feathers. The professor scratched his jaw, shooting the class a wink. "I can't for the life of me figure out why you're all so bloody eager today."

"You promised real magic today," said Bryanna brightly.

"Ah yes," he said with a grin. "Today I'm going to teach

you the tools of the trade. As I've lectured you most endlessly, the most important aspect of the job is your preparation." He tapped on his temple. "But like the agility training in Caer Corsydd, you can't plan for everything when you're out in the bush. In the event that things go pear shaped, the first goal should be to retreat to safety, regroup until you can better assess the situation, but if that is not possible, sometimes you have to act quickly."

While he was speaking, Maxine pulled pink rubber bladders from the wagon and hooked them up to an air compressor, which chugged away as it filled them, until they were round boulders the size of a beanbag.

"During your first year, you learned some marks with Professor Vladimir. This year, you're going to learn hunter's marks. There are five marks you must master before we can enter the field. The 5 S's, in order of priority of use," he said as Maxine kicked a pink ball towards him. It bounced and rolled until it bumped into his leg.

Still facing the group, he cupped his hand and rotated it as if he were petting a horse's head. He performed the gesture slowly, before speeding it up, adding the phrase, "*Upsoka.*"

A faint energy tickled the back of Pax's head, but it mostly made her wrinkle her nose.

"This is the mark for soothe, which triggers the feel-good chemicals in the brain. You can use this mark against any beastie you encounter if they're righteous pissed at ya, get 'em to back down and hopefully head a different direction, but the more intelligent or enraged it is, the less chance it'll work. So don't bother trying it on a person—as you just experienced, it will only create a funny sensation in your mind, and not the hee-haw Bryanna kind." This comment brought a head tilt from the aforementioned blonde second year. "It also won't work on a critter that is naturally aggressive. No manticores or hydras. But if you unexpectedly happen upon a dread wolf as you're creepin' through the bush, you could probably get it to turn away with a well-placed soothe."

Professor Cassius picked up the pink ball and tossed it to Jackson, who stood nearest.

"Throw that at me," said the professor. "Give it a good go like you're playing footy."

Jackson bounced the pink ball on the dirt twice, shook his head, and without warning pushed it at the professor rapidly.

"*Schit!*" said the professor, making two flat facing hands, angling them towards each other, forming the upper portion of a triangle, and pushing forward.

A shimmering field of energy appeared between him and the pink ball, blowing it backwards at Jackson, who barely got his arms up in time to deflect it away to bounce across the dirt.

"That was shield," said Professor Cassius, then without further explanation, he said, "*Skorost!*"

He threw his fists by his sides, then in a burst, closed the distance between himself and the pink ball before it completely came to a rest.

"Can anyone guess that one?" he asked, chuckling.

"Speed," said Liam, but checking back with everyone else as he lifted his shoulders. "Seemed obvious."

Professor Cassius lobbed the pink ball into the air, positioning himself beneath it, then crossed his fists with an emphatic shout.

"*Shayut!*"

The ball ricocheted away in a burst of energy, flying far across the arena to bounce against the wagon. Maxine finished filling a seventh pink ball and held it under her arm while she waited for instruction.

"That was stun," said Professor Cassius. "Once you move to stun, you're either going to have to kill or capture your foe.

Which leads us to the final mark."

He nodded, and Maxine drop-kicked the ball towards him. He watched passively as it bounced across the dirt, and before Pax could blink, he slammed his hand down as if he were slapping a table.

"*Khoplat!*"

The force squashed the ball flat, exploding it, sending little pieces of pink rubber flying across the grounds as everyone stepped away in surprise.

"A good slam will injure the beastie, convince it you're not to be trifled with. If you do it right, it'll hightail it away before you can blink," said Professor Cassius. "But if you give it a proper slam, and it's still ready to tango, you've got bigger problems. But let's focus on these first five. I want you to grab a ball, spread out, and work on your marks. Start with soothe. Once I think you've gotten a feel for it, I'll let you move on to the next."

The rhythm of practice didn't come naturally to Pax, but she was willing to give it her best effort. The pink rubber ball was a nice change from the charging unicorn from last year, but it felt a little weird trying to get an inanimate object to cool its jets.

When Professor Cassius came over to observe, her limbs and fingers stiffened as if they'd been dunked in ice water. Even she knew that her soothes were not as powerful while he watched.

"I was watching you from across the grounds, and your gestures were outstanding for a first day. Tell me then, Pax, why did it look like we replaced your arms with wooden versions the moment I walked up?" said the professor, crossing his arms.

"I get nervous around people. It always feels like I'm on a stage," said Pax.

"Prefer animals, eh?" he asked, nodding.

"For the most part I can tell what they're thinking. People? It's a crapshoot," said Pax, looking at the dirt near her feet.

"I don't know," he said, tilting his head. "You look like you're doing just fine to me."

"Fake it until you make it I guess," said Pax.

"Do you have any idea why you think you don't understand people?" asked the professor.

Pax checked with the rest of class, who were busy working with their rubber balls. The cries of "*Upsoka!*" and the caressing hand motion made it look like they were courting strange pink creatures.

"I don't know...well, maybe it's my parents. They were always really mad at me as a kid, so it was easier to retreat to my shed, where I took care of injured animals," said Pax.

The professor searched her with his eyes, his lips pursed with sympathy.

"I'm sorry to hear that," he said. "My parents were pretty good as far as parents go. We owned an animal preserve in eastern Australia."

"That would have been amazing," said Pax.

"So would have working at the Portland Zoo during my formative years." He sighed, stepping close so only she could hear. "I have a different take on why you struggled to cast soothe when I approached you. While your opinion on the matter is valid, I also think that your attachment to the animal kingdom, supernatural and otherwise, is quite strong. You get nervous, not because you're afraid of what I think, but because it reminds you of what I, and this house, represent. Just like the day you left the feymoor thrasher alone, rather than doing as I asked."

Pax hung her head. "It just felt, you know, wrong that

we were bothering it." She pressed her thumb into the palm of her other hand. "Speaking of, when the thrasher attacked you, why didn't you use a mark against it?"

He didn't answer for a couple of seconds. "Well, it *did* surprise me. And water makes them less effective, blocking the majority of the impact. The base magic behind the majority of them is air, which struggles to overcome water, so typically for aquatic adventures, we use specialized marks. Why?" He scrunched up his forehead. "Would you think I would willingly go into the water with that critter?"

"No. No, of course not," said Pax. "I was just wondering. You know, what to expect in the heat of battle and all that."

He lifted his chin. "Shield."

"Huh?"

He chuckled. "You can move on to shield now. You have soothe down, but you'll have to work on it until it becomes second nature."

After he left, the encounter with the thrasher tied up her thoughts. Not only the professor's behavior, but the way Kali had reacted. What if she was as powerful as they'd suggested? What if she'd muddled his mind so he didn't defend himself with the very tools he was trying to teach them? Or, was it as he said, that he'd been genuinely surprised? She'd thought she'd find more answers coming to Hunters, but it was the questions that were multiplying.

Chapter Nine

The green line train car rattled as it sped around the corner above the rows of three-story apartment buildings at the edge of the seventh ward. Pax hugged the center pole, watching the sunlight glint off the Spire, while Kali took the seat next to Liam, who bounced his knee like an earthquake.

"We're gonna be fine, Liam," she said.

Janelle and Jae-Yong smirked at his bouncing knee, while Liam shook his head, muttering.

"We promised the professor not to investigate the creature until he'd deemed us ready," said Liam with a huff. "I should have stayed with Jackson and Bryanna."

"We're not, Liam," said Pax. "We're merely visiting the bars and restaurants of the seventh ward as people of our age do. If we ask a few questions, it's just curiosity, not an official investigation." Liam crossed his arms. "Relax, Liam. And what's the worst that happens? We run two hundred miles? We did eighty three days ago and that wasn't so bad."

"He doesn't want to disappoint Cassius," said Jae-Yong.

"I'm surprised he doesn't have a poster of him on his wall."

"He's a legend in the hiking community," said Liam, gesturing randomly. "So I've told a few stories about it. Is that so weird?"

Pax could see he was taking the ribbing hard, so she said, "It's totally understandable. While Hunters was never going to be my first choice, as far as head of houses go, he's my favorite."

Liam shot her a look of appreciation, while Janelle said, "Speaking of Cassius, any of you read up on his so-called bane?"

"No," said Pax. "Interesting?"

"More than," said Janelle. "The dragon salamander is native to, guess..."

"Hawaii?" asked Jae-Yong.

Pax scrunched up her face. "Portland?"

"Caer Corsydd," said Janelle eventually.

"Oh shit," said Pax, remembering the conversation between the professor and Lord Asphodel. "I wonder if that's what's behind their disagreement."

"So you think Lord Boggy sent Cassius after a dragon salamander and that's when he ended up in Golden Willow?" asked Liam.

Janelle's eyes opened wide. "What if that's the favor that he'll ask of you?"

"No," said Pax, shaking her head. "No way. He said it wouldn't be a huge thing. Nothing too terrible. Hunting the critter that nearly killed Cassius sounds much bigger than that."

"Good thing for you." Janelle shot them a secret smile. "So wanna hear about the dragon salamander?"

Jae-Yong smirked. "Or more importantly, you want to tell us about the dragon salamander. Not sure how you have time for side projects with all your extra work and rotations at Golden Willow. When do you sleep?"

Janelle rolled her eyes and proceeded to explain while running her finger across the notebook page. Pax knew the motion was for show, because once Janelle wrote it in her notebook it was committed to memory.

"So. The dragon salamander, or *draig y madfall*, is native to Caer Corsydd. Lives in the more rugged areas, away from Lord Asphodel's region, but occasionally one wanders down from there, starts killing his people by dragging them beneath the water and drowning them."

"Wait? You got this from a book?" asked Pax.

"With an assist from Professor Ansel," said Janelle. "I acted like I already knew most of it, and in the back-and-forth, he filled in everything I didn't know about the professor. I'd tried Maxine, but she hadn't heard the story either since it happened when she was only a first year.

"The dragon in the name comes from the extended ridge along their head and back, which gives them a dragon-like profile. They mate like mammals with a single live birth, have sticky hands, which they use for grabbing their prey and drowning them. No claws, and only basic teeth for tearing flesh, no big canines or anything. There's speculation on their supernatural abilities, but nothing concrete. Oh, and they camouflage well, assuming you're living in a bog."

"That it?" asked Liam incredulously. "That's what took down Cassius?"

Janelle lifted a single shoulder. "They're cunning hunters and have home-field advantage. Think about it. The professor always talks about preparation and not taking chances. A big flashy critter like a manticore doesn't hide. They just sit on a pile of rocks and wait for you to come mess with them, because they know they've got a tail full of spikes for you. So you can plan, eliminate the dangers by shooting them with a concoction that makes their spikes fall out for a time, and trick them into a titanium cage using an illusionary mate.

"But a creature that hides in the water, waiting for you to wander by and then pulls you into the depths and just holds you until you drown. That's a good trick. Maybe simple enough to beat Cassius."

That didn't seem like enough to Pax, but she had no time to question Janelle because their conversation ended when the train lurched into the station, spilling them out with the other kids their age coming to the seventh ward to enjoy the idyllic bars and restaurants. The sun had yet to set, so the mage lights glowed weakly from poles, but the air had a dreamlike quality.

Laughter and chatter came at them from all directions as they broke into the main canal area. A watery channel meandered through this section of the ward, carrying tourists and drunk happy hour business folk in their corporate wear on the automatic gondolas.

Inebriated on straight alcohol and alchemical concoctions, delirious smiles were the mask of choice. Janelle led them through the walking paths, over bridges and past gondola loading stations, towards a cul-de-sac of bars unofficially known as the Devil's Horseshoe.

Jae-Yong, wearing a silky blue jacket over a white T-shirt, nodded towards the rowdiest bar, spilling over with college students that had clearly come in from out of the city. They belched illusionary fire after chugging from miniature cauldrons.

"I'm guessing our victim was drinking at Hell's Head Hole," he said.

"I looked them up online. They specialize in drinks that make you breathe fire or sparkles or all manner of things. But no, he wasn't at Hell's Head Hole." Janelle gestured towards the bar on the far end that was the least packed. "The Drunken Imp."

"Oh, thank Merlin," said Pax, wrinkling her nose. "I did not want to jam myself into that sweaty mass."

The bouncer at the front didn't want to let them in, since half the group was underage, until Liam produced a ball of flame in his fist and the guy stepped out of the way, frowning. The inside of the bar was more high-tech than she would have expected, with TV screens everywhere showing a cartoon of an imp dancing around while spilling his drink. While the mascot was engagingly cute, Pax had heard enough stories from upperclassmen to know that summoning demons was forbidden, and even if you managed to successfully pull it off, you were just as likely to die at the taloned hands of said demon.

"Shall we grab a drink?" asked Jae-Yong with a shrug. "You know, plausible deniability should Cassius question us."

Janelle bought them a round of specialty beers. Nothing like the illusionary concoctions at Hell's Head Hole, but Pax's made her face tingle as she looked around the place. There were small groups of kids their age, crowded around tables, sometimes with trays of breaded bar food.

"Now what?" asked Liam, sipping from his glass as he turned his head.

When the bartender collected a few empty glasses near their spot, Pax leaned over, shooting him a grin. He did a double take, a smile spreading across his lips the second time.

"Is this the bar that guy was at that gotten eaten by the monster?" she asked.

His expression fell as he shoved the glasses into a rinsing station. He muttered under his breath, which Pax partially caught as: "fucking tourists."

"He didn't get eaten here," said the bartender eventually.

"In fact, he was probably at all the bars in the Horseshoe that night. A lot of kids come here and do the Devil's Five, where you have drinks at each of the bars in this curve."

"But he was here last before, you know, munch munch munch," she said, gesturing towards her gut.

The bartender sighed heavily. "Look, I know there are all sorts of conspiracy theories about the Mangler. You're not the first to come in here asking questions, some of them were even mages from the school, but no one's learned shit. In fact, if I had to bet, I'd say this isn't a monster, but a run-of-the-mill serial killer who gets his kicks off of eating livers." He paused, shook his head as if he'd realized that he'd gone a little far. "If you want to see where he was hanging out that night, it's in the back room."

Janelle stuffed a bill into the tip jar before they took their drinks to the private room. It wasn't an unusual place: bar table, chairs, imp-related knickknacks on every wall.

"Not much here," said Liam with a shrug.

"Let's go to the place where they found the body," said Janelle.

As they left, the bartender gave them a sour look as he wiped down the bar.

Janelle led them away from the Horseshoe, towards the apartments that ran along the backside of the canal region. They were mostly inhabited by younger residents, who didn't mind the late-night noise, because they were probably at the bars. She stopped them at a bridge that went over the canal. The iron bars had red ribbons tied around the railing, where a waterlogged picture of the kid had been zip-tied. Near a park bench and trash can, the concrete sidewalk had a dark stain.

The four of them stood around the site of the guy's death without speaking. To Pax, it felt like she was attending his funeral by their solemn demeanor.

"Not sure why," said Janelle, "but standing here makes it feel more real."

"Yeah," said Liam, nodding along with everyone else. "Even more important to figure it out now."

"But what about, as the bartender said, if this isn't a creature that we're equipped to handle, but some crazy dude, or worse, a demon or something.? This is the Devil's Horseshoe. You could have some wacked-out Coterie mage who took things a little too literally," said Jae-Yong as he cradled his chin in his hand.

Pax crouched by the stain, wondering if they had anything to add by investigating the deaths. She glanced around the apartment buildings, past the canal to the bars, which were still brimming with drunken students. This didn't look like the kind of place that her hall had something to offer.

Deep in thought, she didn't notice anything was wrong until she heard Janelle yell, "Catch him!"

Pax looked up in time to see Jae-Yong's eyes roll into the back of his head as he tipped backwards. Liam threw himself behind Jae-Yong, breaking his fall, and let him down to the concrete as he gritted his teeth and grunted animalistically. His hands curled, the veins sticking out, as he rolled around, breathing heavily and grabbing at his coat. The contours of his handsome face contorted as if they were being stretched.

"What do we do?" Pax asked Janelle.

"I don't know," she said anxiously. "I just saw him go stark white and foam at the mouth."

"He looks like he's having a reaction to something," said Liam, holding Jae-Yong's head as he thrashed around, clawing at his own chest.

A bulge in his jacket prompted Pax to reach inside, finding a prescription inhaler. When she pulled it out, Jae-Yong grunted and pawed at it, so she shoved it against his mouth and pressed it down, exhaling medicine into his lungs. His eyes fluttered open again briefly, revealing orange-brown irises, before clamping shut again. The shock of his different-colored eyes lasted until he opened them again, revealing his normal brown eyes, which made Pax wonder if she'd truly seen them.

As Jae-Yong came out of his convulsions, they helped him to a sitting position. He cradled his arms around his bent knees, still breathing heavily.

"Thanks," he said, clearly embarrassed.

"What was that?" asked Janelle.

Jae-Yong held his hand out for the inhaler, then shoved it into his jacket.

"Leftover problems from, you know, when I almost died." He looked into their faces. "The professors know about it, so don't worry. Patron Adele wouldn't have let me back into Animalians if I couldn't control it."

"Control it?" asked Pax, eyebrows raised.

Jae-Yong blinked, stared at the concrete before answering. "It's like an epilepsy from the toxins that almost killed me. It probably won't ever go away, so I have this inhaler." No one spoke again. "Can you guys stop staring at me like I have leprosy and help me up?"

When they were all back on their feet, Janelle said, "Sorry, JY. It was just a surprise. You should have warned us."

He lifted a shoulder. "I didn't want you to worry about me. Remember, I'm the new kid where you all already know each other. It's hard coming back to a place that passed you by while you were gone."

Liam bit his lower lip. "Everyone has a sort of aversion to secrets after last year."

"Understood," said Jae-Yong, screwing up his face. "Now, can everyone stop staring at me."

"Maybe this is a good point to just head back," said Janelle. "Not sure if we really learned anything."

"I learned that this is much harder than I thought," said Pax, frowning. "I don't know why but I thought we'd show up and answers would appear."

"Let's head back," said Liam. "Unless you want to stop in Hell's Head Hole for a drink first?"

Everyone looked across the canals at the packed bar, pounding with music, spilling kids out the front like straw from a scarecrow's belly.

"I'd rather go on a two-hundred-mile run with Cassius," said Pax to a round of nods.

Liam put his arm around Jae-Yong's shoulders. "No more secrets, man. Trust me, it never works out."

Chapter Ten

The idea that Jae-Yong had told the truth about his incident lasted until early November, when Janelle came rushing into their room after spending the day at Golden Willow. Pax was lounging on the soft moss, tomes lying all around her, while Kali lay against her side. The foxlike creature sat up at Janelle's wild-eyed entrance, which only grew more worrisome when she put her finger to her lips before spending the next minute putting a silence spell on the room (which once again reminded Pax of how much better at magic her friend was).

"I hope whatever this is, it isn't too terrible," said Pax, shutting the tome on her lap. "I'm so behind on our Traps and Tracking reading. I'm totally going to suck on the test tomorrow."

Janelle didn't climb onto the moss floor, but stayed in the entryway, pacing as she talked.

"Today I did a rotation on the restricted floor at Golden Willow. This is the place people go when whatever happened to them is a danger to others. It's more like a prison than a hospital, but for good reason."

"What? Like werewolves and stuff?" asked Pax.

"Exactly," said Janelle, her nostrils flaring. "Lycan-thropes, possessions, full-blown faez madness, death-head toe fungus...the whole gamut."

Pax stifled a chuckle. "Death-head toe fungus?"

"That's real serious stuff. Until it's cleared, the host can kill dozens of people. There was an outbreak in a Cincinnati gym, after some dude got cursed by a witch he stiffed," said Janelle.

"Someone have death-head fungus in Animalians?" asked Pax.

"No. But since it's so dangerous, they only let me help with paperwork, rather than do rounds with the doctors. I was looking through the records and found a familiar name in the lists," said Janelle.

"Jae-Yong," said Pax.

"Yep." Janelle crossed her arms and screwed her mouth up sideways.

"So...what was it?" asked Pax.

"I wish I knew," said Janelle. "I didn't have clearance to look in the records, only see the names, but after I saw his name, I remembered his inhaler. After a bit of digging, I found that those are used to control transformations."

"Lycanthropy," said Pax.

"Not necessarily," said Janelle. "There are other transfor-mational afflictions that don't involve turning into something else. Sometimes it's just a change in demeanor, like Dr. Jekyll and Mr. Hyde."

Pax stroked Kali's back for comfort. "When Jae-Yong had his incident, there was a moment he was coming out of it that I thought his eyes had changed to a weird orange-brown, rather than his pretty brown eyes."

"I didn't see that, but I believe you," said Janelle, sitting on the edge of the moss floor.

"Maybe it's nothing to worry about," said Pax. "As he said, Patron Adele let him return, and they had to know full well what his affliction was. If they weren't worried, then why should we?"

"This hall is not exactly a model of good safety practices," said Janelle.

"What are you suggesting?" asked Pax.

Janelle sighed, looking away. "I don't know. Maybe we just keep an eye on him. Not let our guard down."

The weight of knowledge hung heavily on Janelle's shoulders. She twitched irritably.

"Kali and I are headed back to Caer Corsydd tomorrow with the professor," said Pax as she stroked her companion's silky fur.

Janelle raised both eyebrows. "Oh, damn. I was hoping we'd be done practicing marks and get to head into the city with him."

"Hopefully soon," said Pax, biting her lower lip. "Sorry I suck at them. I just haven't gotten the hang of slam and stun."

"For a potential Hunter, you are remarkably averse to injuring even a big pink rubber ball representing an animal. How are you going to deal with the real thing?" asked Janelle, clearly worried.

"I don't know," said Pax, crossing her arms across her chest. "Maybe if the pink ball was more threatening, but when I look at them I just think of big, cute, squishy creatures that I want to hug rather than squash."

"So...what about your visit to Caer Corsydd?" asked Janelle.

"He didn't say much, except the last time he promised that the training would be better, which wouldn't be hard since it was a total disaster," said Pax.

Kali looked up at her, pressing her paw against her leg sympathetically.

Pax sighed. "I know, little one, I know."

Chapter Eleven

The first few months of portal travel had usually left Pax nauseous upon her arrival, but after dozens of trips, she could shake off the uneasy feeling and get right to running. On this day, Cassius led, while Kali kept pace behind her as they headed away from the civilized area of Caer Corsydd, which on the surface seemed like a minor change but was the difference between life and death in the realm.

Pax could tell the moment they left Lord Asphodel's territory because of the uneven paths, unexpected pools of water filled with ochre caprarium grass that blocked their journey, forcing them to detour through lily-choked swamps, and the absence of the black birds adding their bored squawks to the sunless air.

Whenever the professor's pace slowed as he scanned the unbroken horizon, the hairs on the back of Pax's neck rose, and she tried to spy the danger to which he had unconsciously been alerted. She never spotted anything, but he had decades of training, and access to magics and concoctions that gave him razor-sharp reflexes and senses that rivaled an owl's, so she just accepted that his sudden changes had saved them from being ambushed by a hidden predator.

At other times, without warning, he paused their advance, crouching to the soggy soil, checking tracks or other signs. She tried to observe them from over his shoulder but saw nothing more than weeds and mud. The only thing that kept her from questioning his start-stop actions were the shots of warning sent from Kali: nothing immediate, but a haze that warned danger was nearby. Without that she might have thought he was feigning since she never saw anything, especially because Professor Cassius had been given two tasks by Patron Adele. The first was to teach Kali how to coexist within the school and not become a mage-eating monster, and the second was to kill her companion if that task proved impossible. And while she loved learning from Professor Cassius, and there was a certain youthful energy and kindness in the hunter, she couldn't fool herself into forgetting that he was a danger to both her and Kali, because if it came to task number two, there was no way she wasn't going to defend her companion, even if she had no shot of winning.

Pax caught sight of a stone structure about an hour after they left Lord Asphodel's lands. It rose above the swamp at an awkward tilt, as if part of the base had sunk into the waters. The stepped moss-covered angles came to a flat platform near the top, and the size of the structure only became apparent when they halted on a grassy rise with a lone dead tree as a sentinel on its crown. The structure had to be at least fifty meters tall.

True to form, Professor Cassius knelt behind a fan of heather, gesturing across the swampland while tiny insects buzzed in their ears.

"*Igamogam y marw,*" he said eventually.

"I assume you're going to translate. Or are you just showing off your knowledge?" said Pax, catching the harshness in her own tone, but not caring to modulate it.

"Both," he said as he scanned the horizon. "Ziggurat of the dead."

"Lovely," said Pax. "Just when I thought we were going to do something ordinary."

The face he made was something she might have expected from her father, if he'd been normal, which took the wind out of her ill mood, a touch.

"So how are you planning on getting us killed this time? Or is it going to be a surprise?" she asked.

Cassius extended his arm towards the ziggurat. "See those lumps along the ridge of the structure?" Pax nodded, and he placed his fingers to his lips and blew an ear-piercing whistle that made her flinch.

"Owww, you could have warned me. I'm practically deaf now," she said, rubbing her left ear.

"Look."

A half dozen dark shapes rose from the pyramid, flapping awkwardly as they circled the structure. Thin, rope-like appendages hung from the back of the lumpy aerial creatures.

"They fly like a seal if you attached wings on them," said Pax.

Cassius snorted softly. "That's an apt description. Hthracks."

Even from a distance, Pax could spot their glistening black skin that shimmered like an oil slick.

"Is that a tail?" she asked, squinting.

"A stinger is more appropriate," said Cassius. "Filled with awful poison."

"Not deadly?"

He furrowed his brow. "Depends on how resilient you are.

But don't worry, we're not headed to there, and the hthracks won't bother us unless we try to enter that structure."

"What are they guarding?" asked Pax, staring at the ziggurat uncomfortably. There was something about the place that put a stone in her gut.

Cassius didn't answer for a time. He squeezed his lips tight. Eventually he hung his head, pinching the bridge of his nose with his thick fingers.

"I'm sure you've heard the story about my predecessor, and Jae-Yong," he said.

"Sure, they got attacked by a spotted wyvern..." She glanced at the hthracks, which had settled back on the moss-covered ziggurat, and reinterpreted his sullen mood. "You're saying they were attacked by those? The wyverns were just a cover story because you don't want us to freak out about this realm."

He nodded.

"What were they doing?" she asked.

"One of the reasons the Hunters get to use this realm as a training location is that we occasionally do favors for Lord Asphodel. He'd asked Ernest for something from inside the ziggurat, and he thought he'd taken all the necessary precautions, but they didn't work, obviously," said Cassius.

"Wait, Professor, you're telling me that our former head of Hunters died here and so did you, nearly, before that?" she asked. "Why do we even come to Caer Corsydd?"

"For the record, my near death was far from here, on a separate task, but that's a good question," said Cassius, shading his eyes momentarily even though there was no sun. "Adele thinks it's useful to maintain this relationship, and honestly, for the most part, it's been smashingly beneficial. Lord Asphodel supplies us with alchemical reagents we could not acquire otherwise. That bone-hardening potion relies on his offerings."

"Merlins abound, you don't think he'll ask me to go into that ziggurat as his favor?" she asked, eyes wide.

"No. Lord Asphodel is a precarious ally, but he wouldn't ask for something he didn't think you could do," said Cassius.

"That's only slightly reassuring," said Pax. "So if we're not going in there, what *are* we doing here?"

"When Ernest came here, he brought an item with him that he thought would help him get into the ziggurat. The amulet is a becalmer. It's a ripper of a soothe mark without having to refresh the spell. But when he died, he dropped the item in the swamp. During the recovery of his body, we found the item missing, but I only recently learned where it'd gotten to."

"This should be good," said Pax, putting her hand on Kali's back.

Professor Cassius nodded away from the ziggurat, towards a swampy region beset with cattails and wide lily pads that Pax knew from experience could hide predators.

"A little ways into that swamp is the lair of a nagazara. This particular nagazara snatched the amulet away, and now we have to retrieve it," said Cassius.

"How will we do that?" she asked.

The professor rose slightly, unbuckled the big bowie knife from his left hip, and handed it to Pax.

"We're going to kill it," said the professor. "Or more appropriately, *you're* going to kill it."

Pax tossed the knife into the grass as if it were on fire.

"No. I'm not doing that," she said emphatically. "I thought we tried our best to trap or relocate a troublesome creature, not murder it in cold blood."

"This is neither a troublesome beast or even a creature, but a cunning inhabitant of the swamp who has already rebuffed efforts to trade or purchase the amulet. And I'm not suggesting that we leap into her camp and stab her with impunity, but the last time I was here, she threatened to kill me if I returned," said Professor Cassius.

"I thought we were supposed to be training together, not learning how to be supernatural assassins," said Pax, gesturing angrily.

"When you joined Hunters, you agreed to accept lessons with me," said Cassius, standing taller with his jaw tight. "If you cannot abide by the agreement you made with Patron Adele, then we can return to the portal."

Her curiosity for the mission in Caer Corsydd turned bitter in her mouth.

The professor's eyes rounded with sympathy as he scooped up the bowie knife. "Look, Pax. I don't normally ask students to go tromping around the bush like this, but this is what you asked for, even if you didn't know it at the time. I hope to the gods, if they exist, that the nagazara changes her mind, but if she doesn't, then I need to know you're going to bloody well have my back."

He held the blade out. Kali looked up at Pax, but gave no indication of her opinion.

"Shit," said Pax, swiping the weapon away from Cassius and hastily attaching it to her belt with shaking hands. "I can't promise I'll kill it, but I won't let it kill us, as much as I can."

"That's all I ask," said the professor as he spread his hands. "There's a trail that winds around towards her mud cave. I'm going to head there. I want you to come behind me in about a minute."

"And then?"

He cracked his neck by rapidly tilting his head. "You do what you need to do."

With a heavy heart, Pax nodded. He disappeared down the path behind a clump of cattails, leaving her with Kali.

"I didn't think it'd be like this," said Pax, lips squeezed.

"I thought training with the professor would be, I don't know, learning new spells or something, but I think this training is just pushing us to see what happens. It's not training, but a test."

A lump rose in her throat. She thought she knew what she had agreed to when she accepted a position in Hunters, but it felt like joining the mob, when every task seemed to get slightly worse. Would she know when she crossed a line?

"What if we just left? I think I could get us back. I'm sure he can handle the nagazara alone."

Kali whined, barked lightly, and trotted after Cassius, leaving her to sigh.

"At least someone's ready to do this," said Pax, unclasping the knife at her hip.

As she wound along the path, she worried that she'd somehow missed the nagazara's lair, leaving the professor to his fate. The twist in her gut turned again, and she scanned frantically, overtaking Kali to sprint ahead, until she saw a lump protruding from the bog brush.

The descriptor of mud cave perfectly described the abode of the nagazara. It looked like the hood of a cobra stuck out from the wet ground. As Pax stepped off the path, her boots sank in the mud atop pale bones, sucking as she pulled them up.

Professor Cassius stood on the far side of the clearing, facing her, while the nagazara had her long scaly back to Pax. The creature was as long as a bus, thicker than a drainpipe, and covered in brownish-gray scales. It had the head of a humanoid, though Pax couldn't see her face.

A gargling speech from the nagazara was met with Cassius' shaking head.

"The amulet isn't yours," he said, his hands on his hips. "If you don't give it back, we'll do this the hard way."

His gaze briefly shot up to her, but not enough to give away her arrival. Kali circled to the left in a low crouch, her tail swishing above the mud.

The whole time she'd been running her heart had been ricocheting around her chest and her mind buzzed with thoughts, but standing behind the nagazara drained away her fears.

Her hand drifted to the knife, but she squeezed it into a fist instead. She wouldn't use the blade unless it was absolutely necessary.

"Amulet. Now," said Cassius, holding out his hand.

The nagazara uncoiled its long body as its upper section stayed in place, facing the professor. The scaled length slithered across the mud, slowly encircling the professor, who soured as he watched.

"I gave you ample warning," said the professor.

The head of the nagazara snapped forward, right where Cassius had stood a millisecond before. He dove over the body, which whipped towards him, sliding across the mud, and scrambled to his feet.

The nagazara shot after him, running into a stunning mark, which ripped the heads off nearby cattails, but barely knocked the enormous creature off target, forcing Cassius to dive out of the way.

"What are you waiting for?" he asked when he got to his feet. "Shove it right behind the head. That's the weakest spot."

Pax pulled the knife, holding it towards the nagazara as she advanced. The creature snapped her head to the right, finally catching sight of her. The nagazara's face looked like it'd been melted in the sun. As ugly as it was, Pax had no intention of killing it, so she shoved the knife back into the sheath.

"*Shayut!*"

Her stun was no match for Cassius' but it made the nagazara flinch before continuing its advance.

"Kali!"

Her companion lurked in the bushes, baring her teeth in a defensive growl. A moment after the shout, the nagazara's eyes clouded with darkness, and the creature thrashed around violently as it attempted unsuccessfully to escape Kali's psychic hold. The enormous tail crashed through the camp, slamming into Kali, knocking her into a tumble until she slid into the water.

Pax ran after Kali, sliding on her knees to pull her away before her companion went under, nearly forgetting about the nagazara. She looked up in time to see Cassius leap onto the nagazara's head, grabbing it with both arms, wrestling her away.

"Kali, please."

Her foxlike companion, covered and matted with mud, snarled as she leapt out of Pax's arms to return to the fray.

"Come on," yelled Cassius through gritted teeth. "I can't hold her much longer."

Her hand briefly hovered over the knife, before she spied a glint of metal in the mud cave. While Cassius was thrown about the camp, like a fireman on a runaway firehose, Pax dodged over the nagazara's long body to enter the cave.

The amulet hung from a fractured thigh bone, which had been jabbed into the earth like a pole. Pax snatched it away.

"I got it!"

"Great, but I can't let go," grunted a mud-splattered Cassius. "Shove it behind the neck. Hurry."

The thought of leaving him to the nagazara once again passed through her mind, freezing her in place with the worry that it was not her own, but Kali's misplaced intention. Which seemed only slightly less worse than if it were hers.

The professor caught her hesitation, his eyes widening as

he read her expression. His reaction spurred her forward as she pulled the knife from its sheath. She held it up, the point aimed at the dimple at the base of the neck. One blow and it would be dead.

No, I can't, she thought as she dropped the blade to a low grip and sliced the nagazara across the side, splitting the scales.

The creature lurched to the side and the tail caught Pax in the ribs, tumbling her across the camp to land in the bushes as the nagazara screamed. Before Pax could shake off the injury, Professor Cassius appeared, scooping her up and pulling her into a run.

With Kali at her side, she sprinted across the swamp, keeping up with Cassius even though her side ached worse than any hit from the whirler. They ran until her eyes watered. Pax could have gone longer, if only to avoid the eventual discussion about her hesitation.

When they finally stopped, her lungs and thighs burned. The sustained full-out sprint was a blur in her mind. She bent at the waist, chest heaving as she sucked in humid air, while Kali cleaned her fur of the stinky swamp mud.

She avoided the professor's gaze, for fear of what he might say.

"Why didn't you shove the knife where I told you? She would have killed you if she could," said the professor.

Pax picked the mud from her shirt as she looked over the swampland. Nothing she could say would satisfy him.

Eventually he sighed as he held out his hand. "Not a textbook fight, but they never are."

Pax was confused until she remembered the amulet chain wrapped around her hand. He washed the item off in a puddle before holding it up for examination.

"Professor...I, uhm, sorry about—"

He waved her away. "It's okay. Battle is unruly, and you didn't know what to expect. The important thing is that we both survived." He looked at his hand. "And we got the amulet."

Pax gave him a tired smile. She didn't know if he was saying that because that's what he thought, or because he didn't want her to know that he'd read her thoughts.

After refreshing themselves with the water they'd carried, and cleaning the mud from their faces, they headed back to the portal. The whole way Pax tried to justify her hesitation to help the professor as an effect of the crag worm poison, or the chaos of battle, but the longer she thought about it, the more she was convinced that it'd come from Kali.

Chapter Twelve

The semester stretched into the cold months, when winds whipped down from the north, bringing sleet and freezing rain. There were fewer trips to Caer Corsydd, which was a shame, since the tepid air was a balm from the face-hurting cold. Even the charms that Pax learned to ward against the weather didn't seem to work as well as they did for others. She buried her face in a thick scarf on runs between the buildings.

Classwork cycled between lectures about tactics with Professor Cassius, mark training with Maxine in the Arena, and more mind-numbing nomenclature memorization. The latter would be a staple of their studies for the entirety of their stay at Animalians, as the number of creatures in the known realms far exceeded the time possible to memorize them.

The creature in the seventh ward attacked no one else, which meant it'd moved on, been killed, or the weather had impacted its ability to move in the city. Pax was relieved, especially after the trip to take the amulet back from the nagazara, which had proved that being a hunter was much harder than she'd thought.

So she was a little apprehensive when Professor Cassius packed the eight of them into an SUV and headed out of the city for a day trip. He wouldn't tell them where they were going or what they would be doing, so the second years tortured him by singing the latest pop hit, "Loca Love Lazer," at the top of their lungs for the two-hour ride, which made the cramped trip bearable, and by the end, downright fun, as if she were at a summer camp, not a second year at a dangerous magical academy.

The singing stopped the moment they passed under the Norris Megathurn Ranch sign, headed to a big house at the edge of a fenced-in area. While her family hadn't been poor, they weren't rich by any means, and Pax knew in an instant the owner was a different level of money.

"Megathurn? Aren't those what that wacked-out mage made when he crossed cows with turtles for their shells?" asked Liam from the back of the SUV.

"If by wacked-out mage, you mean Richard Norris, the owner of the ranch, then yes," said the professor over his shoulder as he turned into the long driveway.

"Sorry, Professor," said Liam, ducking his head between his shoulder blades.

A short guy with a receding hairline wearing a dark green cabled cardigan greeted them near the grand house, which sported a stone turret and looked big enough to comfortably house half of Animalians.

"I guess being a wacked-out mage is really profitable," said Jackson after a low whistle, pressing his face against the window of the car.

"Cass!" said Richard Norris, throwing his arms around the bigger man, who returned the hug. He threw a wink toward the squat fifth year. "Hey, Max."

"Good to see you, mate." The professor jabbed his thumb towards them. "This is the newest crop. We'll try to go gentle on 'em."

Norris let loose a hearty laugh. "Always the jokester. Only three broken bones last year, amiright?"

The professor gave the class a sheepish grin. "Let's get at it. There's a storm moving in tonight and I don't want to have to take a detour to the hospital in bad weather."

Norris led them to a small fleet of off-road vehicles that could fit two in the protected cab. Pax jumped in with Janelle, who wanted to drive, wishing she had Kali to ride on her lap for warmth, but the professor had requested her companion stay on campus for the day.

They drove on a narrow path through the frozen landscape. Snow blew across the ground in gusts, but the sky was clear and crisp, not a storm in sight, but the professor had a nose for weather. Norris and the professor led them through a gate into a fenced area. The barrier was made from steel slats, and the inner wall had gouges at head height.

The journey ended at a concrete pad in the middle of a field. A pile of titanium cage sections gave Pax a clue to their task.

"Alright," said the professor, clapping his ungloved hands as a white cloud exited his lips. "You've been listening to me ramble on about hunting and trapping, but today you have to put those ideas into practice, so I hope you've all been listening.

"Somewhere on the ranch is a megathurn with a white X painted on its side. As a team, you'll have to coax that beauty back to the ranch without injuring her. She's due for her checkups, so you're doing Norris a favor."

Professor Cassius put his foot back into the cab of his off-road vehicle while Norris climbed into the driver seat. "We're gonna head back to the ranch house and sample his bottle shop. But don't worry, Max can answer any questions while I'm gone."

The fifth year crossed her arms and frowned, which made Pax smile inside. She knew jack-all about people, but Maxine was an open book. She liked being a fifth year, and assistant to the professor, but she didn't enjoy babysitting them, but it was the price of her position, so she endured it. Kids at summer camps at the Portland Zoo who had no interest in the supernatural animals had the same look.

"So...what do we do?" asked Liam, staring at the piece of titanium cage.

Maxine smirked, a snort of white mist coming from her nose. "Figure it out. When you become a hunter, there won't be anyone to tell you what to do."

"I guess we can put the cage together," said Pax, crouching down by a section. "We can talk strategy while we work."

No one had a better idea, so they followed her lead, though her intention had been less about the task and more about staying warm.

"Who knows about megathurns?" asked Liam.

"I thought you did," said Janelle.

He shrugged as he grabbed the other half of the titanium cage piece with Jackson to pull it upright so Pax and Bryanna could fit it to the other half.

"*Bos taurus carapase chimeric*," said Pax, squinting. "But I could have that wrong."

Janelle lifted a titanium bar, wrinkling her nose as she rotated it in the air. "For as little as you study the nomenclature tomes, you sure remember a lot."

"I had a big head start from, you know," said Pax, which required no further explanation, since the Portland Zoo was the touchstone that all her stories emanated from. Unlike the others, who had more diverse experiences, hers pretty much always started with, "This one time at the Portland Zoo."

"So spit it out, zoo-girl," said Jackson.

"They are, uhm"—she closed her eyes to picture the book—"they were made to survive in dangerous places, back in the '50s when the realms really became accessible, and people thought we'd be colonizing them, but then Invictus shut down non-hall portal use. But, uhm, the megathurns are really just that. Big, armored cows. Like hippos in platemail. Usually passive, until they've been riled up, then watch out."

Bryanna snapped her gloveless fingers. "Maybe we could ride them into the cage. My mom's family is from Texas, and they say you can ride anything if you try hard enough."

Pax never knew when Bryanna was being serious, so she just said, "We'll add that to the idea list. Anyone else?"

Liam glanced around. "Hey Pax, why isn't Kali here? I bet she'd be a big help."

Before she could answer, Maxine interjected, "She can't cheese her way through every lesson with her companion. Eventually she has to learn how to do it herself."

The naked animosity was a bit of a surprise. The second years shared wide-eyed surprise before Liam kicked the last piece of the cage into place.

Janelle saved the awkward moment by pulling out a notebook.

"Alright, let's not forget our lessons. Terrain, tricks, and trouble. What do we know about the terrain?" she asked, tapping her pen against her lower lip.

"Scattered trees, hard ground," said Liam. "Easy for a megathurn to build up speed, trample someone if they're not careful. Also, easy to escape. We should find a place to funnel her into the cage."

"Tricks," said Jackson. "We should try soothe first, but I

bet that won't work, otherwise this would be too easy."

Thinking about how Kali might help her if she was there, Pax said, "Maybe we could selectively limit her vision? Like using blinders to keep horses on track?"

"Hard to know until we find her," said Janelle. "What about trouble?"

"Getting trampled," said Bryanna, tilting her head sideways. "Flat as a pancake. Or a crepe, which I much prefer, with a bit of strawberry jelly and powdered sugar." She squinted one eye. "I'm hungry."

"We should probably find our target before we decide on anything else," said Pax.

While scratching the back of his head, Liam said, "Maybe we shouldn't have assembled the cage yet."

"Let's leave it," said Janelle. "Find our megathurn."

They got in their off-road vehicles in pairs, except for Maxine, who rode in her own, staying to the back of the group to observe.

"What was that with Maxine?" asked Janelle as they drove deeper into the ranch.

"No idea," said Pax. "I don't think I did anything to her, but it would explain the day at the whirler."

"Maybe she's jealous about your companion," said Janelle.

"Kali never reacts to her unfavorably, so, I don't know," said Pax. "Look, over there. I see them."

The herd of megathurns had clustered around a partially frozen pond, the dark olive green of their shells caked with mud and snow. The big beasts had trampled the ice, revealing water beneath. As the off-road vehicles rumbled up, the herd shifted away, breaking into a run as they headed away from them.

Liam, who was in the lead with Jae-Yong, sped up for a minute, until finally slowing and stopping.

"I think they're afraid of the off-roaders," said Liam, when they gathered outside.

"Makes sense," said Jae-Yong, patting the cab of the vehicle. "Probably nothing but bad happens when these bad boys show up."

"What if we use the vehicles to herd the megathurns back to the cage?" asked Janelle.

"How are we going to coordinate that?" asked Jae-Yong.

"Going to be slow going if we have to move out on foot," said Janelle.

Rubbing her arms, Pax said, "But at least we'll be warm."

When no one had a better idea, they headed out on foot. Bryanna took the lead, headed in the direction of the herd of megathurns. It wasn't hard to follow them. While the snow was thin, there was enough to make tracking easy. Twenty minutes later, they found the herd clustered around an old grandfather oak.

"Our target is at the center of them," said Janelle. "This is not going to be easy. Who's got ideas?"

"We could use the shield mark to separate them without injury," said Liam, cradling his jaw in his hand. "Would be messy but the six of us could manage."

"What did you do your year, JY?" asked Jackson.

Jae-Yong knocked his dark hair away from his face. "This must be a new task. I don't know if Professor Valentine knew this guy."

"What if we blinded them?" asked Janelle. "I know a spell that creates temporary blindness. It might be a little weak without the focal, but I'm sure I could make them sightless long enough we could get in and get one."

"I don't know," said Pax. "I'd be pretty freaked out if I went blind. I'd just be lurching around trying to figure out what happened."

"Yeah, good point," said Janelle.

Bryanna snapped her fingers and jumped into the middle of everyone. "I know, I know, I know." They shared glances because everyone was expecting a Bryanna-ism. "What if we threw a birthday party for the megathurns, and lured them away with cake. Everyone likes cake, right?"

"We need to stop thinking like hunters and more like megathurns," said Pax, repressing a grin. "Isn't that what Cassius says? If you understand your target then you have nothing to worry about."

Bryanna rubbed her belly. "I suddenly have a hankering for grass and a bad case of IBS."

"Right. You were right about the cake, except for them its grass. It's cold and they're probably hungry," said Pax. "Normally farmers put hay in the field for their cows, but I haven't seen any. I bet we could do a lot with food."

"I don't have a better idea," said Janelle. "At least we could get them near the cage. Once there, we could figure out how to separate our target megathurn."

They spent the next ten minutes collecting grass. There wasn't a lot to find, and it was difficult to pull up, but they managed to collect a small pile in that time.

"Now what?" asked Jackson.

"I think someone's going to have to lure them with the grass by hand, because we don't have enough that we can leave a trail," said Jae-Yong.

"I'll do it," said Pax. "It was my idea."

Liam stiffened. "Are you sure? Something riles them and you'll get smashed as flat as a—" He rolled his eyes towards Bryanna. "Anyway. It's dangerous."

"I'll be fine. Probably," said Pax over her shoulder. "Just no one make any loud noises."

Approaching the herd of enormous armored mammals

with two handfuls of grass felt like trying to chop down a tree with a noodle. The further Pax got from her friends, the more her shoulder blades itched.

From a distance the main feature of the megathurns that drew her eye was the armored plates of bone beneath the skin. But closer up, tails swished and big dopey eyes roved, watching her carefully as she approached.

Her friends were *way* behind her. Too far to do anything about a sudden surge from the herd. It was more likely that the megathurns would run away rather than towards her, but that's not where her mind was going as she took tentative steps across the crunchy snow-packed landscape.

"Here, cow, cow, I have some nice grass for you, hand-picked by a bunch of friendly mages," said Pax as she held out a handful like a torch in catacombs.

A big megathurn at the edge grunted and meandered towards her. She lifted her hand so the cow could bend its head down to eat the grass, because it was so damn big. While the megathurn ground the grass in its wide mouth, Pax craned her neck to find the one they had to separate from the herd. She was so busy trying to identify the right megathurn, she didn't notice as they shifted around her, drawn by the grass and the patient chewing of the biggin in front of her.

Before she could shift backwards, the herd had her trapped, teeth extended to pick the grass from every direction. When a younger megathurn pushed forward to get at the grass, her foot got caught beneath the first one she was feeding. The eye-watering pain made her drop the grass, which drove the nearest megathurns to jostle against each other, but she couldn't move with her foot beneath the hoof.

Thankfully, it only lasted a second as the megathurn shifted, but her eyes were still crossed as she side-shifted through the herd to avoid being crushed. She ended up right next to the megathurn with the "X" on the side in white paint.

"Oh, hi baby," said Pax, patting the hard shell of the megathurn.

The smaller megathurn bumped against her chest as if she were hoping for the grass she couldn't get because the larger members of the herd had crowded her out.

"You're hungry, aren't you?" she asked the armored cow as it sniffed at her hands, peeling back its lips as if it were going to take a bite. "I have more grass back with the others."

Pax slipped her hand inside the curl of shell from which the head stuck out, grabbing an edge and gently maneuvering the megathurn away from the herd while speaking softly. She had the creature marching away towards her friends, a triumphant grin on her lips, when the low roar of an engine vibrated against her chest.

She knew what it was before she saw it. A low-flying plane headed over the ranch. She heard the grunts of alarm as the herd spread out, trying to locate the source of the noise, which they interpreted as danger.

Her friends were waving at her to come back to the group, but she didn't want to abandon the megathurn she'd collected. The low plane was headed almost directly overhead, which brought groans from the herd. Before she knew what was happening, the nearest megathurns surged toward her. Using the curl for leverage, she threw herself onto the megathurn's back, right as another smashed shell to shell.

Before she could blink, Pax was bouncing across the landscape on the back of the megathurn as the herd thundered away from the plane. Staying on the back was mostly in her hands, since the slick shell had nothing to grab with her thighs, so she shifted with each bounce.

"Easy, baby, easy, please," she said desperately, her hips jarring with each impact.

After a few minutes of running, the plane disappeared, the Doppler sound fading quickly, and the herd slowed to a stop. Perched precariously atop the megathurn, Pax found herself away from her friends in a snow swept field.

She leaned over and rubbed the megathurn's ear—because every creature loved an ear rub—which brought low moans. When her temporary mount had settled, she slid from its back, hooked her hand in the shell, and limp-marched her away from the herd, grimacing each time her injured foot came down. She took turns using different hands, since her fingers were numb, even after refreshing her weather spell. She kept expecting to see her friends appear out of the scrub, but no one revealed themselves, and when she checked her cell phone she had no connection.

Pax stopped whenever she found grass to feed the megathurn, and to give her injured foot a rest. She only gave enough food to keep the megathurn motivated, not enough to sate her. Eventually Pax found a road, which had fresh tire marks in the snow, and she followed the tracks back to the ranch, which she reached as fat flakes fell from the gray sky.

Two men in winter overalls collected the megathurn from her when she arrived and sent her inside the ranch, where she found everyone else. They welcomed her with applause, ushering her over to the crackling fire, which felt painful after the long exposure.

"Bloody good work, Pax," said the professor. "If we gave grades in Animalians, you'd get an A for that business."

Bone-tired from the long walk, Pax fell onto a chair near the fire, and someone shoved a hot chocolate in her hands.

"What was the point of all that, Professor?" asked Liam. "Besides doing some ranch-hand work. Pax didn't use any magic, or marks."

"That's the beauty of the lesson," said the professor with

a wink. "When I dropped you off by the cage, what did you do right away? You started building it, even without knowing what you were going to do. Then you chased them around in your pretty little vehicles, which only frightened the megathurns. If I've told you once, I've told you a hundred times, your most important tool is your brain. I've seen a lot more students with more magical talent than Miss Nygard, but she has a way with animals, and that matters more than any Merlin score."

"Thanks, I guess," muttered Pax.

"But how is that going to work with dangerous, supernatural creatures? Are we really going to whisper sweet nothings to a manticore?" asked Jackson.

"Not in the least," said Cassius. "But you've got to start thinking like your animals, even if it's just an armored cow. And not just any armored cow, but the specific ones that you're working with. An armored cow in the wild is going to react differently than one on a ranch."

Pax might have felt pride if she wasn't so tired, not to mention her foot throbbed where the megathurn had stepped on it. She was afraid to take off her boot and see how bruised it was.

After a short while, they piled back into the SUV.

"Why don't you ride in front as the guest of honor," said Cassius, patting the seat next to him.

Pax was climbing in before she heard the snort of derision from Maxine, who had to ride in the back. Any other time, Pax might have said something, given the seat back to Maxine, but her eyes had weights on them and the idea of being crammed between Liam and Jackson in the second row rather than having a bucket seat to herself seemed ludicrous. She was asleep before the SUV left the ranch.

Chapter Thirteen

The semester ended without fanfare. Pax's foot healed up after being smashed by the megathurn, but it was still an ugly yellow-gray from fading bruises. Three cheers for the bone-hardening she'd experienced; otherwise, she would have had to walk back on a broken foot.

Returning to Portland for the break seemed out of the question. While she hoped her parents would have forgotten about the kitchen incident, she wasn't ready to find out. So she stayed on campus, along with a few other students that didn't want to return home either.

Liam was there, but he was busy working, earning money to send home to his mom. Pax had been so busy that taking hours at the Menagerie was out of the question, and she had no interest during the break, wanting to stay curled up in her hammock with Kali instead, even though her companion had gained ten pounds over the semester, making it a tight fit. So she was surprised when Professor Cassius appeared in her doorway.

"G'day, Miss Nygard. Care to run an errand with me? Or is staring at the wall your new pastime?"

Pax blinked, gave him a drowsy smile. "Sorry. I'd forgotten what sleep was like. Errand? Like training errand?"

"Not this time," he said, rapping his knuckles on the wooden door. "Headed into Caer Corsydd to drop off some things for Lord Asphodel, thought you'd want to come along."

The raven-cloaked figure could have been a villain in a fairy tale, so she wrinkled her face at him.

"I thought I should be avoiding him so he forgets the favor, or something like that," said Pax.

The professor snorted. "Lord Asphodel does not forget things like that. He forgets nothing, period. But he might go easier on you if he sees you in a better light. We're bringing him some gifts from Patron Adele, picking up a few reagents."

She sat up and stretched.

"You'll get to see the inside of his home, which is worth the journey," he said.

"I'm coming, I'm coming. Just need to wake up is all." Pax shook Kali, who was lying on her back waiting for belly rubs. "Come on, fluffy one. We have business in bog land."

After she threw on her traveling gear—even simple visits were not to be treated lightly—Professor Cassius led them through the portal into Caer Corsydd.

"Anything more ever happen with those people dying in the seventh ward, Professor?" she asked as they jogged on the manicured paths between the watery paddies.

"Not a thing," he said. "Might be our critter moved on. Happens quite often really. They're trying to survive as much as we are. That is, of course, if it really was a critter in the first place. If I had to bet, I'd put a small amount on a bipedal animal."

"I was thinking something flying," said Pax. "It's why no

one could find it. Something like a wary camazotz."

"That's a good thought," said the professor. "Though I'm not sure they're so discriminating."

Without the expectations of training, Pax spent the journey through Caer Corsydd examining the details she usually didn't have time to savor: the little purple flowers that clung to wispy vines, blue frogs that clicked instead of croaked, slender insects that soared through the air on prismatic gossamer wings. If it weren't so deadly, the place could be quite idyllic.

At the edge of the lake, a boatman in a raven mask and gray cloak waited for them. Once Pax settled onto the riser, Kali leaning against her leg, the boatman pushed away from shore using a long pole.

Pax used the journey to study the boatman, the first Gwyllion other than Lord Asphodel she'd gotten to examine. It wasn't long before Pax realized it was a boatwoman, when she pulled away the mask momentarily to wipe sweat from her chin. She had short cropped hair, slender ears that rose to a point, and a mole on her cheek. The boatwoman's calloused hands looked capable of skinning a deer, or wielding a cunning axe.

The toe of a boot caught Pax in the leg. Professor Cassius gave her a look that said, "Don't stare."

Pax mouthed an apology and shifted her attention to the approaching mound, which from the shore had seemed modest in size, but that'd been a trick of perception. A massive porticullis at the front flickered with light. As they slid beneath, Pax realized that she couldn't touch the bottom even using the boatwoman's pole.

The interior had room for fifty small boats. A barge with gilded railings that looked like it could have once floated on the Nile was nestled away in a section away from the main gate. The boatwoman left them on a dock away from the other boats, where another raven-masked attendant ushered them away.

From the outside, the mound looked earthen, dark, damp. Inside, pristine ceiling beams glittered with strange little lamps that cast a warm light on everything, and the dark wood floor resounded with their footfalls like a proper palace. Pax could imagine these elven cousins in grand attire, sweeping down the hallways on their way to a festival.

Kali sent her little mental impressions that matched her own. A bit of surprise and embarrassment at what they'd expected from the "mound." The final image Pax received was of Kali curled before a fire inside the mound.

Their guide led them until they reached a side room, where they found a tall man with a cleaver chopping away at the leg of goliath frog, which was a species of enormous amphibian that lived in the swamps. The creature took up the whole table.

Pax thought they'd been brought to the wrong place until she noticed both their guide and Professor Cassius had clasped their hands in front reverently as they waited. Only then did she realize the tall figure butchering a giant frog for meat was Lord Asphodel in a leather apron.

When he was finished, he left the cleaver on the edge of the table, pulled the apron over his head, and handed it to the guide, who scurried from the room. His reddish-brown skin was splattered with pinkish blood, which he wiped from his arms with a rag.

The whole time he worked Lord Asphodel regarded her keenly, like a lion pleased to find a mouse had wandered into its den. His gaze flickered to Kali briefly, before switching to Professor Cassius, which left her room to take a breath.

Kali shot her a measure of danger—not immediate, but not to turn her back on it—which was entirely unnecessary because she'd had the same impression in that overlong sharing of gazes.

"The task so difficult you need an assistant?" asked Lord Asphodel as he looked down his nose at Cassius. "Or did you bring her for other reasons?"

"Pax is a promising student within Animalians. It's good for her to get as much experience as she can," said the professor.

Lord Asphodel made a dismissive noise in the back of his throat and swept from the room. An attendant handed him his raven cloak, the glistening black feathers like an oil slick in the rain.

When he turned back to them, the blood splatters had disappeared. Pax stilled her face from reacting. Was this fae glamour? Or had he fixed himself with a subtle spell?

With long strides, Lord Asphodel led them back to the watery entrance. Their craft was only slightly bigger than the one she'd ridden into the mound, and he stood at the front, foot on the gunwale like a conquering hero.

"What is your companion's name?" he asked when they were on the lake, gliding across the mirror-like water.

"Kali."

"Where did you find her?" he asked without turning around.

Pax checked with the professor before answering. It was a simple question but her heart jumped around in her chest.

"When I was younger, in Portland, which is, uhm, a city—"

"I know where and what Portland is," said Lord Asphodel with restrained venom.

"My apologies," said Pax, hanging her head, glad that he had chosen to face forward.

Her companion had her paws on the edge of the boat, watching the water glide past, giving no sign that she understood the conversation even though Pax knew that was untrue.

At the far end of the lake, a canal meandered through the bog, dotted with huts on stilts, or on higher ground. The part of Caer Corsydd where the Hunters trained was less populated. Men and women who shared a resemblance to Lord Asphodel in reddish-brown skin tone, dark hair, and general fae-cousin appearance had none of his grandeur, and often sported warts, misformed limbs, or other changes that left Pax curious.

After leaving the boat at a pier that consisted of two long planks between thin poles shoved into the water, which rocked as they traversed it, Lord Asphodel marched to a thatch-roofed hut that reeked of smoke.

An old Gwyllion woman with a crown of steel gray hair and two different color eyes—one blue and one green—ambled from the abode with a stiff limp. Her rough wool dress was speckled with mud, and peeking from a pocket was a doll made of bound grass with painted pebbles for eyes.

"Lord Asphodel. What a pleasure to welcome you to my home. It is an honor and the gift of this meal will be most appreciated," said the woman, flashing Pax a wild-eyed grin and a cackle.

The corner of Lord Asphodel's lips twitched with mirth, while the rest of his face stayed ambivalent. He held his hand to Professor Cassius, who'd removed his backpack and produced a small vial, which was handed over to the old woman. She smacked her lips in anticipation before throwing the mixture down her throat.

"Your Grace," she said with a curtsey. She flipped up the front hem of her skirt before breaking into laughter and returning to the darkness of her hut.

Pax took the professor's stoney-faced lead as they traveled to four other huts, dispensing what she assumed was medicine to Lord Asphodel's people. Two were small families, while the next hut was a blind Gwyllion who spoke to Lord Asphodel as if he were his son.

The final hut smelled like death.

Kali confirmed her suspicion, though it wasn't necessary. Even Professor Cassius' eyes watered with the stench of decay. A spot of bile was quickly swallowed down, and she stopped breathing through her nose to maintain composure.

A younger Gwyllion, the youngest she'd seen by far and ruggedly handsome in the same manner as Liam, greeted them, but that was where the similarity ended. The fae before her had been hollowed out with grief. His face was etched with sorrow, and salt lines streaked his cheeks.

When Lord Asphodel handed over the vial, the young Gwyllion dropped it from his quivering hand, which only made his crying worse. The vial miraculously didn't break, but it lay in the dirt near a patch of violet oryllian flowers, stranded by his inability to stop shaking. Lord Asphodel's lips curled with disdain as if he'd let it slip from his fingers on purpose.

Pax surged forward, collecting the vial and cleaning it with the hem of her shirt before holding it out to the young Gwyllion, but he looked like he was falling apart at the seams.

"I-I-I...s-s-sorry," he sputtered.

Before she lost her nerve, Pax pushed through the wall of stench into the darkness of the hut. She clamped her hand over her mouth reflexively.

As her watering eyes adjusted to the dim light, she was pleasantly surprised by the space of the interior. It was like finding a bohemian apartment inside a trailer. On the far side of the room, a bed sagged in the middle, the source of the stench.

Pax was expecting an older parent on the cusp of eternity, not the bandaged waif with an arm missing and a bloody crust on the edges of her lips. But even through the injuries and the sickness, the girl was a bronzed jewel. Her perfect bow-like lips hung slightly open, tainted with sickness.

Holding the vial before her like a light, Pax approached the bed, watching the hurried rise and fall of the girl's chest, the grit of her teeth as she moaned, delirious with pain.

Kali appeared by Pax's side, looking up with sad, sympathetic eyes. Together they approached. Given the dangerous nature of Caer Corsydd, Pax imagined that the girl had been attacked by a denizen of the swamps.

There were no instructions on the vial, but the others had downed theirs without comment. Pax tried to push the vial against the girl's lips, but she clamped them shut.

"Kali. Can you help?"

Her foxlike companion lowered her head, as if she were embarrassed by her ability, but a moment later, the girl puckered open like a baby bird.

Pax pressed the vial to her lips and slowly tipped it back to let the pale blue liquid trickle down her throat. The fae girl coughed slightly halfway through but otherwise provided no further resistance.

Within the span of a few heartbeats, the girl stilled, her jaw no longer pulsing, and her heaving chest slowed to a lazy ocean swell.

When Pax returned to the sunless sky outside the hut, Lord Asphodel regarded her strangely. She didn't know what to do, so she genuflected as if she'd just arrived at court.

Inscrutable and majestic, Lord Asphodel swept towards the boat as Professor Cassius gave her a nod of approval. It wasn't until later as the boat neared the mound that Lord Asphodel spoke.

"Gilfaethwy was attacked by the creature that you call the dragon salamander when she was collecting bog berries in shallow waters. Pwyll already lost his wife to the swamp, losing his daughter would have been catastrophic," said Lord Asphodel.

His gaze swept over Cassius, dipping the professor's head and squeezing his lips to a point.

"I am aware of my failures," said Cassius as his nostrils flared.

"As we all are," said Lord Asphodel as he stared at the professor. "This idea of a so-called bane has affected your abilities. The dragon salamander is no more dangerous than many other creatures of this realm."

"What happened to the one that attacked her?" asked Pax.

"A band of my people hunted it down. It's not the first that we've had to take care of," said Lord Asphodel.

The repudiation stung in Cassius' eyes, furthered when she met his gaze and he looked away. This wasn't the lesson he'd hoped to impart by inviting her along.

On the lonely pier beneath a dome of brightly lit wood, Lord Asphodel stepped from the boat and the raven-masked attendant pushed away with his pole. Fearing to offend, Pax kept her gaze slightly diverted as they glided back into the lake through the gate, but before they left the warm lights of the mound, she caught Lord Asphodel staring at her curiously.

Neither of them spoke on their journey back to the portal. The professor had been reduced by the comments, his shoulders squeezed small, his rambunctious nature stilled.

Pax wondered if he'd been honest with Pietra, when she'd troubled him about his bane. Clearly, Lord Asphodel thought this superstition a factor in Cassius' failure. For her part, she hadn't decided if she believed in banes, but certainly could understand that some creatures might be a natural foil for your abilities.

Many things she'd thought she understood had been upended by this trip, including her expectation of Lord Asphodel, and warnings about the capricious nature of the fae did nothing to temper her concerns. She'd thought that it'd been Cassius' intention to shine a favorable light on her to lessen the impact of the future favor, but in some ways the trip felt like an audition. Pax promised herself to trust nothing of Caer Corsydd, not that anything had given her cause before.

When they stepped back into the Arena, Professor Cassius tugged his river hat from his bald head.

"You did well with Lord Asphodel."

She squinted. "Was this visit planned between the two of you?"

He was taken aback. "What can you mean? Of course it was. He'd asked specifically for those alchemical solutions, medicines only available in the city of sorcery."

It wasn't what she'd meant. She wanted to ask him why on the first day she'd arrived in Caer Corsydd Lord Asphodel had been waiting for her outside the portal, as if he'd expected her to be there. She'd written it off at the time because the fae were known for their supernatural abilities, but in hindsight, the interaction felt suspicious. But if it had been a setup—for reasons she didn't understand—calling him out on it wouldn't help her figure his motives.

"I guess I didn't realize you two talked so much," said Pax, trying to make it sound offhand. "You know, the political side of magic is a mystery to me."

Her explanation unraveled the knots in his forehead as his face broke with a smile.

"I have to meet the other professors for a meeting. Have a great rest of your break." He winked at Kali. "Try not to get into trouble."

Chapter Fourteen

The new year brought her friends back to campus. Janelle gave her an enchanted bracelet that provided protection against the cold for a Christmas present, while Pax had given her a stack of spiral notebooks with unicorns on the front. The imbalance of the gifts made Pax blush, but Janelle hugged the notebooks to her chest and claimed they were her favorites.

Pax settled into a routine. The blustery winter and intensifying classwork turned free time to a mirage that always seemed to approach during the weekend then evaporate with responsibility.

The second years were subjected to a new round of alchemical brews, which were administered in the infirmary. In the first moments after downing the cinnamon-flavored liquid, Pax curled into a ball on the examination table while Professor Ansel looked on. The debilitating stomach cramps lasted a minute or two, before subsiding, leaving her in a cold sweat that stunk like body odor. The professor suggested a long shower to ease the effects of the potion, which was to help protect them against the poisons and venoms they would encounter in their roles.

To keep from overwhelming the body's immune system, they would only receive a new protective alchemical mixture once a week, but that visit to Professor Ansel's infirmary became a source of dread and pride, the latter only after cleaning off in the shower, as the second years met at the Bantu Queen for celebratory drinks.

During the week they worked on their marks. Professor Cassius warned them using the quick magics needed to be second nature, a task which left Pax feeling inadequate compared to her classmates. They also studied tricks and traps, ways of coaxing their targets into cages or natural capture points like caves, which could be blocked off and filled to incapacitate their targets. While the rest of her class easily bested her at navigating the painful whirling contraptions in Caer Corsydd and using the right mark with hair-trigger reflexes, it was in outthinking her animal prey that she excelled, as shown by the day at the megathurn ranch.

But the schoolwork, studies, and longing for a moment of sleep were set aside on an unexpectedly warm day during the second week of February. A thick, eerie fog had coated the city for days. In another city, the lingering haze would have brought suspicion or conjecture from its citizens, but after all, it was the city of sorcery, and strange events were made commonplace by their regularity. So the fog barely registered to anyone but Pax and her friends, who had speculated that their creature had gone underground during the cold months and would resurface when it warmed.

"The creature's back," said Liam breathlessly as he burst into the Bantu Queen with Jackson and Jae-Yong on his heels.

Pax, Bryanna, and Janelle had been quizzing each other

on the nomenclature. Mugs containing a special brew Dane called Study Sauce, which helped Pax focus for a few hours before leaving her jittery, littered the table along with open books.

Kali lifted her head above the table from her napping spot. Dane had made her a raised bed along their favorite study table, but already the foxlike creature's legs overhung the cushy spot.

Pax uncrossed her eyes from staring at the tome for hours, slamming it shut.

"I could use a break," she said, rubbing her right eye with the palm of her hand.

"Me too," said Janelle, carefully closing her unicorn notebook and sliding it into the carryall that she slung over her shoulder.

"But *mortuus est cerebrum,*" deadpanned Bryanna.

"What creature is that?" asked Jae-Yong as he scratched Kali's ear.

Bryanna offered a maniacal grin. "Me."

Jackson punched him in the arm. "She said she has a dead brain, you goof."

"Sorry," said Jae-Yong with an eye roll. "I hear Latin and all I can think of is the nomenclature. I see it in my dreams."

"Shall we head to the seventh?" asked Liam a hungry gleam in his eye.

From her experiences in Caer Corsydd with Cassius, Pax's appetite for investigating unknown critters was less intense than the others, but she knew that if she were going to be an effective Hunter she needed the practice, and with the six of them it was unlikely they'd get into too much danger.

On the train ride to the seventh, Liam outlined what he knew.

"It happened a few blocks from the canal district. Some

tourist was waiting in the fog for a ghost taxi when it attacked him, but it ran away when the vehicle arrived. He got away with a bite on his leg and a good story for when he goes home," said Liam.

"How the hell did you find all that out?" asked Janelle.

"I called Invictus PD claiming I was a reporter for the *Herald of the Halls*. The official statement is that it was a dog that attacked the tourist, but the guy I talked to gave me the unofficial version too," said Liam.

"Did the tourist see anything? Notice what kind of creature?" asked Pax with Kali lying across her and Janelle's laps.

"Nothing. He was standing on the sidewalk. It hit him from behind, knocking him forward, right in the path of the taxi. Lucky he didn't get run over, and since it was a ghost taxi, there's no way to ask the driver," said Liam.

"I mean, technically, you can *ask* the driver, but you're just not going to get an answer," said Bryanna with a demure hand beneath her chin playfully.

When they reached the seventh, Pax noticed the hopeful cast to Liam's gaze, so she grabbed Jae-Yong as her partner when they decided to split up in pairs. Janelle organized them by assigning an area of eight square blocks for each pair to patrol.

"Text if you see anything, or have a problem," said Janelle, holding up her phone as she and Bryanna headed into the fog.

Away from the others, Jae-Yong glanced backwards. "You like torturing him, don't you?"

Pax spun on her heels to face Jae-Yong as she crossed her arms. "He's torturing himself. I've made my intentions clear. Besides, he broke my trust last year."

Jae-Yong held his hands up. "You're right. That was shitty of me. I know you don't mean to mess with him. Can we move back to the investigation?"

"Yeah, fine," said Pax, shoving her hands into her jean jacket as they strolled along the street in the whiteout, which left everything around them muted. She wasn't expecting to find any sign of the creature, but it was a nice break from studying.

The reinforced silence lasted for a block until Jae-Yong spoke up. "You know, he told me about what happened last year. How he messed up with those criminals, and how you and Janelle rescued him."

"It was stupid," said Pax. "We almost got killed."

"But you saved him, which was pretty awesome, even after you learned that he'd lied to you," said Jae-Yong.

"I'd do it again, even if it was stupid. A sense of self-preservation is not one of my hallmarks, I've learned. You might have made a mistake by coming with me today," said Pax with a chuckle.

Jae-Yong smiled at her earnestly, triggering a little pang of desire. He *was* handsome.

Matching her pace with his hands in his coat pockets, he shrugged his shoulders as he stared into the fog pensively. "I just think it's cool that you all had each other's back when the chips were down."

She normally didn't feel other people's emotions, but Kali reflected Jae-Yong's mire of regret.

"You worry you didn't do enough when Professor Valentine died," said Pax.

With his lips squeezed tight, he nodded. "I wish I knew one way or the other. I'm afraid that I did something to cause his death. I wish I remembered something, anything."

"You know it wasn't a spotted wyvern," said Pax.

He wheeled on her. "What? How do you know that?"

Pax bit her lower lip, realizing she might have spoken out of turn. While Professor Cassius hadn't explicitly told her not to reveal what he'd said about that visit, the fact that they hadn't told him already should have clued her in to their intentions.

"Professor Cassius and I were on an errand in Caer Corsydd last year. We were at the place that, uhm, you know. We were retrieving the becalmer amulet from a nagazara who'd picked it up afterwards," said Pax.

He blinked, furrowed his forehead, and looked away. "None of that sounds familiar."

"You were in a coma for over a year. That certainly messes with the brain," said Pax.

"The doctors tell me my brain is fine now," said Jae-Yong. "But I don't feel that way. I feel like there's a hole in my past, and not just any hole, but one where my action or inaction might have gotten someone killed."

"You can't assume that," said Pax.

He raised his eyebrows. "Tell that to my brain. Is there anything else you can share that might fill me in? Maybe if I knew more that would help me dispel those feelings."

Since Janelle had learned about his attendance on the danger ward of the hospital through unauthorized means, Pax decided that it wasn't worth risking her friend's career, so she kept that news to herself.

"Nope. Nothing more than that," said Pax. "So...do you remember other meetings with Lord Asphodel? Anything about your first, second year?"

"Not really," he said as they resumed their stroll through the fog. "The generalities of the training yeah, but not a lot else about that. I barely remember how I felt about my classmates, and since we haven't talked since, I still don't know. The only thing I really remember is how the swamps smelled and felt, but after spending so much time there training, I guess the place gets into your soul."

"That sucks. For what it's worth," she said, putting her hand on his shoulder, "I'm glad you got to join our year."

Jae-Yong blushed. The intense glance showed that he had feelings for her, but unlike Liam he wasn't as forthcoming with them.

"Thanks, Pax," he said, playfully bumping into her shoulder with his. "And thanks for picking me for your fog partner. It's nice to hang out with you."

There was a part of her that wanted to slow him with a touch, place her hand against his cheek, lean in for a long kiss and make a plan for a rendezvous later. But she didn't know if he was capable of maintaining that separation. She didn't want a boyfriend. She didn't have room in her life for anyone else but Kali, but that didn't mean she didn't have desires.

Their walk slowed as Pax kept glancing over to find Jae-Yong doing the same. Before she knew it they were shoulder to shoulder, and the contact, even through four sets of fabric, sent quivers down her spine.

Even though they were in the middle of the city, the fog made it so they were in a private, enchanted land. The slow rise of her own chest, the heat in her cheeks, she knew she'd convinced herself to kiss him and present her proposition afterwards when her shoes slowed to a stop.

Jae-Yong turned, lips half parted in anticipation. She was leaning towards him when a spike of black licorice came from Kali.

Pax immediately broke away, leaving Jae-Yong bewildered until he saw Kali streaking ahead through the fog.

"She sense something?" he asked as they hurried after.

"Yes."

Normally, a warning came as a quick spike then faded away, but this time, the licorice remained, reinforced with other flavors and sensations that left Pax with more questions.

At the next corner, Kali sniffed at the sidewalk in front of a house. Though it was hard to tell, they were in the middle of a neighborhood of apartment buildings. The house gazed out of the fog with two windows. A muted honk and brief surge of color reminded them of the regular traffic only a few feet away.

"What was it?" asked Pax.

Kali looked up at her, sending a tang of familiarity, confusion, and caution. The cocktail of emotions left Pax no closer to understanding.

"Can you track it?" asked Pax.

When Kali shook her head, Jae-Yong said, "Do you think she sensed the creature?"

"Possible," said Pax, and since he wasn't privy to Kali's true nature, she added, "A thoratic fox has limited psychic abilities. She might have picked up its hunger, or the strangeness compared to the humans in the area."

"I wish we knew what it was," said Jae-Yong. "It might help us find it."

Pax craned her neck back. "I've been thinking that it could be flying. That would explain how it can move around the city without getting caught. The rooftops provide a perfect hiding spot."

He gestured behind them. "There was an alleyway back there. Wanna take the fire escape up to the roof and find out?"

"Oh, yeah," said Pax. "I forget about those."

"I grew up in Chicago," he said with a shrug as he led them into the alleyway. "When we were kids we'd play hide-and-seek on the roofs."

"I thought your family lived in Houston?" she asked.

He ticked off his fingers. "Houston. Albuquerque. Kansas City. Chicago. My parents were first gen Americans. They never really found a place they wanted to call home. I guess it's always made me a wanderer."

The fire escape swayed as they climbed, each creak leaving a twist in her gut. The thick fog dissipated around the fourth floor, so the rooftops looked like islands in a sea of mist while grainy sunlight illuminated the haze to a warm glow. They managed to travel across a half dozen roofs before they ran out of real estate.

"I don't know," said Pax, crossing her arms, craning her head in all directions. "Maybe this wasn't such a great idea. Everything looks the same up here. I was hoping we'd see a nest, or other signs."

In the instant after she spoke, a bloom of fire lit up the fog a block over, the flames reflecting through the pale canvas. Ozone tickled her nose a moment later. Jae-Yong was ahead of her before she could look for the fire escape, banging down the metal stairs, rocking the structure with shrieks and groans. She threw herself after him, her earlier caution lost to the pursuit.

As her boots hit the asphalt, splashing through a leftover puddle, she heard someone cursing ahead in the fog. Kali lifted her muzzle to sniff at the air while Jae-Yong sprinted ahead. Pax yelled at him to slow, not rush heedlessly, but he disappeared into the white.

She heard tires screeching and squeezed her eyes shut, expecting a sickening *thump*, but nothing came. When she and Kali hit the street, a businessman in a blue sedan had his window down yelling obscenities.

When she stopped, the guy looked at her and said, "Damn kid jumped my car like he was a gazelle."

"I guess he went this way," said Pax, slipping behind the car as she cautiously darted across the street using Kali's danger sense for warning.

Pax found herself outside a Wizard's Coffee, near a line of customers waiting to get inside. Her sudden appearance with Kali startled a few who'd been staring into their phones, but they just laughed and commented on the fox, and she left them behind.

At the next alleyway, she climbed the fire escape after leaping up, pulling the ladder down, and then lifting Kali so she could make it to the first level. She was halfway up the metal stairs when she heard that same cursing as before.

"Fuckfuckfuckfuck."

It was Maxine.

Pax almost called out to her, but their strained relationship and Maxine's volatile mood kept her lips shut. Kali whined softly at her heel.

She could almost make out the squat fifth year as she paced, fist held to her chin.

"I almost had that fucking thing. Dammit. This shouldn't be that hard to catch. Oh Maxine, Maxine. Why does everything have to be so hard? Pietra's not going to like this."

The comment hit Pax wrong. She wrinkled her forehead, trying to figure out why she'd mentioned Pietra.

Maxine's outline filled in with details as she headed Pax's direction. Crouched on the second level of the fire escape, Pax kept a low profile, but if the fifth year looked up she'd see her and Kali. Pax wasn't sure why she was hiding from Maxine, except that she'd been eavesdropping.

But the fifth year never looked up and disappeared moments later. About that time, Pax's pocket buzzed.

[JY: Where's everyone at? Got separated. Meet at Wizard's Coffee on Allanon?]

Replies from the rest of the group came fast. She met them at the location, away from the line of customers.

"Thanks for leaving me behind," said Pax as Kali sniffed Jae-Yong's leg.

Jae-Yong rubbed his face with his palm. "I know. I got so

excited, I kinda lost my mind."

He was flushed, still breathing heavily, even though a short sprint shouldn't have affected him that much after all their training.

"Try not to do that again, we're supposed to stay together. Remember, we're hunting," she said.

When the others showed up, Jae-Yong repeated their brief adventure, then Pax added, "It was Maxine. I guess she's hunting the creature too."

"Not a surprise," said Jackson. "She soooo wants to join Pietra at the Phoenix Company but they only take hunters who have experience. I bet she's trying to catch the creature for some cred."

"Hunt all we want, but this fog is making it impossible," said Liam, scratching the back of his head. "Everything looks the same."

"Yeah," said Janelle. "I think I'm done. The break from studying was nice, but we've got that test on the chimeratic kingdom tomorrow, and I still have a rotation at Golden Willow tonight."

Jae-Yong looked like he still wanted to investigate the creature, and the thought of renewing her earlier plan surfaced until she caught Liam staring at her, and then the whole idea of an unwanted love triangle drained her desire.

Stupid boys. Don't know what they're missing if they'd just learn to talk.

"Yeah, I'm done too," said Pax as she crouched down with Kali.

No one spoke on the return to Animalians campus, since they weren't sure if the trip had been a success or failure. But it didn't matter, since homework waited for no one.

Chapter Fifteen

On a Sunday in early March, Professor Cassius found her at the Menagerie signing with Edgar, who had made her a necklace of shrimp carapaces on a string. The aromatic gift hung around her neck while she was thanking him. He got distracted when the professor ambled up, giving Cassius an excited spin before signing *hellohellohello* through the glass.

"G'day, Edgar," said the professor, signing with his words and managing to add his accent to the gesture with a little wrist twist. "Nice necklace. She's a real beaut."

"Oh, you like? I bet Edgar would make you one too," said Pax, quickly signing to the octopus before the professor could stop her.

"No, wait," said Cassius, but the octopus had already disappeared into the enormous tank. "Oh, well. He's a good lad. Better he have something productive to do instead of getting involved with student shenanigans."

The professor raised his eyebrow at Pax, who said, "I would never do such a thing. Without his consent of course."

"Right," he said, glancing left and right as his expression tightened. "Is Kali around?"

"Training time?" she asked.

He crossed his enormous arms. "Lord Asphodel requests your attendance in Caer Corsydd. He's calling in his favor."

"Oh, shit," said Pax. "Any idea what he wants?"

"I'll give you a hint, he asked for me to join you," said the professor.

As if called, Kali trotted into the room despite having no way to open the doors, but Pax had learned a long time ago that simple barriers never stopped her companion.

"Hey, Kali," said the professor, greeting the foxlike creature with an inclined head. She extended her forelegs in a downward dog, which had the semblance of a bow, before returning upright. "We have work to do."

After a stop by her room to gear up, and leave her gift from Edgar, Pax met Cassius at the portal. She was glad that Janelle hadn't been there to ask questions since she was doing her rotation at Golden Willow.

To Pax's surprise, Lord Asphodel was waiting for them on the other side without his raven-cloak, dressed in a light chain shirt, a slender longsword on his hip. The lack of cloak and addition of the sword removed the aloofness from his gaze, as he stared into the distance with the intensity of a soldier before battle.

"Greetings. Professor, Pax, Kali," said Lord Asphodel in what could only be described as a cheery tone, even if it seemed impossible from the source.

Pax shared a glance with the professor, who lifted a shoulder.

"You brought the amulet?" asked Lord Asphodel, resulting in Cassius pulling it from his pocket, rattling the chains for effect.

"We're going to the ziggurat, aren't we?" asked Pax.

Lord Asphodel only nodded sagely, before sweeping towards the path in long strides that forced Pax to jog to keep up. During the journey, black birds roosting in trees watched them pass, occasionally adding their caws to the air—a greeting, or encouragement, Pax couldn't tell.

The run left Pax limbered up, more awake than she was before she passed through the portal. The ziggurat was the same as they'd seen before—dark figures dotting its slope, moss and vines choking the stones, the sagging tilt a sign of its future demise.

Pax glanced to the left path, the one that led to the naga-zara. Lord Asphodel briefly followed her gaze before saying, "She's no longer there to bother us."

"You didn't have to kill her," said Pax.

The tall fae squeezed his lips. "I did not say we did. She is well, as much as her kind can be, in another swamp. But I did not want interference today."

Professor Cassius elbowed her in the ribs.

"My apologies, Lord Asphodel," said Pax, but there was no acknowledgement as he stared at the ziggurat. She cleared her throat. "What's the plan?"

"The plan, as you say, is that together we will enter the *Igamogam y marw*, and within its hall retrieve something that has long been lost to me." Lord Asphodel turned to both her and Kali. "It is my hope that you can make this a less exciting trip than it would be otherwise."

"You want Kali to keep the hthracks from attacking us?" asked Pax.

"Precisely. When your Professor Valentine tried to enter, he only had the amulet and his student assistant. This time, I believe we will be more successful," said Lord Asphodel keenly. "There are many treasures inside, but the one I desire is now within reach."

If there was a path to the ziggurat, it'd long ago sunk into the swamp, leaving them to wade through knee-high waters. Kali rode on Pax's shoulders, which used to be like wearing a living neck warmer, but her growth left her foxlike companion hanging over both shoulders and pushing her further into the mud.

At times, the waters stirred with critters, but nothing dared approach the small party except the tiny insects that buzzed in her ears and kept Kali's snout twitching. Nearer the ziggurat, the black leather wings of the hthracks could be made out as the creatures stared down at them from their angled perches.

Professor Cassius held out the amulet as if it were a torch in the darkness. Pax had no idea if Kali was projecting any calming emotions, but so far the hthracks hadn't stirred from their spots. They reached solid ground without incident, a bump of land protruding from the water as if it'd been squeezed from the sinking structure, which gave her the opportunity to let Kali down. Her companion stared at the creatures on the angled stone. Pax sensed unease as if she'd had previous run-ins with the hthracks, but unless there'd been hthracks in Portland that wasn't possible.

Moldy green vine-covered steps led upward into a dark hole inside the ziggurat. Lord Asphodel led the way, his blade still in its sheath as he made careful advances upward, each step a testing of the hthracks' will to attack.

The steps were small from a distance, but went on for what seemed like forever. Behind her, the swamp was a brownish-green flatland, dotted with dead trees. The mud cave of the nagazara remained in its previous spot, but the swamp was reclaiming it with greenery.

When they reached the entrance, a single hthrack broke

away, winging into the sky, leaving Lord Asphodel to reach for his weapon, but make no other move. The creature circled the ziggurat before disappearing.

"If you must prepare, do it now. Once we enter, I cannot guarantee our safety," said Lord Asphodel.

Professor Cassius handed her a vial and then drank down one of his own, grimacing as he swallowed. She followed his example, the liquid making her jaw tighten, and as soon as it hit her stomach, her heart quickened.

"A bit of protection, and an enhancement," he said.

As she took a calming breath, every faint odor in the area revealed itself, a cornucopia of smells that despite the number did not overwhelm her, as if she could set each one on an individual shelf and admire it singularly.

She followed Cassius' example, giving herself darkvision— on the first try for once—before they followed Lord Asphodel into the ziggurat.

The vines that had plagued the outside of the structure were strangely absent inside as if a barrier prevented them from entering. There was no clear demarcation, but a gradual lessening until no more vines advanced.

Lord Asphodel led the way. Pax would have felt more comfortable with a weapon in her hand, or a torch which she could use to ward away critters. Professor Cassius caught her touching her hip, so he unbuckled one of his bowie knives and handed it to her. She held it against her stomach.

Outside, the humid air always felt cloying against her skin, but the interior of the ziggurat was strangely arid, and at each step the hair on the back of her neck rose higher. They walked until the light of the exit was a mere pinprick behind them, and a sandstone door blocked their passage.

The stone was lined with hieroglyphs unblemished by age, while above the double doors gold-embossed wings accented with rising flames marked the importance of the barrier.

"These look Egyptian," said Pax, reaching towards the hieroglyphs until Lord Asphodel blocked her hand.

"Do not touch."

Pax stepped back, motioning for Kali to do the same as the foxlike creature sniffed at the door cautiously, as if she were checking for a predator.

"Danger?" Pax asked as she crouched.

Her companion nodded her furry head, taking two steps backwards, her black eyes trained on the double doors.

Lord Asphodel continued to stare at the hieroglyphs as if he could read them. He dipped his fingers into a pouch at his hip and sprinkled an ochre dust near the bottom edge. Some of it blew past their feet.

"This is a strange temple," said Professor Cassius as he examined the door.

"It's not a temple," said Lord Asphodel. "It's a tomb."

"Tomb? Like a pyramid, not a ziggurat," said Pax.

Lord Asphodel extended his long arms, motioning for them both to step back. From his lips came a language that was clearly not of Caer Corsydd, but it thrummed with power. There was a moment when she felt a reflection from Kali, as if Lord Asphodel's invocation had bounced off her and impacted the golden flame-kissed wings, because as soon as it had, they glowed with import.

The door cracked with the force of a cannon, exhaling stale air in a rush, knocking her red hair around her face, forcing her to quickly tie it up while keeping her eyes closed from the dust assault.

After a good half a minute of wind, the doors were spread wide, and the glow of the wings subsided. Kali glanced up at her with concern, as if she knew what might lie ahead. The passage that extended through the opening looked less ravaged by time than outside, with stones on the wall providing light.

Lord Asphodel tilted his head to the right as if he were deciding if it were safe to proceed while Kali sent her warnings of unspecified danger.

"Come, let us explore further," said Lord Asphodel.

The passage was wide enough for all of them to walk side by side, Pax taking the far right with Kali between her and Professor Cassius. Pax was about to ask what they might expect ahead when the floor opened beneath her feet—a trapdoor triggered by her weight. In the blink of an eye, the trapdoor slammed shut behind her, and she fell through darkness.

Chapter Sixteen

Pax woke to darkness. Not the grays of darkvision, but true, absolute darkness.

Her body throbbed, the aftereffects of hitting the sand floor from a great height. She recalled bouncing off a wall with her shoulder, then tumbling into the sand. Although it cushioned her fall more than a stone floor would have, only the constant training and the impact-hardened bones saved her from a catastrophic result.

It took a while before the pounding of her heart quieted enough that she could hear again as the potion that Cassius had given her had worn off. Which meant she'd been out longer than a few minutes. She listened quietly, hoping that the others were searching for her, but the only thing she heard was the trickling of water across stone.

She hated using magic in the darkness, but there was no other way to get around her blindness. It took three tries—her head ached with a low-level migraine—before the world bloomed back into existence, revealing a cavern of broken stones.

A chute went up through the ceiling to the passageway, far above, too far for her to even consider getting back that way. The stone structure around her had fallen down, the stones turning to sand.

Cautiously rising to her feet, she carefully stepped towards the sound of trickling, fearful of hidden traps. At a crack in the wall, clear water bounced over chunks of stone, before disappearing through a hole in the floor.

Pax cupped her hand beneath the trickle, capturing a handful of water, which she sniffed before testing it with her tongue. For all she could tell, it was clean water, but she wasn't about to drink it, at least while she had a full pouch in her backpack.

"Let's see if we can find a way out."

The high, curved ceiling suggested a bigger cavern than her direct surroundings, so she climbed over the broken stones until she found herself in a big space. The darkvision spell was limited in its range, so she had to move cautiously as not to run headlong into danger.

Pax found a crack in the far wall, which seemed to travel upward, but the width would barely allow her to squeeze through and could just as likely get her stuck. After a complete circuit of the room, she came back to the crack, which as far as she could tell was the only way out.

"Maybe they can find me," said Pax, craning her neck towards the chute in the ceiling. "Or put a rope down the hole so I can climb out."

The idea seemed obvious, which suggested that it couldn't be done for some reason. Maybe the trapdoor was too heavy to move, or they'd been forced out of the pyramid.

After weighing the risk of making noise versus staying quiet, she placed her hands around her mouth.

"Hello! Professor Cassius! Lord Asphodel! Kali! Can you hear me? I'm down here. I was knocked out, but now I'm fine, well, stuck here, but alive anyway."

Her words echoed through the chamber before returning to silence. No answer came.

She tried two more times before giving up. She'd have to rescue herself.

"Maybe they're looking for another way down," said Pax as she crouched on her heels, picking at sand. A more dire thought wormed its way into her thoughts. "Or they think I'm dead, and went on without me."

But she knew that couldn't be true. Kali wouldn't leave her if she knew she was alive.

"Wait, duh, Kali."

She sent out a mental signal to her companion. Nothing more than *"hey, I'm alive"* but it was enough for now. The problem with their communication was that Pax never knew when Kali received it. Their conversations were two-way, but Kali held all the equipment.

When no answer came, she closed her eyes to focus and sent the message again, harder, with more intensity. But for all she knew she was shouting in a grave with a million tons of stone above her head.

Pax plopped onto her rear and took out a handful of trail mix and her water pouch to sate her grumbling stomach.

"At least I have a source of hopefully safe water. Maybe Professor Cassius went back for help," she said, then popped a cashew past her lips and crunched down.

It wasn't like they needed her to get in and out of the pyramid, only Kali.

Kali won't leave me. Professor Cassius won't leave me.

These were the mantras that she repeated as she finished her snack, prepared to attempt the crack in the wall.

Pax sent out another round of mental shouts before returning to her only potential escape. She left the backpack in the sand next to the crack after taking a long swig from the water pouch.

The opening in the wall was narrow at her hips, which required maneuvering to squeeze past, but then it opened up slightly. Inside, she felt a slight breeze, which gave her hope that there was a way out.

Gingerly sidestepping, Pax slipped through the crack, outward and upward at an angle. A short ways into the opening, the passage narrowed, until the rough, broken stone scraped at her chest and knees, forcing her to extend her arms and suck in her gut.

The crack went for thirty or more feet, but it was hard to tell since she had to fight for each inch. There were two more open sections, and another narrow one, which wasn't just a pinch point to slip past but a long, squeezed passage.

Imagining herself elongated, Pax maneuvered herself into the space, wiggling to edge forward since she had to balance on her tippy-toes to keep her heels from catching. The crack was C-shaped, forcing her to bend slightly, holding her arms over her head rather than to the side.

At the narrowest point, her hips and midsection wouldn't budge, even after wiggling. The more she pushed, the more she was afraid she was wedging herself inside the crack, and she wouldn't be able to get out.

The thought brought a wave of anxiety as the surrounding stone pressed upon her. She imagined a shifting of the earth, grinding her flat over an excruciatingly long time, which only made her take deeper breaths. Each heavy exhale squeezed her lower chest until she could convince herself not to panic.

After she calmed herself and pulled up her shirt to give less friction, Pax worked on squirming forward. The tight space heated up with her breath, and sweat dripped from her forehead. Eventually the effort lubricated her stomach and she finally squeezed free of the crack.

The next hundred feet came with no more close calls, but the going was slow. She was most afraid that another narrow spot would force her to turn back and attempt that same section. She wasn't sure she could make the journey twice.

Eventually the way ahead shone with blinding light, suggesting she was nearing an exit. She thought briefly of attempting a shout, but decided against it until she could determine where she was at. The crack opened up into a lighted space that was still inside the pyramid. Once her eyes adjusted she could make out the interior of the tomb. Half the room was covered in water from which stone figures stuck up, heads barely above the surface, their features crisp as if they'd just been carved. It looked like whoever had been entombed had buried their treasures with them. There were painted vases and bronze spears on the dry, angled part of the room.

Her crack was about twenty feet above the water. Part of the wall beneath her had fallen in. She gathered that the water from this room was what made it to the place she'd fallen.

The tomb was at least a hundred feet in length, maybe sixty wide, with the majority of it underwater. The stone door on the far side, similar to the one outside with flame-kissed gold wings, was half under. Her spot was above the deepest end, and farthest from the door.

There was something else about the room that bothered her, though she couldn't put her finger on it. Her nose tickled as if she could smell the faint ozone of faez as if the air was alive with it. She almost expected to see sparks with each exhale.

Pax was looking for places to put her boots to climb down to the water when she saw the surface ripple with the suggestion of movement. She froze in the crack, half her body sticking out, as she waited for whatever it was to reveal itself.

Patiently staring down, she caught glistening scales briefly slide above the water before returning beneath. Her heart thrummed into gear.

Not only was she trapped in a tomb, but she was trapped with a creature, a very large creature by the glimpse she caught. If there was a time for Kali or Professor Cassius to find her, it was now.

Kali! I'm here!

Gripping the stone hard enough to tear the edge of her fingernails, Pax put every bit of her mental energy into that broadcast.

Kali! I'm here!

Kali! I'm here!

She settled against the stone crack, taking the weight off her arms when a response came through.

<Pax>

The voice came as a whisper. She wasn't entirely sure she'd heard it. It felt more like a tiny wet kiss on the end of her nose than her spoken name.

Who is this? I'm trapped in the tomb.

No answer came. Pax strained her thoughts, desperate to hear signs of someone else.

<Kali>

Pax furrowed her forehead, checking with the dark waters beneath her to make sure she wasn't hallucinating. But as she rolled that response over in her mind, she decided it felt like her companion.

Kali? You can talk?

Silence. Pax shifted her foot, knocking a pebble away from the wall, and it bounced into the water with an audible *bloop*. She held her breath as the scales surfaced again, speeding towards the location the stone had entered. She squeezed herself back into the crack desperately, ignoring the rough edges tearing at her arms and knees.

<Pax>

The voice was stronger this time, and Pax was distracted by the V-shaped line in the water, which told her she wasn't hallucinating. The disturbance on the surface dissipated as the creature shifted deeper. Judging by the angle of the room and the demolition of the water, the pool had to be at least ten feet at the deepest corner, maybe more.

<Kali talk>

The same wet nose kiss words returned, and Pax was ever more sure that it was her foxlike friend. They weren't words she was hearing, not spoken directly from Kali, but since she could project images and sounds into the minds of others, it was like taking edited clips of a TV show and using them for speech.

This is amazing, Kali. Where are you? I'm trapped in the tomb. There's something in here.

The words tumbled out of her mind. Pax had always assumed that Kali understood her by reading her emotions and intentions, and used that to define the message, but now she knew that she was actually hearing her words. The thought both excited and terrified her.

<door no>

While her companion had learned "speech," her execution was understandably lacking, but in this case, Pax understood what she meant.

You can't get through the door?

A few seconds later the scent of warm apple pie entered her mind, which was Kali's usual way of saying "yes."

Are Cassius and Lord Asphodel with you?

Another pause.

The description of Professor Cassius nearly made her snort. Only her precarious position left her squeezing her lips shut with her free hand.

<stern raven yes>

The second description checked out with Lord Asphodel. But on this mental image there were other, subtler intentions, too nuanced for Pax to make out.

Did you tell them I'm here?

<yes>

What did they say?

<open door>

I can't. Big snake in the water. You open door?

There was no response for a long time. Pax imagined there was a discussion on their end about the meaning of a big snake. Or maybe Lord Asphodel was aware of it and explaining how they might defeat it.

<no door Pax open>

Can't.

Pax added extra concern to her mental message, hoping to convey that she was stuck.

<Pax open>

She rested her forehead against the rough stone. The alternative was to head back through the crack, but the thought of remaining in those tight quarters for a few more hours while a quick and easy exit was within sight gave her stomach cramps.

Okay. I'm going to try to get to the door. But can you tell me anything about the snake before I try?

After a short time.

<snake bad>

Her eye roll was wasted on the stone wall.

Fine. Heading to door. Wish me luck.

The boulders beneath her provided a bridge to a shallower section of the tomb, provided her balance was excellent. While she no longer had the potion thrumming through her veins that helped with physical acuity, the months of training on the whirler and other contraptions had given her a sense of balance she never had before.

Her fingertips were raw from the journey through the crack, but she managed to find enough handholds to lower herself to the first boulder above the water, being careful to settle her weight slowly and not create the slightest ripples.

The first step was the hardest. She had to extend her right leg to a narrow stone a few feet out, and then pull her weight across the gap without creating turbulence. Blessed with long legs, Pax reached with her leg, gingerly setting the toe of her boot down before following with the heel. Straddling the gap, and so far not even making the stone tremor, Pax prepared to haul the rest of her body across.

The surface behind her bubbled.

She weighed the options of attempting a mad dash to the door, which would require wading through waist-deep water, or leaping back to the wall and climbing into her crack, but she knew the latter would mean that she'd lose her chance to escape. Neither option was palatable, but if she stayed still, the creature might spot her.

From the depths, a massive reptilian head surfaced facing the opposite direction. The head was as big as her midsection. It glided across the water, tongue flickering at the air. At this distance, if the snake turned, she'd only have a millisecond to react before it struck.

\<Pax\>

Can't talk.

For a moment, Pax thought the snake would turn its head, but then it disappeared beneath the surface of the dark waters, leaving her to silently sigh.

Willing her trembling legs to move again was a challenge, but she managed to pull herself to the other side of the boulders, which gave her a straight shot halfway across the room. She moved like a glacier, testing each placement of her foot as if she were disarming a bomb.

When she reached the end of the boulder path, she only had a thirty-foot section of water before she could reach dry tomb and the stone door.

Nearing door. Can I open?

The last thing she wanted was to reach the door with the giant snake on her heels only to find that she couldn't open it from her end, or that it required time or a magical spell.

<Pax yes>

Easy to open? Might not have time.

The answer took time.

<easy open>

Pax straightened from her crouch, only to hear the follow-up answer.

<no easy>

Easy or not easy? I need to know.

Standing on the final stone, surrounded by dark waters that hid a giant reptile, waiting for an answer was the longest minutes of her life. One minute. Two minutes. Time stretched past what she could reliably count.

Kali?

<door spell>

Pax balled her hands into fists. *You could have told me that before I left the safety of the wall.*

<sorry Pax>

The pathetic answer brought longing to curl up with her companion on the moss-covered floor of her room, forget about the favor for Lord Asphodel, which currently was doing a very good job of putting her life in danger.

Not you, Kali. I know you're just relaying a message. Mad at friendly hairless bear and stern raven.

An image of Pax on her back, hands and feet in the air, while Kali rubbed her belly nearly made her snort.

\<Pax\>

Yeah, Kali?

\<faez room\>

Yes. It's faint, but there's faez here.

\<temporal lock leave faez stern raven say make faez boom open door\>

Processing the jammed together string of messages took a moment, but she gathered what Lord Asphodel was trying to say eventually.

They want me to ignite the excess faez in the room to open the door?

\<yes\>

The ache in her stomach took another twist. She sent the picture of herself on her back, but with a big chocolate shake in her hand, which she sucked through a long straw. The return picture had Kali on her back next to Pax and also with a chocolate shake.

Deal.

Pax glanced back at the dark pool in the back of the tomb. She could explode the faez while crouched in the water, or run up to the door and trigger the explosion. It wasn't a lot of faez, so she wasn't worried that she would blow herself up, but such magical expenditures came with unforeseen consequences.

Okay. First I'm getting into the water, close to the door as I can, then I'll trigger the faez.

\<all kill snake\>

Yeah, yeah. Kill the snake. Let's get the door open first.

Pax lowered herself into the water slower than grass growing, worrying the whole time the giant snake could smell her through dark liquid. When it was up to her waist, her boots touched the stone floor, bumping against a long shaft. She pulled up a bronze spear before deciding against the flimsy weapon.

Crouching until only her arms were out of the water, Pax cast a simple fire element spell. The flame wavered across her hand before dousing itself with a steamy *ptthh.* Refocusing her effort, she cast it again, this time projecting the flame across the room, pouring as much faez as her meager ability could muster.

The flaming ball that arced across the room was barely a Roman candle, but it was enough to ignite the unspent faez, sending crackles of flame and electricity through the air. Pax dunked herself into the water as the wave blew over her, then immediately thrust herself above the surface and waded towards the door, hoping that it would open first try.

Pax wasn't even two steps before the dark pool at the back of the tomb exploded, the giant snake sliding over the rocks and boulders at a rapid pace directly at her like a spring-loaded scaly missile. There was no way she would make it to the door, so she hit the snake with a stun mark.

"*Shayut!*"

The miniature force wave hit the giant snake right between the eyes, stopping it momentarily as its hood extended out, and it shook its scaly head. In the brief pause, Pax waded through the last section of water, nearly falling when her toe clipped an underwater vase. She reached the door as a drippy mess, eyebrows slightly singed from the faez explosion, flinging it open as the giant snake sped towards her unprotected back.

Chapter Seventeen

The moment the doors swung wide, a splash of water directly behind Pax filled her ears. The shadow of the enormous creature flashed across the wall, while the muscles in her shoulders tensed for the impact.

She'd been too slow. Too slow to reach the door, and now the snake had her.

<duck>

Pax threw herself to the floor as Professor Cassius leapt over her, punching the snake in the jaw. The creature emitted an ear-splitting hiss, which forced Pax to throw her hands over the sides of her head.

The giant snake retreated to the middle of the tomb, curled over the boulders, and slapped its tail against the water. The gray-black hood pulsed with opening, and it displayed its anger with hissing fangs.

Lord Asphodel strode into the tomb, his blade singing from its sheath. The clear-eyed Gwyllion placed himself in direct opposition to the giant snake while the professor helped

Pax to her feet. The desire to throw her arms around Kali was tempered by the dangerous creature coiled for a strike.

"It can't be," said Lord Asphodel in anger and disgust, his lips rippling. "You're supposed to be dead."

The hooded snake flared up, showing a milky white underbelly, then to Pax's surprise and horror, extended leathery wings.

"Lord Asphodel," said Cassius with urgency as he held his hands out with the threat of a spell. "What is this creature?"

"Aepep."

It sounded like a name, rather than a nomenclature, which along with Lord Asphodel's surprise suggested a long history.

The standoff between them and the giant winged snake ended the moment Kali stepped between her and Professor Cassius. The winged creature had appeared appropriately defensive at the mutual threat, coiling across the boulders, ready to strike at a breath, but as her companion came into view the long, glistening body of Aepep rippled, hood stretched until it was a hateful moon, fangs excreting venom in anticipation.

When Kali went hunting for mice and other critters, Pax sometimes caught echoes of her mood, which usually involved a raid on the pantry for snacks. But the feeling she got from Kali as Aepep rose towards the ceiling for a strike was one of cornered terror. Memories of ancestral fear, the roles of hunter and hunted reversed as slithering scales stalked through the gilded halls of ancient palaces, left Pax feeling like she could see through time.

But her companion was made of sterner stuff, and even though the presence of the giant snake had hollowed out her thoughts, Kali stepped forward, lowering herself into a crouch, teeth bared in a growl.

Professor Cassius struck first, slapping his hands together.

"*Khoplat!*"

The mark hit Aepep as it surged, knocking it sideways, but not slowing its forward progress. The giant snake headed straight for Kali, but Lord Asphodel's arm blurred, and a spray of hot blood splashed across the wall. His triumphant sneer ended when the long tail of Aepep caught him in the midsection, tossing him across the room, and his blade disappeared into the water with a *bloop*.

The next few seconds of the fight was a stop-motion blur. Pax could do little more than avoid being smashed or bitten, while Cassius used successive marks to keep the giant snake at bay. Pax sensed that Kali was attempting to blind the snake, but the creature was resistant to her mind-altering effects.

A shaken Lord Asphodel stumbled out of the water, his fists balling and his handsome face stretching with a shout.

"Aepep!"

A fell energy emanated from Lord Asphodel. The scent of swamp lilies and bog cherries filled the room as he extended his arms, capturing the giant snake with a hidden force. The two were matched. "Get my sword." The tall fae shouted his instruction through gritted teeth.

Pax stumbled through the water, digging around for the weapon with her bare hands with the full understanding she could just as easily grab the supernaturally sharp blade and slice off a finger. She managed to bump the hilt with her boot, and she snatched the weapon out and held it between two shaking hands because she had no earthly idea how to wield a sword.

"Kill it! Moorlight will guide you," said Lord Asphodel, still locked in his invisible wrestling match with the giant winged snake.

True to his word, the blade made her hands tingle with the

expectation that it was guiding her, but she restrained herself.

"What is it? Why does it deserve to die?" she asked.

"There is no time, kill it," said Professor Cassius.

Even Kali willed her to wield the blade against the giant snake.

She hated the idea of killing a sentient creature, even if it'd tried to kill her. After all, they'd broached its hiding spot, and more so, she worried that if she gave in to the calls to kill, it would only encourage the Bad Thing that existed inside her. By staying true, she might find a way to fix her parents—and herself.

But the incredulous faces at her inaction, and the immediate threat of the enormous winged snake—one known by a fae lord—suggested that it was time to put aside her pacifist ways. This wasn't like the thrasher they'd accosted in the swamp, or even the nagazara who'd stolen the valuable amulet and wouldn't return it. This creature seemed to come from a bygone era, when monsters roamed the realms, and mages were sometimes worse than those they hunted.

Pax raised the blade above her head as she splashed through the water, a war cry on her lips.

But her brief hesitation had cost her her valuable advantage. Before she could reach the immobilized snake, Aepep broke free, and instead of striking out against one of them, it beat its leathery wings, knocking Pax out of the way as it propelled itself. She managed to swipe at the appendage, tearing the edge of the membrane, but not slowing the enormous supernatural creature as it fled the tomb.

Silence intruded, an after-hush in which contemplation of other results reigned. Shaking and soaked from head to toe, Pax let Lord Asphodel take the blade from her hands, his inscrutable mien leaving her unsure of his judgement.

"Why did you hesitate?" asked Professor Cassius, aghast

and dripping wet with disappointment. His jaw pulsed.

Pax didn't answer at first, as she threw her arms around a wet and pathetic looking Kali.

The leftover adrenaline and harsh recrimination brought forth an unexpected rage to her lips.

"I'm sorry, I didn't know I was an expert in using a fae sword. I guess that was a class I missed while Maxine was knocking the crap out of me on the whirler."

The expression of angered authority softened as Professor Cassius glanced at the room, the shattered vases, the blood splatters on the wall, then to Lord Asphodel.

"You're right," said Cassius, letting his anger release with a sigh. "This was no normal fight, not for a second year, not even for a professor I guess."

While the rest of them looked wrecked from the battle, Lord Asphodel somehow appeared ready to enter a tavern for a mug of ale.

"What was that? Aepep?" asked Professor Cassius.

"A legend," said Lord Asphodel, shaking his head as he slipped the blade back into his sheath. "I was probably incorrect in my assessment. It looked like a creature known in our history as Aepep."

On the dry portion of the tomb, Pax spied a clay-fired vase with a curious picture that drew her near. She reached out to the container, which showed a pictograph of an Egyptian cat stalking a winged snake, but as her fingers brushed it, the vase fell into pieces, leaving her unsure of what she'd seen.

"How did a giant snake even live in a place like this without food?" asked Professor Cassius.

"The temporal field in the room likely sustained it, though it appears that it was breaking down as the pyramid sunk into the swamp," said Lord Asphodel as he waded into the water towards the back of the room. "This is the final resting place of my ancestor, Lady Nymphaea, the last of our kind to rule an intact kingdom, not the watery doom that we currently inhabit."

The sadness, the barest shame, that inhabited Lord Asphodel's face was a glimpse into that fell fae that she knew she would not under any other circumstances see, and for her own safety, could never acknowledge. He erased it behind a stern façade, but she was eternally aware that he labored towards a future he knew was no longer possible.

At the front of the tomb, while Lord Asphodel searched through deeper waters, Professor Cassius quietly approached her.

"I'm sorry, Pax. This turned out to be much more dangerous than I thought. As your professor, and teacher, I have failed you," he said.

Pax wiped the water from her face. "You couldn't have known what was going to happen. Merlins tits in a wringer, even Lord Stern Raven didn't know about Aepep."

"Stern raven," said the professor with a chuckle.

"That's how Kali thinks of him," said Pax.

Professor Cassius crouched next to her foxlike companion. "Stern raven, eh? That's a good one. Whatdya think of me, mate?"

"Friendly hairless bear," said Pax, barely repressing a grin.

The professor slapped his knee and scratched Kali behind the ear.

"Not wrong. You're not wrong." He stood, putting his hands on his hips as he watched Lord Asphodel search. "When Kali entered the room, was it just me, or did Aepep react to her as if it knew her?"

The incrimination made it hard to meet his gaze, but she kept it, nodding slightly. "Not her, but maybe their kind have a history."

The professor glanced down at Kali, a question on his lips, but then a noise of self-congratulation drew them to Lord Asphodel, who was wading back towards them with something in his fist, his eyes alight with wonder.

When he reached them, he held out his hand, revealing a jeweled diadem with a sapphire at the center of the gold band.

"Diadem of the Scarab. I did not expect to find it, even though my heart hoped. It has long been lost," said Lord Asphodel. "Come, let us leave this place."

Outside the structure, the calm gray-blue sky was unchanged despite the events inside. But as they moved through the shallow waters, Pax noted the hthracks no longer dotted the vine-choked stone.

When they reached the portal, Lord Asphodel turned to them with a magnanimous smile on his lips and bowed deeply to her and then Kali, giving her foxlike companion an uncharacteristic wink.

"Your debt is paid," said Lord Asphodel, before sweeping away without further comment.

After he was gone, Professor Cassius frowned. "I feel like I'm missing something."

"That makes three of us," said Pax, though she wasn't quite sure she could speak for Kali in this case. "I feel a little used."

"Aye. Bloody hell, I do," said Professor Cassius.

"Where do you think Aepep went?" she asked.

"Not the slightest clue," said Professor Cassius. "But I'm sure that won't be the last time we hear about that creature." He patted her on the shoulder. "Come on. We've had a long day. Let's reflect on this adventure another time, because I'm hungry enough to eat a whole bison."

Her stomach rumbled in response to the thought of food. "Deal."

Chapter Eighteen

The "adventure in the swamp," as her friends came to call it, was told and retold dozens of times in the weeks after her visit to Caer Corsydd. Her close friends listened with a twinkle in their eyes, showing pride at her survival of such a brutal and awesome event. The older students listened to the story with a skeptical mien, their lips squeezing, barely restraining an eye roll at the action.

"The patron wouldn't let a second year go on such a hunt," said a few students.

Or she heard, "That's a great story, but what really happened?"

Of course, she left out a lot of personal details, like Kali's abilities and Aepep's recognition of her companion, even with her closest friends. She wasn't ready to admit that Kali was changing, in case they took those new abilities as a threat. Having Kali as a companion was like carrying an unstable bomb with her.

So when she told the story, she treated it like a regular

hunt, excluding the fantastical elements. So it wasn't a stretch for them to think that she might be exaggerating because most hunts were overprepared, planned to the last detail to reduce the danger to the hunter and hunted.

So as the weeks passed, she began to doubt the details of her own story. Not the broad strokes, but maybe Aepep wasn't as large as she remembered, or the crack she crawled as narrow. Even Professor Cassius treated her exactly the same as before, no knowing winks to the adventure they'd shared. Nor did he confirm what had happened when the other students asked him, only lifting a single shoulder, his expression saying, "Maybe so, maybe not." The only thing that changed was her and Kali's relationship, since her companion's discovery of using clipped pictures as a form of communication had opened her up to a whole new level of commentary that had only come across as vague feelings before.

But on a fine spring day in April, Pax had none of those thoughts as they waited for Professor Cassius to appear at the portal for a training session with the whirler. She was looking forward to her next attempts, because she was *this close* to making it through the whirler without getting knocked off. Everyone else in her small class had made it through at least once, leaving her the only outlier.

"Did we get the schedule wrong?" asked Janelle, who had her hair back in a ponytail as she shifted from foot to foot, the anticipation of training no longer a burden.

"I saw Professor FHB yesterday," said Jackson, using Cassius' new nickname, which meant Friendly Hairless Bear as he bent at the hip, leg extended in a pre-run stretch. Pax had let the nickname slip when she was telling the story, and had to take credit for it to hide Kali's new ability to communicate. "He said we were going to do a short training session then work on trapping a thrasher for tagging."

Pax was only halfway listening to the others as she crouched on her heels, picking burrs out of Kali's tail. After nine months of training, they no longer looked like college students but professional athletes getting ready for a high-stakes match. She'd never been much for fitness, but the general well-being she'd gained was a nice bonus, even if it came with a lot of sore muscles and awful-tasting potions.

"Where's JY?" asked Bryanna, forehead furrowing as she sat in the dirt, legs extended as she stretched her quads.

Everyone looked to Liam, who shrugged. "I haven't seen him since Saturday, but that's not unusual. He disappears sometimes for a couple of days. Probably his checkups at Golden Willow."

"Something's wrong," said Janelle, shaking her head. "No professor, no Maxine, and no JY."

When Professor Ansel pushed through the foliage, no one was surprised, and everyone climbed to their feet, except Pax, who was about to pull out her belt knife to cut out a particularly troublesome burr from Kali's fur.

"Is the professor okay?" asked Janelle, eyes rounded.

Professor Ansel tugged on the front of his white coat. "Cassius is fine, but I'm afraid Maxine is in Golden Willow. She was in the seventh ward when she got attacked."

"What?" asked Liam. "Was it the Mangler? Is she okay?"

The others questioned Professor Ansel, crowding around until he held up his hands.

"Maxine is...stable, but unconscious. Look, I don't know much more than that. I just came by to tell you that class is canceled today," he said.

"But where's Professor FHB...I mean Cassius," said Jackson, receiving a raised eyebrow from Professor Ansel.

"I believe he went to the seventh ward to see if he could track down the creature, but he made it explicitly clear that no students should be attempting to find the creature themselves. Maxine is an experienced fifth year. If she had trouble, then no second years should be getting involved. Is that clear?" asked Professor Ansel to a round of nods.

After he left, Liam spread his arms as he addressed them. "We're headed to the seventh ward, right?"

"Uhm, are you crazy? Cassius will be there, so it's not like we can go sneaking around without getting caught," said Janelle.

"Damn," said Liam, punching his fist into his other hand. "You're right."

"We should go visit Maxine," said Pax, bringing everyone's head around. "So what? We don't get along. I still don't want her to be hurt." Pax glanced sideways. "Plus, we can learn something from her injuries, and if she wakes up, maybe more."

After a short trip through the city, the five of them—minus Kali since she wasn't allowed in the hospital—entered Golden Willow. The nurse attendant wasn't going to let all of them visit Maxine until she recognized Janelle.

"They're your charges," said the nurse with a smile. "Keep 'em in control."

"Thanks, Amber," said Janelle as she led them to Maxine's room. "We won't be too long."

"They sure do like you here," said Liam.

"I try," said Janelle with curtsey and a wink. "But mostly they're just glad to have the extra help."

While Janelle usually played off her excellence, Pax knew better. Her friend was easily the best student of their year, driven by her older brother's death.

The room barely fit the five of them, crowding around Maxine's bed. The fifth year was hooked to a mess of tubes and wires, machines patiently beeping at a serene pace. Janelle interpreted the chart at the end of the bed for the rest of them.

"Burns on her right arm, head contusion, and a large bite to her midsection," said Janelle, frowning at the information on the sheet. "It says she's been unconscious since she was discovered. There are toxins in her bloodstream, but there's no results from the lab."

"How long does that take?" asked Jackson.

Janelle lifted a shoulder. "Days. Weeks. And then no guarantees that they'll learn anything unless it's a common venom or poison. They're not equipped for the strange supernatural critters we're used to dealing with."

"Great," said Liam, putting a hand to his forehead. "We're still no closer to figuring out what this creature is."

Pax dug into the bag underneath the only chair in the room, pulling out a pair of high-top sneakers. She picked out sawdust from the treads and held it up for her friends.

"She was somewhere they were doing construction," said Pax.

"That could be anywhere in the seventh," said Jackson. "There are always people moving in and out, rehabbing the old houses, or the ones trashed by the kids living near the bars."

Pax sniffed the sawdust, catching a brief scent that she couldn't quite identify. It was familiar, but not enough to trigger a direct memory.

"Where did they find her?" asked Bryanna.

"Good question," said Janelle. "Let me go ask, it's not on the chart."

A minute later she returned with the explanation. Maxine had been found in the seventh ward near the canals. Invictus PD found her wandering down the sidewalk, delirious and bleeding profusely, with burn marks across her clothes.

"She has singe marks on her hair," said Bryanna, touching the crispy edges. "That doesn't sound like our creature unless she blew herself up."

"That's not Maxine," said Pax. "She's tough and smart. Better mage than I am, but that's not saying much."

"All signs point to the creature living in the canals," said Jackson.

"There's too many people there," said Janelle. "They would have seen something big enough and nasty enough to take on Maxine."

"We're going to investigate this, right?" asked Liam.

"Of course," said Janelle. "But not today when the professor is there. We'll pick our spots, but carefully."

After they agreed to continue their investigation into the creature, despite the warning not to, the rest of the group headed back to Animalians, minus Pax and Janelle, who wanted to ask a few more questions of the nurse. On the way out, after learning nothing new, they ran into Jae-Yong in the elevator.

His right arm was wrapped with a bandage and he had a gray pallor, and most certainly, he did not look excited to see them.

"Hey," said Jae-Yong, tilting his head. "Why are you here? I didn't think you worked today."

"You haven't heard? Maxine got attacked by the creature in the seventh ward," said Janelle.

"Oh shit, that's terrible," said Jae-Yong, glancing at his shoes.

"What happened to your arm?" asked Pax.

Jae-Yong blushed, gesturing at the bandages. "Check-ups. I get these weird rashes at times from, you know. They kept me through the weekend for observation."

"Sure, sure," said Pax. "Wanna head back with us?"

Jae-Yong's eyes widened before squeezing shut. "Oh, crap. I just remembered, I forgot something up at the, anyway, you know."

He stepped out of the elevator, gave them a sheepish wave. "I'll see you back at the Arena."

After the door closed, Pax and Janelle shared a look.

"That was strange," said Pax.

"Too strange," responded Janelle, looking like she'd smelled a skunk. "Did you catch the hint of burning on him?"

"No," said Pax. "But why was his arm bandaged? He hasn't had rashes before."

When they got out of the elevator, Janelle led them to a computer station, navigating through the system until she pulled up the entry and exit times for patients. She jabbed her finger onto the screen when his information appeared.

"Bullshit," said Janelle. "He wasn't at Golden Willow all weekend. He came in this morning. Something ain't right."

Pax's stomach roiled with the implications. "You said he was on the danger ward, the one for transformations and stuff."

"Yeah?"

Pax shifted her mouth to the side. "What if he turns into something occasionally? A lycanthrope of some kind. What if he's the one killing people? That would explain why Maxine's hair and skin was burnt. JY's pretty good with fire magic. Hunting a creature is one thing, hunting a mage is a completely different challenge."

Janelle looked like she was going to be sick. "Oh, no. You're not wrong. But I just hate to think that."

"There could be other explanations, but this is one possibility. Should we tell the others? Liam?" asked Pax.

"No," said Janelle, shaking her head. "I don't think it's JY. Why always in the seventh ward? What about the bite marks? Transformations aren't usually that quick and simple. Even lycanthropes take days to recover. It's not like they just transform in the blink of an eye."

"I'll take your word for it. We won't tell Liam then," said Pax.

"But we'll keep an eye on JY. Just to be sure," said Janelle.

"Just to be sure," repeated Pax, even though she didn't feel sure.

Chapter Nineteen

A week later, classes with the professor resumed, but with a different fifth year, Darren Akio, who was ill-prepared to be Professor Cassius' assistant. He had no plans to be a hunter, focusing on trap design and general research, which left a lot to be desired in instruction.

The hunt for a thrasher to trap ended in failure, as Darren kept sneezing from the damp swamp air, and the professor, who seemed continuously distracted, either by Darren's ineptitude, or his failures at catching the creature in the seventh ward, kept letting loose a litany of curses every time their target got away.

"Let's call it a day," said a thoroughly dejected Professor Cassius. His eyes had dark circles. "Bloody well couldn't get any worse."

They marched back to the portal with Darren apologizing every hundred yards.

"Not your fault, Darren, I'm a shit professor today," said the professor at the final apology back in the Arena. The fifth year hung his head as he left the portal tree to head to his room on the upper floor.

"Any luck finding the creature?" asked Janelle hopefully as Professor Cassius threw the moss-covered snare ropes onto the ground for disassembly.

"Slippery as a crocodile dunked in butter," said the professor, crossing his enormous arms. "The city is making it too damn hard to hunt. I can't lay any of the usual traps, my cameras get fried by the privacy charms people use, and now that they're calling the creature the Canal Killer, everyone's jumping at shadows and the report line at Invictus PD sounds like a D-movie creature feature list."

"We could help," said Pax.

Professor Cassius shifted his mouth to the side. "I'm sorry. Patron Adele forbade any more students from investigating the creature. She threatened to kick me out if I allowed any more of you to get hurt."

"But you didn't get Maxine hurt, she did that on her own," said Liam.

"Not true, lad. I gave her permission to hunt the creature, thinking she was up to the challenge. But I'm thinking whatever it is, is more dangerous than I first thought," said the professor.

"What do you think it is?" asked Pax as she brushed grass from Kali's back.

The professor inhaled deeply, his mouth shifting to the side. "I can't say."

His eyes shot up, and Kali tensed under her hand. A flash of glistening black sliding into dark waters briefly intruded into her mind, followed by the acrid taste of shame. The flashed image was clearly from the professor. Kali hunched her little shoulders in apology.

That was HFB?

"Or don't know really, but it doesn't matter because none of you are stepping foot into the seventh ward," he continued.

"Not even to have an innocent drink at the Drunken Imp?" said Bryanna brightly.

"*Especially* not there," said Professor Cassius. "I'd rather drink from a swamp rat bathing pool than the Drunken Imp. But either way, no seventh ward, not even a toe." He shifted his mouth to the side as thoughts passed across his gaze. He gestured towards the gear. "Be a cobber, would ya? I need to go check on something."

After he left, Pax volunteered to take the bait back to the Menagerie with Janelle. Everyone was glad to let her do it, since it stunk like dead fish.

As soon as they were away from the others, she said, "He knows something about the creature he's not telling."

"How do you know?"

Pax gestured towards Kali, who sat on her haunches and looked up at Janelle. There was an air of embarrassment from the foxlike creature.

"Kali? She can read minds?" asked Janelle, mouth agape.

"This is new for me too, but I guess she got a glimpse," said Pax.

<Kali sorry>

When Janelle's eyes became the size of moons, Pax knew the message had been sent to both of them.

"Wh-what? She can talk?" asked Janelle.

"Yeah," said Pax sheepishly. "More like using cutout pictures for words, but it works the same. She figured out how to do it when I was stuck in the tomb."

<Kali afraid Pax>

The foxlike creature looked up with wide, expressive eyes.

"I get that," said Janelle. "So, it's not just talking, but also reading minds?"

<strong emotion picture>

"You can see something if there's a strong reaction?" asked Janelle.

Kali nodded her furry head.

"Whoa, that's crazy powerful," said Janelle, cupping her chin in her hand. "Anyone else know?"

"You're the first, maybe only," said Pax, feeling a little dizzy as she spoke. "Well, the professor knows. But I don't want anyone else to, in case they worry about her."

Janelle crouched in front of Kali and placed her hand on the foxlike creature's shoulder.

"You don't have to worry about me," said Janelle straight to Kali. "I know you're good, just like I knew Logan was a piece of shit and Pax was getting screwed over."

"You're the best, Janelle," said Pax. Her stomach twisted with worry that her best friend was wrong, but she wasn't about to argue.

"You're damn right I am." Janelle stood. "So what did you see?"

The image returned to Pax's mind: a flash of glistening black sliding into dark waters, followed by the acrid taste of shame. Janelle spit on the concrete pathway afterwards.

"Was that Caer Corsydd?" asked Janelle.

"Felt that way," said Pax. "I think the professor still carries his failure for Lord Asphodel with him."

Janelle strolled away momentarily. "I get that. It's hard to shake the past sometimes." When her friend looked back, Pax could see the force that was her brother's death in her life. "Sometimes I don't feel like myself, but a collection of mistakes masquerading as a person."

"I wish he'd let us help," said Pax.

"I thought you were all done with adventure after the fun

in the tomb?" asked Janelle.

"Bull in a china shop," said Pax, gesturing towards herself. "Remember?"

"Or you really are a good person," said Janelle, giving her a sassy headshake.

"Rumors only. When you dig down deep there's only nomenclature," said Pax with a self-satisfied snort.

"*Bovem sina pax.*" Janelle screwed up her face. "Pax. Kinda hilarious that your parents named you peace."

"You're not the first to make that joke," said Pax, resuming the walk to the Menagerie.

"What are we going to do about the professor's vision?" asked Janelle.

Pax stuttered to a stop. "We should go to the seventh. Me, you, Liam, and Kali. I don't want to get the others in trouble."

"But we're fair game," said Janelle with a laugh. "I'm in, but when?"

Pax tapped on her chin. "We need to find out when the professor won't be on the hunt, so there's no chance of running into him. And we should be more prepared. Just wandering around the ward like last time isn't going to do anything."

"I can work on that. So first chance we get, when HFB is busy," said Janelle with a head nod.

"Deal. The hunt resumes."

"For Maxine," said Janelle with an eyebrow raised.

Pax paused. "For Maxine *and* for the professor."

Chapter Twenty

Pax was alone at the Bantu Queen memorizing niche spells from their *Hunter's Tricks and Traps* tome, feet up on the bench, while Kali lay on the floor under the table. A few other students had been in and out during the day, but otherwise it'd been quiet. She barely even saw Dane, who'd been reading a romance novel behind the bar until he disappeared upstairs for a nap.

When Liam strolled into the Bantu Queen, eyes searching, she knew he was looking for her. The rolled-up sleeves on his khaki shirt made him look like he'd just come from a long hike, even though he smelled as fresh as summer rain.

"Hey Pax," said Liam, gesturing towards the spot across from her. "Can I join you?"

The eagerness of his expression made her stomach flip.

"Sure, but watch out for Kali," she said, pulling her feet to the floor.

"Hey you," he said, crouching down to pet her companion as Kali's tail thumped against the wood.

"What's up, Liam? This doesn't look like an accidental visit," said Pax with her eyebrows raised.

"I, uhm, yeah. I wanted to talk to you and Janelle both, but it's been so hard to find you two not at the Arena," said Liam, green eyes flashing.

"Us both? So this isn't another attempt at us dating?" asked Pax.

He bit his lower lip, then gave her a carefree grin. "Only if I still have a shot." Liam threw his hands out right away. "I'm just kidding. I get it. I hear you. You're not interested. I'm trying to do a better job of listening, of being an adult."

"That's good to hear," said Pax. "So what's this about?"

Liam scooted forward, inclined his head, and lowered his voice. "It's JY. He's been weird lately. I think you've noticed he's missed class more than a few times due to his checkups. Do you think there's anything wrong? Should I be worried as his roommate?"

If Pax hadn't known Jae-Yong's lies about being in Golden Willow, she might have thought this was an underhanded ploy to subvert her flirting with his roommate. It was Pax's turn to bite her lip. "Yeah, actually. Well, I don't know if you should be worried, but you should keep an eye on him."

Pax explained what they'd found at Golden Willow after the visit to Maxine. Liam slapped his hand against the table.

"I can't believe you didn't tell me already. I thought we weren't keeping secrets," said Liam, face flushed.

"It wasn't that we were keeping secrets, but we decided it was most likely *not* JY who was the Canal Killer, and we didn't want to worry you," said Pax, cringing as she told the story.

"Not the Canal Killer? I wasn't even thinking about that," said Liam as he looked out the bay window at the busy street. "Why would you think he could be?"

After she explained her reasoning, Liam just looked at the

ceiling. "Aww, shit. That could totally be the case."

"I don't know, or don't think so. It doesn't all line up. And I can't imagine that the patron would allow a dangerous therianthropic student to be in the mix. It has to be a coincidence." Pax tapped on the table. "But yeah, I can see now that we should have told you."

"No, I understand. I still feel like such an asshole from last year," said Liam, sitting back in the bench.

"How's your mom doing? No more trouble with the criminal elements?" asked Pax.

"Everything's fine. Between our misadventure and whatever the patron did afterwards, there hasn't been a peep. I should have brought it up sooner," he said, looking her straight in the eyes.

Pax could only meet his gaze for a few seconds before looking away to the street outside the window. Two men walked by pushing a stroller. An airplane droned overhead.

"What should I do about JY?" asked Liam.

Pax lifted her shoulders. "Keep an eye on him? Knowing what you know now you should be able to tell if something's happening. Even just knowing when he's coming and going might help us. You know, if he's away from the room during one of the killings, then we should suspect him."

Liam ran his fingers through his lush brown hair. "I can't believe I could be rooming with the Canal Killer."

"Allegedly," said Pax, then realizing how bad that sounded added, "and only possibly, but probably not really. Okay?"

Liam puffed up his cheeks and blew out a big breath. "Yeah, allegedly. I thought you'd tell me not to worry about anything, it's all in my head, that sort of thing. Not, you know, the killer is in the house, or in the room in this case."

Pax batted her eyes at Liam. "You should know by now that everything I touch becomes infinitely more complicated."

He reached out as if he were going to touch her hand, but quickly pulled it back into his lap.

"I should get back to campus. I'm doing a shift at the Barn helping Vlad with the monoceros," he said.

"Unicorns," said Pax with a grin. "Or stabby horses, if you prefer."

Liam chuckled as he rose to his feet. "You're weird, Pax. An awesome kind of weird, but weird. Never change."

After Liam left, it was Pax's turn to blow out her cheeks. "That's what I'm afraid of."

Chapter Twenty-One

Finding a night when Professor Cassius wasn't in the seventh ward proved nearly impossible because he was *always* in the ward. It was nearly the end of April, and Pax worried that they'd never get a shot, but then Patron Adele returned from a trip, and all the professors were meeting during a Tuesday evening.

Janelle had rented a storage locker in the seventh because they didn't want to be seen carrying gear out of the Arena, inciting questions they didn't want to answer. They got looks from the other customers as they strapped knives to their hips and threw enchanted nylon ropes into backpacks.

"I'm more nervous about this than I was going into the pyramid," said Pax, tightening the buckles on her backpack as they stepped outside onto the sidewalk. The descending sun reflected on the tip of the Spire, setting the clouds to glow with pinks and purples. A woman walking a Labrador moved to the far edge when she noticed the unleashed Kali, who was bigger than the dog by a few pounds.

"Death is always easier to face than disappointing those you look up to," said Liam.

The comment brought stares from both Pax and Janelle. He rolled his eyes.

"Okay, a little dark," said Liam as he fished into his backpack, pulling out three bracelets. "One for each of us. In case we get split up. They work like the kids hot-cold game. When they get nearer, they get hot, away, they get cold. Just squeeze the circular section to turn it on and off. If someone triggers theirs, it turns all three on."

"Awesome," said Janelle as she handed them each a pair of sunglasses. "Put these on."

"I know we're cool," said Liam, "but it's going to be hard to find the Canal Killer if we can't see anything."

"Just put them on, you big oaf," said Janelle as she slid her pair over her ears.

"No fair," said Pax as she examined hers. "This style makes me look like a bug. You look great in them."

"Next time you enchant the glasses and you can pick the style," said Janelle as the corner of her lips twitched.

Curious, Pax slipped hers on, recoiling the instant she saw the colored mists floating in the air along the sidewalk, a particularly thick dark green cloud trailing after the Labrador that had passed.

"Pheromones," said Janelle, before Pax could ask. "They look for non-human pheromones."

"Wow, that's crazy," said Pax as she craned her head in both directions, examining the myriad of trails on the sidewalk. "It looks like a jungle here, but I only see people and that dog that just passed."

Janelle bit her lower lip. "It's not perfect. The spell is trickier than I'm used to, but it works."

"This is amazing, where'd you get the idea?" asked Liam.

"Professor Cassius," laughed Janelle. "I saw him walking around campus in shades the other night and when I asked him, he told me what they were for. He was testing them out. It's a spell that Pietra taught him from the Phoenix Corporation. I called her a few nights ago and asked if I could have a copy, explaining it was for a project with the professor."

"Awesome work. What did you bring, Pax?" asked Liam, bumping her with his shoulder playfully.

"My willingness to do stupid things, oh, and Kali, of course." Pax shifted her mouth to the side. "Which reminds me. Kali, can you do the thing for Liam?"

The handsome second year tilted his head at the foxlike creature, and within a second, his eyes widened. "Was that you, Kali?"

She nodded her furry head.

Squinting, Liam stared at Pax. "When did this happen?"

Pax gave him the brief rundown about the pyramid. "But don't tell anyone else. The professor knows, and you two."

"And Lord Stern Raven," said Liam, shaking his head. "Now I know where those nicknames come from."

"Alright," said Janelle, clapping her hands. "The plan is to wander the seventh ward. I figure we can stay within sight. Trigger your bracelet if you see something important."

The three of them split up, with Pax and Kali going to the other side of the street. They avoided the Canal district since the place was packed, and it was unlikely the creature would be on the prowl.

Kali stayed by her side as they strolled along the sidewalk, keeping their heads on a swivel. They generally enjoyed a wide berth, as her foxlike companion created subtle, but confused stares. Even without her mind-reading ability, Pax knew they were trying to figure out what kind of fox she was.

Notice anything?

Pax didn't quite understand until Kali projected an image of a foaming mug of beer in her mind. She must have been reading the happy hour crowd.

Yeah, funny liquid, though it doesn't always make you funny.

<humans strange>

Pax was about to respond that calliduses were strange too, but Kali was the only one of her kind, at least that they she knew of.

Do you remember your parents? Anything before we met?

<Kali small hurt Pax love>

Love you too, little one, and yes you were small when I found you.

It'd been a while since she'd thought about those early years. While she couldn't remember the exact moment Kali came into her life, she could recall the black-and-silver furry ball that could fit in her two hands and licked her chin for all she was worth every time she moved her face close. It was love at first sight. Pax remembered lying in bed with Kali curled against her stomach as she caressed the pink beans on her paws. It was a time of such bliss and content, while a sea of rage roared around her. Kali made her parents bearable, a sanctuary against the shouting, the insults, the constant verbal attacks.

She couldn't imagine what her life would be like without Kali. Even Baba for all her interventions could not stop her parents from harming her. Years later, Baba had admitted she'd tried to get custody, but her status as a citizen made it difficult, and the courts had sided with her parents.

I wish I had different parents, and you didn't have any at all.

<Pax parent>

The comment brought Pax to a crouch before her furry friend. She stroked Kali's fur, a warm smile on her lips.

"Thanks, Kali. Maybe we were parents for each other. Us against the world, right?"

Kali pressed her head against Pax's chest, and she would have stayed in that position forever except she caught a glimpse of a strange creature on a leash down a side street.

Sensing her distress, Kali pulled away, pointing herself in the direction of the creature. Pax triggered the bracelet, motioning in the direction of the alley before setting off after. Janelle and Liam headed on an intercept path, while Pax and Kali came up from behind.

The alley had water-filled grooves in the asphalt from the heavy garbage trucks. It'd rained the day before and the storm had moved northeast along the coast. They hurried to the corner, peering around to see the rumpled rear of the creature. The guy holding the leash wore a black leather jacket and walked with the easy confidence of someone who never had to worry about their safety.

What if the creature is someone's pet?

<strange hound>

From their angle, it was hard to tell what kind of creature it was on the leash. She needed a better look to decipher if it was capable of the damage that had been found on the bodies.

At the next block, the man pounded his fist on a door heading into a three-story brownstone with restoration scaffolding on the back. As they waited for someone to answer, Pax got a good look at the creature, which she recognized as a kretch hound. They weren't a hound at all, rather a mammal-like equivalent from a nearby realm. A kretch hound had vicious teeth and a trainable disposition. They were the go-to guard creature of the otherworldly criminal set.

<bad hound>

"Yeah," whispered Pax. "That's a problem."

Before the man went into the house, he glanced down the street. Pax barely pulled behind the corner in time to avoid being seen.

Once the man went inside, Pax and Kali slunk down the alleyway, keeping to the wall in case anyone was looking out a window.

When she was half a block away, she pulled out her cell phone and texted the description of the house to her friends, and the presence of the hound.

[Canal Killer?] came back the reply.

[maybe?]

It was certainly plausible. A kretch hound could do serious damage. Had it gotten off leash, or was there another connection between the victims that she hadn't quite yet discovered?

Nearing the corner of the house, she spied a lump of wet sawdust. The house was under renovation, as were a number of houses in the neighborhood. This could have been the area that Maxine had been investigating, and the burn marks could have come from a human.

Anyone near the back door?

<no>

Pax tested the handle, finding it open. She pushed it slowly, expecting a squeaky hinge, letting out a sigh when it opened smoothly. The interior of the building had been gutted. Sawhorses and stacks of wood were everywhere.

Beyond an interior wall came muffled voices. Someone was not happy, but she was too far away to hear. Pax wished she had one of those potions Cassius had given her before they went into the pyramid.

Can you keep us safe from the hound?

How many in house?

<two floor one up>

The man probably expected the kretch hound to detect anyone sneaking up on them, which might give her the opportunity to move closer to hear. If she could learn anything that would indicate this was the Canal Killer, she'd get the hell out and follow him to a safer location before contacting the professor.

With Kali at her side, they crept deeper into the building, staying alert for a stray squeaky board.

"Look, if you can't take this kind of supply, I've got five others who'll pay me top dollar," said a voice who she assumed was the man she'd followed.

"Bullshit," said another man in a heavy accent. "You liar. My price is good, I check."

A chill went down her spine as she thought about what she was getting involved with. It sounded like a drug deal, which meant they both probably had guns.

Let's get out of here. Men bad.

<yes>

She'd barely lifted a foot when the stairs squeaked, sending her into a panic. Whoever was on the second floor was coming down.

"...someone in the..."

Before Pax could make it to the back door, a dark-skinned man in a black T-shirt slid around the corner with a gun trained on her.

"Do not move a muscle or I will spray your brains across the wall," he said.

From the other side of the interior wall, the man with the kretch hound approached, while a blonde woman with a data pad in her hand gestured above Pax, where a camera was located.

"I don't know who the fuck you are, but you shouldn't have come here," said the woman severely.

The kretch hound bared its teeth, but stayed at the man's hip.

"I'm in the wrong house," said Pax, holding her hands up. "I thought this was my friend's place."

"Don't lie to me, girl," said the blonde woman. "I saw you sneaking in the door, expecting not to be noticed."

The man with the hound leaned back around the interior wall. "Do we kill her?"

The dark-skinned man was frowning at Kali. "What the fuck is that thing?"

When he trained the gun on Kali, the other two focused their attention on what they probably thought was a giant fox.

Now!

The man with the gun shifted his head to the side as if he were nodding away a buzzing insect. Pax stepped to the side, right as the wall exploded from a gunshot, spraying her shoulder with brick shards.

"*Shayut!*"

The mark dazed both the man and the kretch hound.

The blonde woman didn't hesitate. A massive pistol appeared in her fist. Pax knew she was too late to stop her, and Kali was busy with the first man.

"*Khoplat!*"

"*Khoplat!*"

The twin slams threw the woman across the sawdust-covered floor, blood leaking from her forehead.

Janelle and Liam appeared around the corner, but Pax yelled, "Run!" as the dark-skinned man fired his weapon randomly as he shouted.

Pax and Kali fled out the back door. She nearly fell as she hit the uneven asphalt. They made it to the next set of buildings before she heard a growl from behind.

The kretch hound bounded towards them, slaver on its muzzle. It looked like an enormous pug made of mottled pink flesh with a set of oversized canines in its mouth. The man with the gun had stumbled from the building.

Kali couldn't stop both the kretch hound and the man with the gun, and her friends had fled out the front of the building, leaving her vulnerable. Pax couldn't even use her marks because Kali had positioned herself in front, to protect her from the hound.

There was little she could do to stop the man from putting a hole in her chest from thirty feet away, so she was confused when his eyes widened and a tumbling ball of flame arced over her shoulder, slamming into the brick wall, forcing him to dive out of the way.

A blur went past Pax. Professor Cassius crashed into the kretch hound like a charging rhino, throwing the creature across the street to slam into a rusted blue dumpster. Before the guy could get back on his feet, the professor kicked away his gun, and with one punch knocked him out.

"Come on," he said as he fled back in her direction.

She followed him for a dozen blocks. When they finally stopped no one was on their trail.

Pax caught her breath while Professor Cassius stared at her, nostrils flaring.

"I messed up."

"You more than messed up. You and the other two. Send them a message, tell them to meet us here," he said with his enormous arms crossed over his chest.

When Janelle and Liam rounded the corner, their expressions of relief turned to disappointment. Liam looked like he was going to be sick.

"What were my instructions about the seventh ward?"

Professor Cassius asked them as they crowded together for safety. Even Kali pressed against her leg in solidarity.

"Not to come here," said Pax, eventually.

"You three are either too insolent to take instruction or too stupid to understand them. Which is it?" asked the professor. "You're second years. Wet behind the ear second years. Thankfully you just stuck your nose into a run-of-the-mill drug deal. Coming face-to-face with our creature friend could have turned out much worse."

"Couldn't it be the kretch hound?" asked Pax, regretting opening her mouth by the weaponized eye roll that he gave her.

"I assure you that it is not a kretch hound. I'm fairly certain I know what's going on, but I can't figure how he—" The professor remembered they were standing before him. "But none of that is a concern for you since you're not supposed to be in the seventh ward!"

His volume rose, leaving nearby pedestrians to either take a wide berth around them or turn the other way in fear.

"I cannot even begin to express the depths of my disappointment in the three of you. Do you not realize how lucky you are to even be in Animalians after last year's shit show? Arse over tit. Patron Adele is going to fire me and then she's going to kick the lot of you out," said the professor as he paced. "What did you think you were going to accomplish?"

Pax forced herself to meet the professor's withering gaze, but had to look away after only a second.

"We're trying to be hunters," said Liam.

"Trying to be is the right way to put it. I'm trying to be a fucking runway model, but you see where that's gotten me," said the professor.

He rubbed his jaw as he contemplated what he was going to say next. He extended his finger directly at Pax.

"I don't think you know if you should even be in this hall.

Your failure to take instruction is worse than a hungry croc in a kiddy pool. Every single one of my training sessions with the both of you was a complete and utter failure. I'm beginning to wonder if that was on purpose," said the professor as he glared at Kali.

Pax stepped in front of her companion. "That's not her fault. It was my decision."

"I'm beginning to wonder if you know the difference," he said. "Or have you forgotten that I had two tasks this year regarding your companion."

A cold chill went down Pax's spine. She'd leave the university before she let the professor do anything to Kali. There was a brief moment that she thought the professor was going to make a grab at Kali, but he closed his eyes instead, taking a deep breath.

"This is my final instruction to the three of you. Return to campus. Do not for any reason leave the campus, except by my explicit permission. That will be your home for the rest of the semester. I'll be installing a tracker on your phones just to make sure you're not disobeying me, and if you cannot follow my instructions, then it'll be the streets for the lot of ya. While it would be a shame to lose three promising students, there's no use if you're just going to get yourselves killed."

When Pax hesitated, the professor said, "Go. Back to the campus. Now."

As they walked away, Janelle looked up, eyes rounded, and said, "We're very sorry, professor."

"Then listen for once," said the professor.

The whole way back to the campus, Pax wanted to scream in frustration. She couldn't decide if she was mad at herself for getting caught, or mad that she couldn't listen. There was a brief moment when she wondered if the professor was right about Kali, but quickly dismissed it. Kali was her best friend.

Nothing would come between them. Not even the university.

As they trudged back to the Arena from the train station, Liam said, "Man, we screwed up."

"No, I screwed up. It's my fault for getting you two involved," said Pax.

"No," said Janelle, shaking her head. "No. I came willingly. It's on all of us."

Liam nodded. "I have no regrets. If we hadn't been there, they would have killed you."

Pax put a hand to her forehead. "Maybe I'm just not that great of a mage. I keep screwing up over and over."

"You survived the giant snake in the pyramid, and helped get me out of a jam last year," said Liam. "You don't get points for style, only surviving."

"Face it, Pax," said Janelle, putting a hand on her shoulder. "You're stuck with us. And I truly mean stuck with us, since we can't leave campus."

"Yeah," said Pax, glancing at Kali. "But that's not what I'm worried about."

<Pax love>

I won't let him hurt you.

Janelle and Liam shared a glance, but said nothing. If they had thoughts about Kali, they weren't sharing.

Chapter Twenty-Two

In the weeks trapped on campus, Pax relished their visits to Caer Corsydd, even if she couldn't pass the whirler without getting knocked off. The bruises became a map of her failures, which she recited on the mornings before.

"Don't worry," said Janelle as they waited outside the portal tree. "You'll get it eventually."

"I'm the only one from our year who hasn't passed the whirler. Bryanna was last back in January," said Pax as she adjusted her running shoes.

There was no further discussion when Professor Cassius appeared, rather than Darren Akio, their substitute fifth year. Cassius was no longer the jovial teacher. The events in the seventh ward and his failure to catch the Canal Killer weighed on him, especially since two more people had been killed, their half-eaten bodies discovered near the canal district.

They entered the portal without comment, falling into a brisk run that pushed them to keep up. By the time they reached the training area, everyone was soaked with sweat.

"This should be fun," said Liam with an eye roll.

"Come on," said the professor grimly. "There's no time to rest on a hunt. This isn't preschool. I've seen one-legged crocs move faster than you blokes."

Bryanna raised her hand tentatively. "No potions today?"

"You won't always be able to rely on alchemy to save you," said the professor.

Since there were only six second years, there was little time to rest between attempts. On Pax's first shot at the whirler, she made it three steps before the spinner took her out at the knees, and she landed hard on the grass.

"Up and at 'em, Miss Nygard," said the professor. "You can sleep when you're dead."

The strained relationship left Pax with a hole in her gut as she climbed to her feet. The professor's good-natured demeanor being replaced by something she'd expect from Professor Vladimir felt like betrayal, echoes of her experiences with her parents.

While the rest of the class struggled to make it through the contraptions consistently, they did manage to pass, even if it was less frequently than previous training sessions. Pax, on the other hand, never made it past the first obstacle.

Back in line and rubbing her arm, Pax hung her head.

"You're too tense," said Janelle, looking on with sympathy.

"I know," said Pax. "But I can feel how mad he is at me. It's like my parents. I just want to curl into a ball."

Janelle opened her mouth briefly, but could only reach out and squeeze Pax's shoulder before it was her turn. Her friend nimbly danced and spun across the beam, avoiding the whirling and spinning poles, until she reached the other side.

"Good work, Janelle. At least someone can actually get through it," said the professor.

When it was Pax's turn, she edged onto the beam, rocking back and forth trying to get the rhythm of the whirling poles. She surged forward at what she thought was the opportune time, only to catch a pole in the back, summersaulting her off the beam into the grass. She managed to land on her back, which was at least a consolation prize, compared to the grass in her teeth from previous impacts.

As she stumbled back to the line, Jae-Yong made his attempt. He had the balance of a dancer, rubbing his hands together as he watched the spinners with wide eyes. At a moment that Pax thought he would get creamed, he darted forward, pausing between two whirlers, then leaped into a forward roll, landing on his feet—just in time to get them taken out.

Jae-Yong landed on his shoulder hard. His eyes rolled into the back of his head and he stiffened like a board.

Pax was the first to him, pulling the inhaler out of his pocket and shoving it to his mouth. The hiss of medicine relaxed his arching back as the rest of the class crowded around. She was mostly focused on his labored breathing returning to normal, but noted the way his arm rippled as if something was straining to get out, but as the medicine surged through his system the roiling flesh settled back to normal.

"Good work, Pax," said the professor with a nod, the earlier animosity absent. "Let's give him some room." He looked across the marshy landscape where a flock of black birds soared. "Actually, let's take a ten-minute break."

The professor stayed with Jae-Yong, who could eventually sit up, arms draped over knees, while the rest of them grouped by the whirler.

No one spoke, but she knew what Janelle and Liam were thinking. The unfiltered comment that Professor Cassius had made when he chewed their butts had never sat right with her.

Pax made a show of doing leg stretches so she could maneuver closer to the professor and Jae-Yong, the former who had his back to her.

"...know what's going on. You can't hide it much longer," said the professor.

"I can control it."

"If you don't then you'll have to go back," said the professor. "Or worse. Know that I am watching you."

With his head down, Jae-Yong nodded. "Understood."

Pax scurried back to the group as the professor rose and wandered back to the contraptions with his hands on his head in a heavy contemplative pose. She didn't know what to make of the professor's comments, or maybe she didn't want to believe that she'd heard it the way she had. Were they right to suspect JY? But then why would the professor hunt in the seventh ward while JY was back on campus? She felt—no, *knew*—she was missing something.

When they returned to the whirler, the restless distraction, the tension, had drained from Pax, so she approached the device on her turn with a calm eye.

"Come on, Pax, you got this," said Janelle, crouched over, clapping her hands supportively.

"Feel that rhythm," said Liam, pumping his fist.

The other second years gave equally supportive invocations, but Pax pushed their voices from her mind.

It wasn't the whirler that she was focused on, but herself. The professor watched from the side with his arms crossed, but it didn't bother her for once, only reminded her that the reason he was disappointed in her was that she wouldn't listen to his instruction during training.

But it wasn't that she didn't want to listen. She craved his praise, much as she did with her parents. Professor Cassius was a good and just person, but he didn't see the world like she did. They wanted to control Kali, control the animals, kill the dangerous ones if they had to, but that's not what she wanted.

The fen thrasher, the nagazara, even the big snake called Aepep—she'd hesitated to strike because that's not what she wanted to become. But how could one be a hunter if you weren't going to hunt?

On the other hand, she'd felt no remorse at tricking the men into releasing the incoxal vipers last year. They'd deserved what they'd gotten. Which made her wonder if she even wanted to hunt the creature in the seventh ward, or save it from the city that was probably not its home.

"Any day now, Miss Nygard," said the professor, who watched her curiously.

"Right," she muttered to herself.

She knew the whirler had been designed for a purpose. To educate the body into nimble evasion, but it'd only become a torture device. Pax examined the bruise on her arm, rubbing the spot beneath her hardened muscles, where her bones had been turned to steel.

Pax stepped to a point right outside the reach of the first whirler, waited until it was screaming toward her chest, and punched out, snapping the pole at the midsection. The impact cracked the skin across her knuckles but the destruction was cathartic.

Her friends, who'd been steadily cheering her, fell to silence. She moved to the second pole, broke it with her forearm while keeping centered on the beam, then without further hesitation, Pax systematically dismantled the whirler until she reached the last obstacle, a point she had reached dozens of times, but never passed.

"*Khoplat!*"

The final spinner cracked and fell off its pillar, dancing

across the grass as poles bit into the ground, landing at Professor Cassius' feet.

Pax strolled across the final length of beam, expecting recrimination from the professor, but receiving a curious head-tilt instead.

"That concludes today's training," said Professor Cassius in a level tone that didn't acknowledge the destruction of the whirler.

Her wide-eyed friends greeted her with the corners of their mouths twitching.

"That was amazing, and also peak Pax," said Janelle, clapping her on the shoulder.

"You always do things your way," said Liam. *"Bovem sina pax."*

The pace back to the portal was leisurely, suggesting the professor's earlier anger had dissipated, or the events with JY and the whirler had put him on a different foot.

The day's strangeness continued when they found Lord Asphodel was at the clearing. He wore his raven-feather cloak, the mantle of royalty resting regally on his shoulders. Her friends made private smirks at the thought of Lord Stern Raven, but she was focused on why he'd come to visit.

Away from the group, Lord Asphodel handed Professor Cassius an ornate box. The exchange was brief, and then the tall fae swept from the clearing, leaving a confused professor to stare at the box as he approached them.

"I didn't know Caer Corsydd had a meal delivery service," said Bryanna, who always saw awkward silences as a challenge.

The professor, forehead still rippling, said, "It's a get well gift for Maxine."

"Maybe he's not such a stick in the butt as we think," muttered Janelle.

The class returned through the portal tree, laughing and joking as if they'd been on a summer picnic, but Pax couldn't shake the mystery of why Lord Asphodel would care about a fifth year.

Chapter Twenty-Three

A light rain blanketed the city on an early May weekend evening, but what did it matter since Pax was stuck in her room. It could have been a sunny day, for all that it mattered, she still wouldn't be able to go out. But at least Kali was there, curled next to her feet, snoring softly, while Pax read a nomenclature tome for the umpteenth time in preparation for an upcoming test.

Liam came rushing into the room, startling Kali onto her feet and getting Janelle to poke her head out of her hammock in distress. Pax set the tome on the moss.

"Are you okay?" asked Pax.

"JY is gone," said Liam, stone-faced.

Pax raised an eyebrow. "And? Isn't he gone all the time at Golden Willow?"

"If he really is at Golden Willow," said Janelle.

"JY and Bryanna went to the seventh ward to snoop around," said Liam breathlessly.

"That's on them," said Janelle. "I'm not risking my place

in Animalians to keep them in check. And anyway, I'm sure it's not a big deal. JY has got that weird thing going on, but he's not the Canal Killer."

"Yeah," said Pax, nodding toward Janelle. "He wouldn't tell you that he was going to the seventh with Bryanna if he had nefarious intentions."

"He didn't tell me. In fact, he left me a note earlier that said he had a checkup at Golden Willow, so I went to talk to Bryanna since she was going to help me prep for the test tomorrow, but there was a note from her saying she went to the seventh with JY," said Liam.

"That's worrisome," said Janelle as she slid out of her hammock.

"Yeah, but...it's still probably not him," said Pax.

"What if I told you that I found sawdust on his sneakers and he's been sneaking out at night alone. I'm a heavy sleeper, but I woke up to take a leak and found him gone," said Liam. "Look, I'm probably wrong, but we can't let Bryanna go out there with him if he's the killer. It might not even be on purpose. Maybe whatever is wrong with him takes over."

The vision of his arm rippling as if something wanted to burst from his flesh returned to her. The conversation with the professor didn't help either.

"As much as I hate to say it, you're right," said Pax, receiving nods of agreement from Janelle. "But how do we find them? And how do we not get in trouble with the professor?"

"For one, we leave our cell phones in the room," said Janelle. "We can start with the area where those two recent deaths happened."

"Great. I need to grab my gear. Meet me in ten minutes near the zoo exit," said Liam as he hurried from the room.

Before they left the Arena, Janelle handed them vials of light blue frothy liquid.

"Is this what I think it is?" asked Pax.

"I snuck some out when I was helping Professor Ansel in the infirmary. Thought it might come in handy for moments like these," said Janelle.

Pax smiled. "You're the best, Janelle."

As the potion trickled down her throat, her senses came into focus. Within a few seconds, she could sense a tiny burr on the tip of her sock inside her shoe and vowed to remove it once they reached the train. Other details of her surroundings revealed themselves—like the faint scent of perfume on Janelle's jacket—as they hurried from the Arena.

Pax didn't bother putting her hood up or trying to hide the fact that she was leaving campus. Kali made it too difficult to fool anyone. She just hoped that the professor would understand why'd they broke the rules.

The rain left smears across the windows on the train as they sped around the city. Pax couldn't stop bouncing her knee, even when Kali put a comforting paw on it.

Janelle met her gaze and pursed her lips. "If we run into this creature—JY or no—just promise me you won't just charge in Pax-style."

Her comment reduced the tension in her shoulders, allowing her to lean back.

"It's never the creatures that I'm worried about," said Pax.

Her friends didn't know how to take her answer as the train lurched to a stop, depositing them in the seventh ward. The gray sky reflected the city lights while a drizzle left her red hair misty.

Feeling an urgency, they didn't hide their search, jogging through the streets in a pack of four, splashing through puddles and dodging around older couples beneath their umbrellas on an evening walk. Kali's fur glistened with tiny watery beads, reflecting streetlamps, as she took point on their run.

After a half hour of jogging Pax's blood was hot and she thought about suggesting splitting up when they heard a muffled scream from a few blocks over. Had it not been for the potion, they would have never heard it. They sprinted to the location of the scream, ignoring the stares of pedestrians.

Much like their previous failed excursion, they found themselves in a residential section of three-story brownstones in various stages of rehab.

"Where did it come from?" asked Liam.

<follow>

Kali darted beneath scaffolding along a brick wall. Pax could smell the freshly tuck-pointed mortar, the bitter scents awoken by the wet air. Her four-legged companion dodged around a pair of work trucks left on site, headed across the alley to a warehouse. As Kali stopped at the heavy steel door, Pax caught a greasy smell and looked around for the source, but saw nothing.

As Liam pushed through the door, a heavy thump sounded from the second floor, along with injured whimpering.

"Find the stairs," said Janelle as they scurried through the office portion of the warehouse, looking for a way up.

Pax followed Kali to a door, which revealed a stairwell. At the second floor, a sudden primal dread ricocheted through Pax, leaving her shaking until she realized it was coming from Kali. Her foxlike companion had frozen by her side. Her stasis ended when she heard a groan from the room to the right, and upon entering, found a gruesome scene.

Jae-Yong stood over a fallen Bryanna, his inhaler discarded on the ground, blood covering both of them. A vicious wound on Bryanna's side was leaking crimson liquid into a pool.

"Back away," said Pax as Kali growled at her side, teeth bared at Jae-Yong.

The only thing that kept her from hitting Jae-Yong with a stun mark was the horror and surprise on his face.

Janelle and Liam found them moments later, the former sliding down to Bryanna to stop the bleeding, while Liam stepped between them. Jae-Yong backed against the wall.

"It wasn't me. I was attacked too. It left the room right before you got here, I swear," said Jae-Yong, eyes rounded with alarm.

"I didn't see anything," said Pax. "And if you got attacked, why is Bryanna the only one injured?"

"I...I don't know," said Jae-Yong as he listed around, staring at the blood on his arm. "I was in the hallway when it got Bryanna. We'd tracked it into the warehouse. When I came running in, it knocked me down. I thought it was going to rip out my throat, but then it just sniffed my head and then left. Maybe it heard you come in."

"Likely fucking story," said Liam, fists at his side. "Then why'd you tell me you were at Golden Willow? Or the other nights you lied to me, telling me that you were at the hospital. You were out here, stalking people to kill."

"No, no," said Jae-Yong, holding his hands up. "I was searching for the creature. I swear. I've almost caught it before, I can sense it, even though I don't understand how. I asked Bryanna to come with me, thinking that the two of us could corner it. I would have asked you all but knew you couldn't come because of the professor."

"Is she okay?" Pax asked Janelle, who was cleaning the wound with bandages from her pack. Bryanna continued to moan, but less so after Janelle applied a pain blocker spell.

"The bite is deep, but didn't hit any major arteries or organs. I think she'll be okay," said Janelle.

"Could the bite have been JY?" asked Pax.

Janelle looked away in thought before shaking her head.

"Too wide a mouth."

"That doesn't mean he's safe," said Liam. "What if he's working with this creature?"

"Liam," pleaded Jae-Yong. "What the hell?"

With his face bunched up, Liam said, "We can't be sure until we know what's going on. Look at it from my end. You've been lying about going out, all this weird shit with Golden Willow, the inhaler."

Jae-Yong crossed his arms, the betrayal on his face bone-deep. "I thought we were friends."

"We are," said Liam coldly. "But what if what keeps happening to you is related? Why didn't it rip your throat out when it had you down?"

Jae-Yong opened his mouth, but couldn't find the words to answer. Eventually he backed against the wall, leaned there as if his legs could barely hold him up.

"What now?" asked Janelle as she set her bunched-up hoodie under Bryanna's head. The blonde second year stared back with hazy eyes.

"Do we take her to Golden Willow?" asked Liam.

"And admit to the professor that we disobeyed him?" asked Janelle.

Pax sniffed at the air. "We need the professor here. Injury or not, the creature was just in this room. I can still smell it."

"Good luck with that. Who knows where he's at in the ward," said Liam.

"Maxine might know," said Jae-Yong suddenly. "I heard that she woke up yesterday. The professor was going to ask her about the attack."

Pieces of the puzzle shifted together, forming a hazy picture for Pax. Kali looked up at her as if she sensed her thoughts.

"I'm going to see Maxine, with Kali, of course," said Pax.

"I'll come with," said Liam.

"No," she said. "Stay with Janelle. Sorry, JY, but we don't know if you're safe yet. And I think it's best if I talk to Maxine alone. I think there's some things she hasn't been telling anyone, but I don't know why."

"Are you sure you want to go alone?" asked Janelle from Bryanna's side.

Pax nodded.

"Be safe," said Janelle.

Pax paused at the exit. "Safety is an illusion."

Chapter Twenty-Four

"You can't bring that dog...wolf? Fox? Whatever it is, it's not allowed in the hospital," said a nurse at the floor desk, looking up from her computer with a pencil in her teeth.

Pax paused mid-stride.

"Animalians. I'm here to visit Maxine. Kali is our nurse fox. She'll help Maxine get back on her feet so you can free up a bed for someone else," said Pax.

The nurse rolled her eyes. "Whatever." Then muttered under her breath loud enough for Pax to hear, "Damn mages."

Maxine was sitting up in bed, staring at her hands as if they held uncomfortable truths. The rings around her eyes left shadows in the hollows of her gaze. The brief wrinkling of her nose at Pax's arrival was not a surprise to Pax, especially when she noted Lord Asphodel's gift on the table next to the bed.

"It was you, wasn't it?" said Pax. "You brought a dragon salamander to the city."

Maxine's once-full lips twitched. She either looked relieved at the accusation, or had already fessed up to her crimes. "How did you know?"

Pax nodded towards the gift. "I couldn't figure out why he would care about a fifth-year student's injuries unless they'd performed an important task for him. You helped his people capture the dragon salamander, but you relocated it here. Is that so you could capture it again and get a job with Pietra and the Phoenix Corporation?"

Maxine pressed her thumb into her open palm. "Not completely, but it was an added bonus."

"Then why?"

Maxine's gaze drifted to Kali, who had stayed near the door as if she was allergic.

"Kali?"

"Because I know what she is. A callidus is one of the most dangerous creatures known to mages. This is a fact of history, a fact of our hall. How could the patron let one into Animalians unless it'd captured her under her spell? The professor too. I know he had reservations. I overheard them argue, but Patron Adele ordered him to work with you and that, that... thing," said Maxine, not bothering to disguise her disgust.

"Kali is not a danger, not any more than you are," said Pax sharply.

Maxine flinched, looked away. "It wasn't supposed to happen like this. It wasn't supposed to escape, and...I didn't know it was Professor Cassius' bane."

"What did you really think was going to happen? A dragon salamander isn't supposed to live in a city full of prey. It's unfortunate that they hunt Lord Asphodel's people from time to time, but you just dropped one in a place full of vulnerable people."

Maxine wrinkled her face. "You sound like you have more sympathy for the dragon salamander than the people that it's killed."

"The people it killed because of you," Pax shot back. "Don't corner a dangerous creature and then blame it because it attacked you. Why are you even in this hall?"

"I would say the same for you," said Maxine. "This is the Society for the *Understanding* of Animals, not worship of them, and the dragon salamander is the natural enemy of the callidus. Or didn't you know that?"

The fear that reverberated through Kali when they'd first entered the hallway became clear. But it wasn't the only time. When they'd first entered the pyramid in Caer Corsydd there'd been unease, but then later, in the presence of Aepep, the winged serpent, abject terror. It was a primal fear, echoing through the centuries from when both of them lived in ancient Egypt. Pax recalled the clay vase in the tomb. It'd shown a cat, but even Imhotep's writings had mentioned his callidus as a feline, a precursor to the goddess Bastet.

"You're finally figuring it out," said Maxine. "Lord Asphodel's people once lived in Egypt, interacted with the pharaohs, until something happened and they fled to Caer Corsydd. The dragon salamander went with them. It'd probably been bred to hunt her kind, but the reason for her existence is lost to history."

Pax knew she wasn't going to persuade Maxine to change her mind, but there was one reason she'd come to Golden Willow.

"Whatever you think about me, or about Kali, you just sent Professor Cassius after the dragon salamander, and while I don't know if I believe in banes, I don't want him to get hurt, and I don't think you do either," said Pax.

Maxine hung her head and shook it lightly with lips squeezed white.

"Tell me where you sent him. Where the dragon salamander is hiding, and maybe you'll get what you want after all," said Pax.

The beeping of the medical equipment interspaced the awkward silence. Pax could see that Maxine didn't want to help her, even now, because to do so would acknowledge once again that she'd brought the dragon salamander to kill her and Kali.

"Or did you want the professor to die so you wouldn't be in trouble anymore?" asked Pax.

"No," said Maxine forcefully. "I didn't want it to work out this way. I thought I could control how it all went down, then it got out and started killing people, and I couldn't find it again so I could kill it or bring it back to Caer Corsydd."

"Where is it?" asked Pax firmly.

Maxine stared back, but looked away after a few seconds of raw eye contact.

"There's an old aquarium in the sixth ward that was decommissioned a few years ago. It's all boarded up, a perfect cage for the dragon salamander. They don't hunt where they live, so it was heading into the seventh for food when it couldn't find rats or mice," said Maxine with her head hung.

Pax and Kali were almost out the door when Maxine spoke again.

"You shouldn't be here. No matter what I did this year, it was for the right reasons. Your little friend is a danger to everyone in this school. Everyone," said Maxine defiantly.

Pax placed her hand on the back of Kali's neck and stroked the black fur protectively.

"And she thinks *you're* the one who is the danger."

They left before Maxine could work up a retort, and by the time she'd reached the edge of the nurses desk, Maxine was out of her mind. Patron Adele would take care of her, but Pax had a creature to hunt. Not only was it the bane of her professor's career, but it'd been bred to kill Kali.

Outside the hospital, Pax crouched before her companion, whose black fur reflected the buzzing hospital lights.

"Are you okay with going on this hunt? Now that we know what it is, I'll understand if you don't want to go," said Pax.

Kali put a paw on her bent knee, leaned forward, and licked her chin.

<Pax love>

"I love you, too, Kali. Let's finish this."

Chapter Twenty-Five

The scene at the warehouse in the seventh ward hadn't changed much since she'd left it, except that Bryanna was awake and Jae-Yong sat against the wall in the corner, his arms hung over his knees.

"How is she?" asked Pax.

Janelle looked up from her position on the floor. "Doing better, but I think we should take her to the hospital to get checked out."

"I was thinking the same thing," said Pax.

"What happened with Maxine?" asked Liam.

"The short of it is that she brought a dragon salamander to the city. It's in an old aquarium in the sixth, which is why we haven't been able to track it down," said Pax.

"Maxine was behind this," said Janelle incredulously. "I wasn't expecting that."

"She probably wanted to take it down so she could get an interview with the Phoenix Corporation," said Jae-Yong from his spot along the wall. It wasn't the truth, but Pax wasn't

200 Thomas K. Carpenter

about to correct him.

Liam shot his roommate an uneasy glance before clapping his hands. "Let's head there right now. We can help the professor take down that creature once and for all."

"You should help Janelle get Bryanna to the hospital," said Pax, sucking in her gut in anticipation. "I'm taking JY with me instead."

"What?"

The chorus of voices was one short, but Pax imagined that Bryanna would have added hers if she'd had the energy. Her forehead wrinkled with confusion from her spot on the floor.

"It's not JY, remember? And he's the best person to help, based on something I learned, and Janelle can't get Bryanna to the hospital on her own." Liam's head dipped, so she quickly added. "But you can head there as soon as she's safe and being cared for."

"Are you worried about him transforming or something?" asked Liam.

"No," lied Pax. "But I think whatever is going on with him can help us with the dragon salamander. Come on, JY. We need to get moving if we want to help the professor take down his bane."

<Kali bane too>

The sweet defenseless expression on her companion's upturned face nearly broke Pax, but she held it together in front of her friends. Was she right to bring Kali into this? Wouldn't that put her in danger? Her concerns lessened when her companion sent a second message.

<Kali hunt>

Pax shot her a wink.

"We'll be there as soon as we can," said Janelle as she helped Bryanna sit up while holding her hand under her head.

"I'm counting on it," said Pax as she led Jae-Yong and

Kali into the street, breaking into a jog. She figured they had a twelve-block run to reach the old aquarium.

"Are you going to tell me why you changed your mind about me being safe?" asked Jae-Yong.

"I don't think that you are safe," said Pax, who saw how everything was sliding down a rail towards one hellava confrontation, but also saw how she might be able to get them all out of it. Just maybe. "But as long as you have your inhaler, I'm willing to chance it."

"That's great," said Jae-Yong, shaking his head. "But could you let me in on it?"

"When you were in Caer Corsydd on an errand for Lord Asphodel, I think you were bitten or stung by a dragon salamander. Or something else that the dragon salamander respects or fears. I don't know, I haven't worked it all out yet, but otherwise, why would it sniff at your head then run away? And you mentioned that you could sense it sometimes. That makes me believe that you're related now," said Pax.

"That's a lot to take in," said Jae-Yong, shifting his mouth to the side. "But it makes sense. Even if it sounds crazy."

The old aquarium was much bigger than Pax expected, and they had to run along the boarded-up windows looking for an entrance for a city block. The building was light blue, chipped murals of sea life on the walls, trash on the sidewalks. It was the kind of place she would have loved to have visited as a kid, if her parents had been into actually taking her places. Another reason the zoo had been her home—what else was there to do for an animal-obsessed kid who lived in a retirement neighborhood with no one else her age? In some respects, she shouldn't be surprised that she gravitated towards animals, though she supposed it could have been anything, as long as it didn't require her parents' involvement.

The front of the aquarium was a gated arch, the place

where customers came through with their tickets, but the booths and kiosks had been boarded up, gang tags spray-painted on them. A mural of two parents holding the hands of their child between them poked out from the wall. A not too small part of her wanted to flip off that painting.

Kali led them to a side gate, which had been propped open, bent at the side, suggesting brute strength.

"It looks like the professor came through here," said Pax, touching the warped metal.

The lock on the inner door had been snapped in half. They placed night vision spells on themselves before entering the aquarium. Inside, long defunct escalators went up and down to the other levels. The air had a musty, wet smell.

"This is a big place," said Jae-Yong, cringing at his own voice. "Going to take a while to search."

"Hopefully we can find the professor quickly with Kali's help," said Pax, finding herself crouching for no reason. "Up, down, or straight ahead?"

Jae-Yong gestured to the right to a map of the aquarium on the wall.

"I assume we want to find water," said Pax. "But I'd think that the pools would have been emptied before they closed it down." She glanced at him. "You getting any feelings?"

He frowned. "No, but I think we should stay on this level. If we hear the professor, we can more easily get to him."

"Good idea," said Pax.

Kali took the lead, crouch-walking forward with her head craning in all directions as she sniffed the air, while Jae-Yong held a mop handle he'd rescued from a janitorial closet. Pax kept her hands free, but felt like a gunslinger ready for a duel as her fingers kept brushing the hilt of her belt knife.

Every tick of pipes, drip, and squeak of their boots on the tile was a car horn to her ears. They found tracks frequently, but since the dragon salamander had been living in the aquarium for months, they couldn't be certain how fresh they were.

They passed grand empty tanks, mold or dust covering old rocks. An enormous model whale hung above a central area, where Pax could imagine families gathering as they decided which exhibit to attend. The aquarium contained mostly mundane creatures, but a sign on the wall pointed to a Cthulhu jelly exhibit, but the poster gave a date that was nearly six years old.

When the mid-level bore no fruit, they descended to the bottom level, finding the floor covered in an inch of water, which made moving silently nearly impossible. Her ears picked up dripping water from multiple locations.

They headed down a tight hallway towards the old beluga exhibit. Pax kept checking behind them as her shoulder blades itched. Occasionally she raised an eyebrow to Jae-Yong when he glanced over, only to receive a noncommittal shrug.

Anything, Kali?

<bad smell everywhere>

As the hallway sloped downward, the water rose. Dust and dead bugs floated in the murky water. Somewhere ahead she could hear splashing. A pipe was probably broken.

"It's close," said Jae-Yong suddenly, his face contorted with memory. He reached for his arm, massaging the muscles as if he were trying to work out a cramp.

"Everything good?"

He patted the pocket of his jacket, where his inhaler was located. "I'm fine."

The hallway spilled into a wide, watery chamber. What had once been an auditorium where sea creatures performed tricks for visitors had been flooded by a broken pipe. Jae-Yong identified it right away, gesturing towards a water fountain that had been mauled by powerful jaws.

"It probably only wanted a drink, it got a swimming pool for its troubles," whispered Jae-Yong.

The water was as high as Kali's chest, but they weren't going any further. They stood at the top of the auditorium with the seats going down underwater. There was a balcony above them, but she saw no stairs, which meant their access came from another hallway. Pax kept her head on a swivel looking for signs of movement. Her whole body was on alert, and not only because of Jae-Yong's warning. It bothered her that they hadn't found signs of Professor Cassius yet, but she didn't want to voice those concerns and spook Jae-Yong.

"I don't like this place," said Pax. "Let's go back, find a better spot for an ambush. I feel exposed here."

"Agreed," said Jae-Yong.

She turned right as a shape dropped from the balcony, wet jaws open for the kill.

Chapter Twenty-Six

The flash of fear seared the image of death into her mind: the dragon salamander's open jaws, lined with a solid ring of teeth. It had leapt from the balcony, headed right for her head.

The months of drilling was the only thing that saved her.

"*Schit!*"

The weak barrier would have received a sarcastic remark from Maxine but it was enough to deflect the dragon salamander from clamping onto her shoulder as it fell.

The oily black creature bounced off the brief shimmering force as if it were sliding across a tin roof, knocking Jae-Yong into the deeper waters. The dragon salamander slammed into the nearby seating, back bending over a chair as it shrieked with pain. It quickly flipped itself onto its feet, taking up the entire space between the rows. The dragon salamander had Kali by at least fifty pounds. Its tongue came flickering out, tasting the air, before reorienting onto Kali, who cowered by Pax's side, simultaneously shivering and growling.

<Pax help>

If Kali hadn't been there she would have used a speed mark to escape the auditorium, but she didn't want to leave her companion alone with her bane. The dragon salamander, which had initially attacked Pax, flared its glistening black nostrils, wet with steam as it advanced towards Kali.

"*Shayut!*"

The dragon salamander flinched away her stun and kept pushing through the seats, bending them outward.

Before the creature could escape the narrow confines, its eyes rolled back, covered in darkness. Kali had blocked its vision.

This came at the moment Jae-Yong came splashing back out of the water. He'd gone under, then pulled himself into the upper level with the exposed rail. Pax grabbed his hand and pulled him towards the exit.

The three of them splashed down the hallway. The dragon salamander ambled after them, its speed slowed by its shorter legs.

"Turn and stun together," said Pax. "Now!"

The mark blew a wave of water down the hallway, slamming into the dragon salamander, giving them a chance to climb to the middle level. Pax stopped them at the top of the stairs. High ground would give them an advantage if it kept up its pursuit.

"What are we doing?" asked Jae-Yong, holding his hands before him, the proper position to cast a spell.

"I don't know," said Pax, wiping the water from her face, staring into the dark tunnel where she expected the dragon salamander to emerge. "Do you sense it?"

<no>

"Not at the moment," said Jae-Yong. "But it's hard to tell. I'm jacked up on adrenaline from when I fell into the water. I kept expecting it to drag me down into the deeps and drown me."

"Valid," said Pax. "I don't think it's coming, or it's headed another way around."

"This is not going as planned," said Jae-Yong as he wiped water off his face.

"Wasn't much of a plan, but we found it at least," said Pax. "Let's move from this spot. Too many directions to watch."

They jogged past a cafeteria, but the many tables weren't appealing, since they could hide the advance of a dragon salamander. A rotunda with a bronze statue at the center was the location they stopped. Pax climbed onto the wide base and helped Jae-Yong up, while Kali easily jumped onto the safer spot.

"Now what?" asked Jae-Yong.

"What happened to your pants?" she asked, noticing that his right leg was exposed.

"They got caught on something sharp in the water," said Jae-Yong. "That's why it took me so long to get out. Practically tore them off in the escape."

"That's not how I imagined it would happen," said Pax, catching her breath.

"Flirting in a time like this?" asked Jae-Yong speculatively.

"A bit of humor to take the tension off. My arms are practically shaking themselves out of the sockets."

Jae-Yong blushed, looked away.

"Sorry. It's not that...you know," she said.

"No, I get it. I'm the one that should be apologizing. This is a rather insane time to flirt. I should have known better." His hand went to his jacket pocket. "Shit. Inhaler's gone. Must've fell out in the water."

His eyes rounded with alarm, and the fear of what he might become. Pax reached out, squeezed his shoulder.

"Are you okay? Do we need to leave?" she asked.

He blinked. "I'm fine. For now. I took a hit before, and it usually lasts for a while, but on the other hand, I've never been in a situation like this."

"Maybe we should head back to the entrance, wait for the others," said Pax.

An explosion from deeper in the compound brought their heads around. Even from a distance, the sharp scent of ozone hit their noses.

"That's the professor," said Jae-Yong.

"Shit," said Pax.

"Back to the entrance or head towards him?" asked Jae-Yong.

"We can't leave him," said Pax.

Jae-Yong nodded, knocking his dark, wet hair from his face.

Kali took the lead as they headed in the direction of the explosion. The many hallways and rooms made it difficult to determine the exact location, so they had to backtrack twice, finally stopping when they found a titanium cage at the center of an exhibit on ocean life.

It was a rune-triggered cage that would slam the door shut once the creature passed through the opening. A small pile of dead fish sat at the back, but not close enough to the edge that the dragon salamander could get at it with its short, powerful arms.

"Maxine must have brought the cage here, but the fresh fish means he's trying to use it to lure them," said Jae-Yong. "Good spot, too. No way around this location from the back of the aquarium."

When Kali's hackles went up as she faced down a side hallway, Pax turned to see a dragon salamander staring back at them from the next room over. It was bigger than she remembered, but their brief battle in the flooded auditorium made events tricky to recall.

"Big fucker," said Jae-Yong as he positioned himself in front of Kali, moving towards the creature, which seemed slightly repelled by his presence, backing away. "Come on down. You know you want some fresh fish."

The casual saunter of the dragon salamander as it tilted its glistening head at Jae-Yong seemed important to Pax.

"No, it doesn't. It knows what the trap is. It's smarter than that. Has no interest in the fish, or coming in here where we have the advantage," said Pax.

But that wasn't entirely right either, she surmised. There was something in the way that it was looking at them that was off to Pax. It seemed neither aggressive or concerned about their presence. Curious maybe.

Jae-Yong cupped his hands around his mouth. "Professor Cassius! Professor!"

Pax put her hand on his arm, which silenced his calls.

"What? We can see the dragon salamander. We don't have to worry about calling it to us," said Jae-Yong.

"I don't know," said Pax. "Something's not right."

"Look, we know it's alone," said Jae-Yong. "Maxine only brought one, and we know they require exogestational fertilization, which means even if it's a female and laid eggs, there's no males to make babies happen."

"Yeah, I know," said Pax, frowning.

The dragon salamander ambled out of view. Pax had the urge to chase after, but knew that was a mistake. It could be setting her up for an ambush.

Jae-Yong continued his yelling, alternating between "Professor Cassius!" and "It's JY and Pax!"

"What if that was just a leftover trap that the dragon salamander triggered? He might not even be here," said Pax.

"I hate to say it but you might be right," said Jae-Yong. "Let's head back to the entrance."

"You good?" asked Pax her furry companion.

<home dry>

Kali trotted towards the hallway that led back to the front. Pax kept glancing behind her, wishing she had a big weapon to hold onto rather than relying on her magic.

The hallway led past the cafeteria, which drew a double take when she saw the dark shape crouched on top of a table, watching them.

"How did it get past us?" asked Jae-Yong.

"It must have figured out how to use the employee passages, or maybe the duct system," said Pax.

"This place is getting worse by the moment. I feel like it's hunting us and not the other way around," said Jae-Yong, standing at the entrance to the cafeteria, watching the dragon salamander.

"Agreed, on all accounts," said Pax as she placed a comforting hand on the back of Kali's neck.

<leave danger>

"Yeah, I get it, Kali. Let's get the hell out of here. Or at least get the others before we mess with it. I hate that we haven't found the professor yet. I worry what that means," said Pax.

She shared a glance with Jae-Yong. "Me too."

His handsome smile was erased as he knocked her out of the way screaming, "*Shayut!*"

As Pax fell forward, a belch of flame went over her back, followed by screaming. She rolled over to see Kali positioned in the way of a dragon salamander as smoke trailed from its open mouth, while Jae-Yong fell to the ground, the air reeking of burnt flesh.

From her knees, she managed a forceful, "*Khoplat!*"

which drove the dragon salamander away, but by the time she reached Jae-Yong, he was writhing on the ground. At first she thought he'd suffered terrible burns, but his wet jacket had protected him and it was mostly the water in his hair that had been turned to steam. He held his arm protectively. When he turned towards her, his eyes shown orange-gold.

"Get away!"

He lurched to his feet, running in the opposite direction. Pax had no time to follow as the dragon salamander made a second advance, which was only blocked by a growling Kali, even though the creature was much larger than her.

A second stunning mark gave her and Kali the room to escape but not in the direction she wanted since the dragon salamander blocked the path back to the front. Instead, she ran down an unknown hallway, stopping at the chained doors of a movie theater, turning and heaving with spent breath. She rattled the door.

"Is it following?"

<no yes no>

Kali stood at the edge of the hallway, hackles up, staring down the length. Her companion's vision was better, which left Pax guessing at the danger. After a minute of watching the edge of darkness, she knew that the dragon salamander was no longer pursuing her, but now there was a bigger problem. Not only had Jae-Yong run off in the throes of his condition, but Pax was almost certain that there was more than one dragon salamander.

Chapter Twenty-Seven

"There was no way that dragon salamander got around us," said Pax as she crouched at Kali's side while they watched the hallway. "Which means there's more than one and the only way that could happen is if our little friend can pull the virgin birth trick." Pax punched her open palm. "Parthenogenesis. Just like the speckled locanath."

Kali looked at her expectantly. "Yeah, I know. You don't care about the words. But it means that the first dragon salamander, separated from its kind, decided to clone itself, or fertilized its own eggs somehow. Life finds a way. Either way, this is very bad for us. One dragon salamander would be a challenge, but multiples is a damn nightmare. It seems our friend is also capable of other tricks."

She thought about Jae-Yong, and how the dragon salamander hadn't attacked him. It would have made sense if he'd been attacked by one in Caer Corsydd, but it'd been a hthrack at the pyramid.

"Unless..."

There were some creatures that could borrow the DNA of others, use it when it suited them. Were the hthracks just relatives of the dragon salamander?

"This is only getting worse the more I think about it," said Pax. "We need to find the professor, if he's still alive. Or find a way out."

Kali pressed her forehead against Pax's chest.

<Pax Kali leave>

The brief greeting ritual helped calm Pax's nerves. While her mind was racing her limbs had a quivering soreness as if she'd been on a hundred-mile run.

But the planned escape ended the moment she saw the three dark shapes at the end of the hallway. The dragon salamanders had them trapped. They sauntered with the expectation that they would make quick work of their prey. The one on the right had a taller ridge on its neck, and the other two were slightly different, but not enough to discern in the heat of battle.

"These three look the same size," said Pax. "Which means that one we saw near the cage was the parent. Lot of good that does us now."

She rattled the chain on the door to the movie theater, but it held fast, and she knew no spells to break it. Pax growled, a warning to the dragon salamanders, but they refused to heed it, ambling forward with their tongues flickering into the air.

"Is this our last stand?" she asked as she took position by her companion's side. "I'm shit-all at magic. Maybe I could hit them with a stun or two and you could escape, Kali."

<Kali stay Kali fight>

"Yeah, I get," said Pax. "But better one of us escape, and I think you have a better shot at it."

<Kali stay>

Pax was readying herself for a battle when she caught the

square grating out of the corner of her eye. A vent duct ended in the room, high near the ceiling, so she hadn't noticed it before. The dragon salamanders were only twenty feet away. She jumped up and pulled the vent covering away.

"Kali, come here, I'll lift you up."

Her foxlike companion leapt into her arms, and she shoved her forward into the vent.

The dragon salamanders, sensing escape, surged forward, their tails banging against the walls. The first came around the corner, right as Pax gripped the edge of the vent and pulled herself up.

The snap of teeth behind her heels provided an extra shot of adrenaline. Pax threw herself into the narrow vent as the dragon salamanders crowded outside, a blast of flame chasing her deeper, only her wet clothes keeping the fire from burning her skin.

At a turn, Pax managed to glance back to see the glistening black head of a dragon salamander peering into the vent, having hoisted itself up the wall. She hoped their short arms would keep them from making it into the vent, but wasn't about to stay around and find out.

Kali led them through the vents, sniffing at junctions, but Pax was too tired to offer guidance, letting her companion pick the pathway. At times, the metal vent was suspended over empty rooms, and she worried that their weight would bring it all down, but they managed to traverse a good distance before finding a spot to climb out without having to drop too far.

Back on the carpeted floor, Pax rubbed her knees, bringing the life back into them after crawling for what seemed like a mile.

"Where next? I don't recognize this part of the complex," said Pax.

Through an open door, she saw a glass tank, the lower

viewing area to a pool. Kali sniffed at the carpet, heading towards a closed door, which looked like a maintenance area.

"In there?"

<funny smell>

Pax tested the door, at first thinking it was locked, but giving it an extra yank to pop it free. It was a claustrophobic space with pipes, narrow passages, and lots of hiding spots. But it also went a ways back.

"This is probably where they treated the water before piping it to the various areas of the aquarium," she said.

Pax took the lead, creeping down the grated floor, which creaked as they walked. When she saw the hastily drawn runes on the entrance to a deeper section, Pax cupped her hand around her mouth.

"Professor?"

A moment later, a reply came: "Pax?"

"Yes, it's me and Kali. We came to rescue you, though it hasn't been going as planned," she said.

"You're bloody right about that," said the professor's voice from deeper in the room. "Watch out for my rune trap. You can bypass it with the basic deactivation spell from class."

"Why don't you come out? We can leave together," said Pax.

"I'm gonna need your help for that," said the professor. "My plan went pear shaped and I got myself pinned beneath a pipe."

She approached the runes with apprehension. There was no way to tell if the trap was actually deactivated by the spell. One just had to know that you'd performed it correctly before moving through.

"What's this one do?" she asked.

"It'll blow the whole section of pipes down on ya," said the professor.

"Great," she muttered to herself. "Kali, stand back."

She limbered up her fingers, practicing the spell in her mind a few times before making the attempt for real. It felt right when she cast it, so she edged forward, pushing her toe through the threshold. When nothing exploded, she motioned for Kali to hurry behind her.

It was more pipes and tanks on the other side of the trap. Pax found the professor in the back of the room, pinned beneath a heavy pipe. He looked exhausted, blood streaks on his chin. A lumpy black tail stuck out from beneath a collapsed tank.

"Is this what the explosion was a little bit ago?" asked Pax.

"Aye," said the professor.

"I see you got one," she said as Kali sniffed at the appendage.

"Unfortunately, no. Our pretty little friend is a true salamander. Biter's tail came right off and it scurried away to lick its wounds," said the professor. "Now, can you grab that broken pipe over there and use it to leverage this one off my leg? I only need a little room to squeeze out."

Following his directions, she managed to lift the structure half an inch, which was enough for him to free his leg. Once it was out, he squeezed through the opening, joining her. He gave Kali a pat on the back.

"I should be mad at the both of you for disobeying my orders, but at this point, I'll take any rescue possible. We can sort out the rest later. Now let's get the hell out of here before they all come back. They were working themselves up to come all at once, when they suddenly left, probably to investigate your arrival," said the professor as he limped around the room testing his leg.

"That's a problem," said Pax. "JY was with me, but he lost his inhaler during one of the attacks, and he ran off."

The professor put his hand on his bald head. "That's not good, Miss Nygard. He won't last long against six dragon salamanders. Merlin's tits on a stick, I've barely survived."

"Six? Shit," said Pax. "I thought only four."

"Yeah, the five kids and Mom. I call them Flamey, Ridge, Swimmer, Claws, and Biter, the last one without a tail," said the professor, then sucked on his water pouch and wiped his forehead with the back of his hand.

"We saw Mom near Maxine's cage. Flamey was the one that triggered JY. But I think he'll be okay. The dragon salamander that attacked Bryanna didn't bite him. I think he's been transformed to be like them somehow," said Pax.

Professor Cassius attached his water pouch to his belt and put his hands on his hips. "Bryanna too? You're going to need to tell me the whole story. Quickly."

Pax ran through the events of the evening, then added her theories about the relationship between the dragon salamander and the hthracks.

"I always did think they looked a little similar. Winged salamanders with oily black bodies. Should have seen it earlier. I just wish I knew how Mom gave birth when they're supposed to use exogestational fertilization," said the professor.

"Parthenogenesis," said Pax. "Like the speckled locanath."

"Make sense," he said with a nod. "Kleptogenesis and parthenogenesis. A nasty combination in a critter. No wonder I've had a devil of a time with them."

"Makes you wonder if they were created, not natural," said Pax.

The professor paused with thought, then nodded.

"Enough speculation, we need to get out of here before they come back," he said. "If we can meet up with Janelle and Liam then the five of us can search for Jae-Yong together."

Before they left the maintenance area, the professor disabled his traps so Jae-Yong didn't wander into them by accident, but before they could head out the way she came in, the familiar sound of dragon salamander feet on metal grate echoed back to them.

"Dammit," said the professor. "We should head through the tank room. If it were only one, I'd say we could double team it, but they like to travel in pairs or more."

The next room over was flooded, forcing them to wade through the water. Kali rode on Pax's shoulders, keeping watch behind them. Her weight made the carry difficult, but her companion wasn't a great swimmer. They reached a wide-open area.

Professor Cassius gestured towards a door on the far side, which was above the water line on a platform.

"That leads back to the entrance by way of the cage room. Let's cross this and then we have a straight shot out of here."

<salamander left>

"Well, ain't that a piece of bad luck," said the professor, sighting the creature the same time as Pax. "That's Swimmer too. Has a long powerful tail."

The dragon salamander stood on a different platform above the water, crouched forward like a championship swimmer at the ready.

"We need to go for it. You go straight for the platform, I'll take Swimmer when he comes for us," said the professor, pulling a vial out of his inner pocket, thumbing off the lid with practiced ease, and throwing it down his throat.

The veins on his neck and forehead strained as they popped out, the effects of the potion coursing through his body.

"Is there one of those for me?" asked Pax, hopefully.

"Not this time. If you haven't built up a tolerance, they'll do some damage to you," said the professor as he dropped into the water. "Now go."

The dragon salamander he'd called Swimmer slipped into the water at the same time Pax dropped in. The water was nearly up to her armpits, making the wading slow. Every step was a struggle, but adrenaline kept her legs churning forward.

The professor kept to her right, holding his big knife in his teeth, as he put himself on an intercept with Swimmer. The long-tailed dragon salamander undulated across the water, moving like an agile crocodile.

"*Khoplat!*"

Even with the knife in his teeth, he managed a forceful mark, and for a brief moment, Pax had hopes that he'd knocked out the dragon salamander, but it dove under the surface, head turned in her direction.

"Come on, Pax, come on, Pax," she said as she pushed through the water, but the platform was so far away. She dared a glance back to see that two more dragon salamanders had entered the room from behind.

Before she could stop her, Kali leapt from her shoulders and doggy-paddled towards the platform, which gave Pax more speed. At every step she kept expecting the powerful jaws clamping onto her ankle, fueling her flight.

The professor dove beneath the water, knife still in his teeth as the two dragon salamanders at the rear dropped into the water in pursuit.

"Come on, come on."

The nearer she got to the platform, the more she expected to get dragged back before she reached it. At almost five feet away, escape felt tantalizingly in reach, and then the water exploded next to her.

The bald head of the professor, along with the oily black body of the dragon salamander, burst from the surface in water combat. Despite her exhaustion, Pax managed to hook her fingers into the grate and yank herself up, helping Kali's feeble attempt up afterwards. Her foxlike companion looked more like a drowned rat, but Pax turned to the water, where the two combatants had disappeared.

The surface roiled with suggestions of what was going on underneath, but she didn't see either Cassius or Swimmer. While this raged, the other two dragon salamanders made their way over at a good pace.

With shaking hands, Pax blasted them with stun marks, but the water kept the worst of the magic from hitting them. Her head ached from the constant anxiety and the strained use of faez, a combination that gave her a migraine worse than a heavy training day.

Kali slowed one of the creatures with her mind-blanking ability, but it carried on swimming, even as its eyes were rolled into the back of its head. As the other two dragon salamanders neared, Pax worried that the professor had not prevailed or that the addition of the other two would spell his doom. But then he burst from the water, startling her, as he yanked himself onto the platform like a beached whale.

He was covered in black, watery blood, but didn't appear injured, only tired as he hurried them through the door. They slammed it shut behind them, throwing the lock in place.

"It won't slow them long," he said, limping beside her. "There are too many ways around this place, and they know them well."

Dripping wet, they ran down the hallway, which took them back to the regular areas.

"Did you kill it?" asked Pax when they stopped at a cross hallway to catch their breath.

"No. Injured it some, but it swam off and I lost my knife," he said.

A part of her felt relief that it hadn't been killed, even if that put her life in further danger. The professor led them back to an open area that she recognized would lead them to the cage.

<salamander follow salamander ahead>

Pax informed the professor, and he nodded. "They're herding us. We need to kill a few to even the odds."

A hard shell formed around her thoughts. She squeezed her hands to fists as her heart pounded against her chest.

"We should trap them," said Pax emphatically.

The professor's expression soured as he stepped back. "Your affinity to animals is going to get someone killed. I'd prefer that to not be me."

"It's not their fault they're here. It was human intervention that created this situation. They're just being themselves," Pax pleaded.

She didn't like the way the professor studied her, a hint of accusation to his gaze. Pax unclenched her hands, even though in her mind, she'd donned heavy armor ready to go to battle for the dragon salamanders.

He crouched down as he talked, marking a line in the hallway with a series of trap runes.

"I really don't want to argue with you in a time like this, but if you have a plan, I'm willing to listen. Capture is preferable to killing, but I'm going to defend myself if I must."

She took a deep breath, her thoughts unloosened by his acknowledgement. It didn't take long to come up with a plan, even if it was probably going to get her killed.

"There's an illusion theater on this level, the door was chained, but it would make a good place to trap them," said Pax.

"There's going to be an emergency exit," said the professor.

"Can you teach me how to block it?"

He wrinkled his nose. "I can. Are you ready for it?"

She nodded. "Me and Kali can lead them into the theater. There's a vent in the hallway outside. If you hide inside, then pop out and block them behind me, we can trap them in the theater, then figure out how to get them back to Caer Corsydd safely."

"It might work, but let's get to the theater and then see if this place will hold them. They're resourceful. If there's a way out, they'll find it," said the professor.

The way to the theater wasn't blocked off by the dragon salamanders, which either was a very good or very bad thing. The chain snapped easily in the professor's massive hands.

There'd been an illusion theater at the Portland Zoo for no-risk viewing of dangerous supernatural creatures. Pax hoped that it was set up similarly, and wasn't disappointed. The circular auditorium had a platform in the center, where the illusions would be generated, much like the Memorial Stone in the Bantu Queen. There was a single emergency exit behind the booth where the attendant would trigger the show. If there'd been power in the aquarium, she might have tried to trick the dragon salamanders with lifelike illusions, but that was a step more complicated than necessary.

"This might work," said the professor. "But how are you going to get them here?"

"The dragon salamander isn't just your bane, it's Kali's too. That's why Maxine brought it here. They seem to orient on her. I'm sure she can get them to follow her into the theater."

"It's worth a try," said the professor, nodding. "But you need to learn this blocking spell first. It's nothing special, just freezes the metal components of the lock in place, but the door can still be knocked down. I can add some higher complexity spells once they're trapped which will give the structure strength to withstand their attacks, but you're going to have to keep them from breaking it down until I reach you and add more powerful blockers. Just reapply shield mark to the door until I arrive. Can you do that?"

"I will," said Pax.

"You'll need to. I might as well be traveling through the Outback to get around to this door. You'll have to hold it for three, four minutes, tops," he said.

The spell was relatively simple. Three gestures, a mental pattern, and a trigger word. The hardest part would be pulling off the spell after getting chased into the theater.

The hallway was surprisingly empty when they returned. Pax had half expected a few dragon salamanders waiting for them.

"Can you fit in that vent?" she asked as he placed his hand on the front edge.

"You'd be surprised. I've squeezed into smaller areas. The trick is to think small thoughts," he said with a wink. "Good luck, Pax. Don't put yourself in danger if you don't need to."

Before she left, she muttered, "*Bovem sina pax.*"

At the atrium, which led to the rest of the aquarium, Pax stopped at a round seating area and climbed on the back of it.

"Okay, Kali. When I start shouting I want you to contact them mentally, piss them off if you can. It doesn't matter as long as they come here," said Pax.

<yes, angry slippery biters>

"On the count of three, one, two...three!"

With her hands cupped around her mouth, and rotating like a radar station, Pax screamed, "Come and get me! Dinnertime!"

She continued until she was dizzy from the effort, getting worried when no dragon salamanders showed up. The hair on the back of her neck went up.

A tailless dragon salamander ambled into the room, its gait halting without the counterbalance at its rear. Two more followed from the other direction, one with a limp, which she assumed was Swimmer, the injury coming from its battle with Cassius in the water.

Pax waited until the nearest was only ten feet away before leaping off the seats.

"*Skorost!*"

The burst of speed took her to the entrance of the hallway, nearly overshooting it in her haste. Kali caught up, her tail low to the ground as she scurried forward.

Two more dragon salamanders appeared from the escalator, but Pax hurried to the theater rather than stay and analyze which critters had joined the pursuit. When she got to the door, she let Kali hurry inside, then fired a weak earthen blast down the hallway, not to injure the dragon salamanders, but to hide any lingering smells from Cassius with a jet of leftover faez.

"Come on, follow me," she said as the lead dragon salamander hesitated at the room before the theater, its head turning towards the vent, either from memory of the previous escape or it'd smelled the professor.

"*Shayut!*"

The mark staggered the dragon salamander. It shook its head, hissing with rage upon recovering, pounding its oily black feet on the carpet in pursuit.

Pax leapt down the first flight of stairs, using the rail to slow her impact, crossing around the theater to the attendant station as the first dragon salamander entered. Her mark had properly pissed it off, and maybe a little too much, as it came barreling around the theater. If she left too quickly, the rest might not enter, so she had to slow it.

"*Upsoka!*"

The soothe put a hitch in its step, but otherwise did nothing to calm it down.

"Can you help me, Kali?"

Her foxlike companion had been watching the entrance, but pointed her muzzle at the charging dragon salamander. The creature's eyes rolled into the back of its head, and it roared with distress, thrashing in the tight quarters, rattling the nearby seats, snapping hard plastic.

To keep it subdued, Pax hit it with a stun mark, which knocked the fight out of it, as it slumped onto the carpet between the broken seats.

"Come on!" she yelled at the two dragon salamanders at the threshold of the room. "Come and get me! We're right here, a nice little snack."

The first dragon salamander, Ridge by its extended crest, peered in both directions, expecting a trap, while the other, the tailless Biter, hurried around the other direction. The entrance of its brother encouraged Ridge, who lost its hesitation.

"Three in, two more. Come on! Come on!"

The dragon salamander between the seats stirred, wobbly on its short legs, a testing hiss coming from its wide mouth. As the other two circled, she feared she wouldn't have time for the others to enter, but then two more shapes appeared in the doorway.

At a glance, she knew it was the kids. Mom was nowhere to be seen, but if they could capture five of the six, hunting down the final dragon salamander would be less fraught.

"You know you want some of this! Come on!"

She fired a weak earthen spell up the seats to the entrance. The spell went wide, but the impact goosed the dragon salamanders to head down the stairs, which was the shortest path to her location.

The excitement at luring the five dragon salamanders into

the theater quickly lost its luster as she realized that if she didn't get out quickly she was going to shortly be lunch. Right as the door banged shut, the waft of ozone from Professor Cassius' spell following, she lunged to the exit before Biter and Ridge could reach her.

Already her hands shook in anticipation of the spell. If she didn't complete it on the first try, they'd burst through the door, and the pursuit would be on again. She kicked open the door, right ahead of Kali, and leapt through, only to land a few feet from the sixth dragon salamander.

Chapter Twenty-Eight

The elder dragon salamander, a sleek powerful creature with a cunning gaze, had a good fifty pounds on her offspring. The mother had anticipated the trap, moved to cut her off. Dread trickled down Pax's spine like hot lead.

Waves of raw fear rolled from her companion, a primal terror that shook bones, but despite the mind-blurring emotion, Kali lunged forward with teeth bared. The door guardian snapped her wide mouth, forcing her companion back into the room.

"Blind her," said Pax.

Kali trembled with intensity. The whites of the elder dragon salamander hazed momentarily, but then the orange-gold irises snapped forward and the beastie lumbered to the attack.

Pax threw the door shut as Biter rumbled over the short staircase, catching a stun mark in the face, which gave them a brief opening.

"Run!"

She leapt over the oily black creature, still quivering from the spell, with Kali on her heels. They skirted around the edge as Swimmer lumbered through the seats, tearing the plastic from their rusty hinges.

The dragon salamanders had moved quickly down the stairs, their heavy bodies providing ample momentum, but ascending proved more difficult, and they gronked their displeasure. The uneven chase gave Pax a chance to reach the door, and she slammed into it with her shoulder when the lock refused to budge.

"Professor! Professor!"

She pounded on the door, kicked at it, shaking it for all she was worth, realizing that Cassius was headed around the outer area to help her block the lower door. Pax placed her back against the door, hands flat behind her, and watched as the five dragon salamanders made their way, each one blocking a potential escape route. If she could only keep them from catching her for a few minutes, it would give the professor a chance to scare off the mother dragon salamander so they could escape, but not even half a minute had elapsed.

"Can you blind them all for the next few minutes?" she asked Kali, who huddled by her side.

<many many bad>

"Yeah, that's what I thought," she said.

As Ridge crested the middle stairs, Pax popped a slam in its face, tumbling it backwards. She stepped forward to the potential opening, only to have Flamey send a wave of flame across the seats, blocking her path. The routes of escape were rapidly dwindling.

When Biter came around the circular wall, Kali lunged forward with teeth bared only to catch a swipe from the dragon salamander's claws, eliciting a painful yelp. The cry was a knife to Pax's gut, her skin hardening as if she were being encased with rock.

"*Khoplat!*"

The spike of faez sent blinding white light through her vision. Her head felt like it was splitting in two, but when she opened her eyes, the dragon salamander was lying prone against the wall, blood leaking from its eyes as it heaved from the concussive blow. The pure rage that had slipped from her mind left Pax shaken. She hadn't killed it but she'd come close, and the knowledge brought bile into her mouth.

The brief delay of her defense gave the others an opening. Pax spun around as two dragon salamanders closed the final distance. She knew she wasn't going to escape, and raised her arms in anticipation of the horrible end.

The door exploded, flying off the hinges and knocking the first dragon salamander sideways. Pax coughed from the smoke as she lurched to the doorway, expecting Professor Cassius.

"Maxine?"

The powerful fifth year limped into the room and quickly scanned the situation, blanching at the sight of multiple dragon salamanders. The incredulousness disappeared beneath a mask of practicality.

"Come on, before they recover," said Maxine.

The three of them sprinted from the room, though Pax had to slow her pace as the fifth year labored by her, hand on her side.

Pax turned on her. "You're not well."

"A simple thank you will do," said Maxine, grimacing.

"But why?"

Maxine blushed, looked away. "You can admonish me for being a terrible human being later, for now, let's get the hell out of here."

Their long legs, even with Maxine's injury, outpaced the squat dragon salamanders, until they were back in the big room with the enormous whale hanging from the ceiling.

"I still don't understand," said Pax as she leaned over on her knees to catch her breath.

"After you left, I was walking around the floor, stretching my legs, when your friends Janelle and Liam brought Bryanna into the hospital." Her lips tightened. Maxine looked close to tears. "I guess seeing what damage I'd caused, to someone I know, made it more real than it had been before that."

Pax wanted to spit. That Maxine had to see someone injured with her own eyes before she could empathize made Pax sick with anger.

"Wait? Are they here?" she asked.

"Somewhere," said Maxine, looking down. "But why are there so many dragon salamanders? I don't understand."

"Parthenogenesis. She cloned herself. And now we have a pack of six to contend with," said Pax.

"Shit," said Maxine, looking away. "Liam and Janelle are only expecting one. I'm sorry. I've really fucked this up."

"I swear, if you get my friends killed..." said Pax, fists at her sides.

<hallway>

Kali made a yip of alarm as the dragon salamanders ambled into the room.

"Come on," said Maxine. "I sent them to the cage area. We can meet them there and then try to find the others."

She took the lead, jogging with a limp while holding her hand on her side. She was clearly hurting, but wasn't going to let the injury slow her down. They headed down a narrow hallway to the room with the cage, keeping an eye on the pursuing dragon salamanders.

<ahead>

"Maxine, ahead—"

Pax barely got the warning out, when the mother dragon salamander burst from around the corner and caught the fifth year right in the middle, followed by a sickening crunch.

Chapter Twenty-Nine

Maxine's screams could have punched a hole in the moon. Kali lunged forward to snap at the side of the mother dragon salamander, but the agile creature turned, placing Maxine in the way as it ripped through her sides with its powerful mouth.

Pax slashed at the head of the dragon salamander, getting it to release Maxine, but the damage had already been done. The dragon salamander lunged at Pax, forcing her to leap backwards, while Kali harried her side. Maxine lay in a pool of blood, her mouth opening and closing like a fish out of water.

In the narrow hallway, the dragon salamander had complete control of the space, backing Pax towards the others, which had finally caught up. In a moment she'd be caught between two sets of predators. Kali tore at the enormous glistening tail of the mother, but she was focused on finishing off Pax, who was deciding if she could chance a leap without getting her legs bitten.

Pax flinched when the oily black shape moved past her,

belatedly realizing that it was a two-legged form, rather than the low-slung dragon salamanders. Jae-Yong positioned himself in front of the mother, who tilted her head and snapped her mouth, not at him, but as a warning to move away.

"Run behind me," said Jae-Yong, his voice watery.

She scooted along the wall, then past the lifeless form of Maxine, who stared blankly at the ceiling, and reached the room with the titanium cage at the center. The image of Maxine burned into her mind. One moment she'd been running in front, the next, she was staring at the ceiling, never again to close her own eyes.

Liam and Janelle appeared from the other side of the room, eyes looking past them to fall upon Maxine's lifeless body before settling on the dragon salamanders headed their way.

"What the actual," said Liam, the words tumbling out of his mouth as his eyes rounded, close to tears.

"We need to get out of here, there's too many of them," said Pax.

Janelle had dialed onto Jae-Yong, hand reaching towards his glistening arm.

"Are you okay?" she asked, receiving a headshake, slow at first, then faster. "We're still your friends."

"Move it, down the hall," said Pax.

The dragon salamanders had gathered at the threshold of the room. It was like being hunted by agile, intelligent crocodiles, but Pax and her friends were quicker, and put distance between them.

They ran right into Professor Cassius. His expression was filled with disappointment.

"At least we're all bloody together right now," he said.

Pax tightened her lips. "Not Maxine. They got her in the hallway."

"Shit," said the professor, closing his eyes momentarily before pulling up his sleeves. "It's time to put this to rest. I want your best offensive spells. Everyone behind me."

"No," said Pax. "It wasn't their fault that they were brought here. We need to capture them."

Liam turned on her, wiping at the corner of his eye. "Fault or no, I don't want to die. We should listen to the professor."

"I don't want you to die either. Look. They're hunting Kali. She's their natural enemy. We can use that against them," said Pax.

"I thought they were the professor's bane?" asked Janelle.

"The more the merrier," said Pax. "I won't make anyone else put themselves in danger. But if we can capture the mom, we can subdue the rest."

"How do you know they won't go into a killing rage? Pax, I get it. You want to protect them, but there's six of them and six of us. We're never going to get better odds," said Liam.

"The mom is wary. If we hit them, she'll disappear, and I wouldn't be surprised if she didn't leave the aquarium, make a new brood. If you don't kill them all right away, then we'll have another problem later, and more people will die. We're hunters, not killers," said Pax.

"I thought those two were the same thing, but whatever," said Liam.

"She's right," said Jae-Yong. "They'll protect the mother. We can use them."

"You okay, mate?" asked the professor.

Jae-Yong held out his arms. "Not the kind of summer tan I normally go for."

A round of laughter broke the tension of the room, though darkness lurked beneath their gazes.

"What's the plan?" asked Janelle.

"Circle back to the whale room. Me and Kali will stay in

the center of the room. The mother will be in back. When they come for us, you go after her, stun her. If she's immobilized, they won't risk her life," said Pax.

"And if they don't?" asked the professor.

"Then it was nice knowing you all," said Pax. "Promise me you won't kill them, unless in self-defense. Even if we're in danger."

"That's a messed-up thing to make us promise, but if you want," said Janelle, her forehead knotted.

The others agreed, albeit reluctantly.

Jae-Yong gestured towards Kali, who'd stayed near her. "She's okay with that?"

Pax crouched down in front of her companion. The foxlike creature stared back with gold-red eyes.

"We might need to slow them so they can take out the mom. Can you do this?" she asked.

Kali nodded, sending a feeling of warm apple pie.

<Pax Kali together forever>

An image of a tree trunk with K + P in a heart formed in her mind, which brought a smile to Pax's lips.

"Together forever," said Pax, patting her companion's head. She stood up. "Follow me. I'll take us back to the whale room."

A short run later, they stood on the couch at the center of the room. The area was wide open, except for the furniture that they stood on. The others went into a side room, closing the door enough to hide themselves, but they were far enough away that if something went wrong, there'd be little they could do. The professor gave her a nod before he disappeared.

"If this works, I'll get you all the ice cream you want this summer," said Pax.

<caramel chocolate salmon>

"Whatever flavor you want," said Pax, chuckling.

The dragon salamanders didn't disappoint. The pack of six meandered into the room, spreading out, but not moving further, each one tasting the air with their long tongues. The cautious demeanor put a stone in her gut.

Slow them with your mind blanking if they get near, she told Kali.

Seeing all six of them together gave her a good idea of how different each one was. Ridge, on the far left, had a high spiny extension on the back of his neck, twice as large as the others', and almost dry skin. Flamey had blackened lips from the exhalation of flame, while Swimmer on the far right was long and powerful like an Olympic athlete. Claws and Biter could have been twins except for the differences that gave them their namesake, and the damage they'd sustained—Claws wobbled unsteadily on his legs, while Biter had no tail.

The last was the mother.

"But you're not really a mother," said Pax. "They're your twins, I guess, with clever modifications. You're trying to stay alive, and here we are in your home, hunting you, while you hunt us."

The eldest dragon salamander ambled forward, tongue tasting the air as her head oscillated, keen eyes searching. Her approach brought a tightness in Kali. Her companion pushed against her leg in solidarity.

"You're looking for the others, you know this is a trap," said Pax. "It is, but I swear it's not a bad one. We'll send you back to your home, where you can hunt in peace, not in this strange concrete jungle."

<danger>

The warning made Pax glance around the room in expectation that she'd missed something. The air had a heavy, wet smell, like an ocean wharf.

"Come on, Kali, we do this right and we can go home,"

said Pax, crouching beside her companion.

The next thing that happened brought light to the ancient enmity between the callidus and the dragon salamander. Linked to Kali in ways she didn't quite understand, Pax felt the tension between the two, an echo through the ages, when they hunted each other in the sandstone halls of the pharaohs. There was something more, deeper, a connection impossible to unravel in that split second, but Pax knew that whatever transpired would not be the end of it.

Pax snapped upright when the elder dragon salamander made barking noises in the back of its throat, and the others peeled off towards the door where her friends were hidden.

"Shit."

When the mother's orange-red eyes drilled upon Kali, Pax said, "Blank her."

Kali stiffened. For a moment when the mother surged, her eyes rolled into the back of her head. But the eldest proved resistant to Kali's psychic abilities, shook it off, and shot forward at a surprising speed.

The impact threw Pax backwards off the seats to land hard on her back. The air fled her lungs as she looked up at the enormous model whale hanging from the ceiling. Time had not been kind—long chips laid its belly bare, and the colors had faded.

She rolled onto her side, trying to gather strength to return to the battle. Kali stood on the apex of the furniture, teeth bared, snapping at the larger dragon salamander that was halfway up, reaching with its nimble, wet hands.

Faez thickened in the air at the double doors, where her friends fought to deflect the charging dragon salamanders with successive marks, which ripped the paint from the walls and blew ceiling tiles to smithereens. The dragon salamanders would be no match for her friends, but they were still trying to adhere to her promise, limiting their spells to the non-fatal marks.

It was only then she realized that Kali was doing the same. In the raw, unadulterated connection, her companion could not hide her feelings. She wanted to rip the throat out of the eldest dragon salamander, unleash her abilities on her ancient foe, but she was holding back because of Pax.

She reinterpreted her days of training with Professor Cassius in this new light. She'd thought that Kali shared her reluctance to interfere with the lonesome thrasher, or the aloof nagazara, but it was Pax alone that was tempering her companion's instinct. The times that she'd felt Kali's fear when encountering the dragon salamanders, or the fearsome winged Aepep, had been more a reflection of her own fears than Kali's.

This realization that Kali was more the killer than she thought distracted both her and her companion, and the dragon salamander lunged forward, grasping Kali's forelegs. Only the awkward peak of the couches prevented the mother from bringing her teeth to bear against Kali's throat.

A blind rage sent Pax at the dragon salamander like a missile, oblivious to peril, oblivious to the sounds of battle, oblivious to anything but her companion's safety. The knife felt good. She grasped the handle with two hands, plunging it downward into the neck of the dragon salamander as its wide, toothy mouth closed on Kali's shoulder.

The tip of the blade went through the oily black flesh before the mouth closed. The dragon salamander made an awful screech and released Kali, but Pax couldn't stop her arms, and she plunged the blade into the creature repeatedly, pink blood splattering across her face and arms.

The other dragon salamanders turned to avenge their mother-twin, and in a moment of awful clarity, without a trace of fear or hesitation, Pax blasted the hanging whale with a well-placed slam mark that dislodged the hanging wires.

The whale fell in two moves, first snapping away, extend-ed fin rotating towards the speeding dragon salamanders, then as the leverage broke the remaining wires, the whole thing fell upon the siblings before they could reach her. A wave of dust cascaded outward, making Pax squint.

As Pax cradled Kali to her chest, examining the torn fur on her forearm from the grasping claws of the dead dragon salamander, her friends subdued the siblings not killed in the impact of the whale.

It didn't feel like victory when her friends joined her. A cold wind traveled through her, even though she had Kali's furry body against hers.

Professor Cassius crouched before her at eye level. She looked up, knowing her face was covered in pink blood.

"You did what you had to do," he said. "I know that wasn't easy."

She couldn't smile, because she didn't share his concern. Once she'd unleashed herself, it *was* easy. Pax looked into Kali's sweet, furry face, wondering whose rage had reverber-ated through her.

<Pax love>

It came with warm, face-tingly feelings. Pax sent them back, pressing her forehead against Kali's.

"Are you okay?" asked Liam upon approach.

Pax wanted to respond that she would never be *okay* with killing, that having to do so, even to defend her companion, had torn a hole in her soul. And more so, she worried that having the taste of it might change Kali. This conflict between ancient foes could have woken her companion, in ways that she might not be able to control.

But while his question sparked a brief rage in her heart, she knew that it'd been well meant, so she smiled with her mouth, leaving her eyes to portray the true answer.

"As okay as I can be," said Pax. "I'm just glad no one else got hurt."

When she could move again, Janelle gave her a long hug, and then she was able to see the extent of the destruction. The falling whale had killed Claws, Flamey, and Biter. Professor Cassius injected the other two with a toxin that immobilized them so they could be dragged to the cage for later transportation.

No one had a working cell phone, so Liam ran back to the campus to gather the other professors for cleanup. He also picked up another inhaler so Jae-Yong could return to his original form.

Patron Adele arrived first. Tall, ebony, her keen eyes fell first upon Pax as if she suspected she was the source of the destruction, but she said nothing and headed right to Professor Cassius.

Even without saying a word, Patron Adele's presence alone admonished Cassius, whose shoulders tilted inward at her quiet intonation. The two of them went off into the other part of the aquarium to collect Maxine's body.

No one had given Pax anything to do, and the night had been hardest on her, so she left, taking the train back to campus. The ride felt surreal, normal in its late-night busyness, packed with the after-bar crowd. She reached to her face to make sure she'd wiped off the dragon salamander blood when drunken riders stared blankly.

When she arrived in her room, she sat against the wall, while Kali lay by her side, form slowly rising and falling beneath her hand, quietly resting or sleeping—Pax didn't know— while she contemplated the ending to the evening. Was she a killer now? Had it been her restraint that had stayed Kali's instincts? These questions lingered with her long through the night, when sleep was never an option, and time stretched with thought.

Chapter Thirty

The funeral was held three days later on the outskirts of the city. Maxine's family was inconsolable as they draped themselves over her coffin. While they had to have known that her choice of profession might deliver the ultimate consequence, they might have also hoped the bill would never come due.

Both Patron Adele and Professor Cassius paid their respects to the parents. The father was a bulky firefighter, his fellows taking up the front half of the church, while the mother looked like a corporate lawyer with short clipped hair and a tailored pearl-blue jacket.

Patron Adele delivered her condolences with the grace of a monarch while the professor looked hollowed out by the task. He returned to his spot near Pax's bench and stared at the floor with tears locked behind a mask.

When it was Pax's turn to say one last goodbye, Kali stayed by her side as she approached the coffin. She wasn't sure how she was going to feel. After all, it'd been Maxine's animosity that had triggered the events that had eventually led to her death. If she'd had her way, it'd be her and Kali in her place.

But there was no trace of that pain on Maxine's serene face. The mortician had done their job well. The harsh barking during training sessions wasn't visible in the smooth brow.

Pax dared to place her fingertips against Maxine's arm. Here was someone who'd let their rage goad them into fatal mistakes. She worried that Kali's nature might do the same for her. Her foxlike companion looked up, whining softly.

<Kali sad>

"I know, little one," said Pax.

It was a contradiction to think that they could both feel sad for the person that had tried to get them killed. Just as Pax could feel the ultimate love for Kali, but be concerned that her strange nature would lead to complication.

"She loved being in Animalians."

Pax hadn't even heard the mother approach. She fixed a single strand of hair that had slipped out of place.

"She did," said Pax, not sure how to interact with a grieving parent, so she stayed still like a mouse trying to avoid a hawk.

With squeezed lips, the mother said, "I always worried that it would come to this, but you can't make logic of love."

Pax glanced at Kali. "No, you can't."

"Thank you for coming," said the mother. "I know she would be happy to know that so many people thought well of her. She was always so hard on herself."

As she turned away, Pax reached out, stopped her with a light touch.

"Maxine saved lives at the end. She saved mine," said Pax.

The mother took her hand and squeezed it briefly, eyes brimming, before turning away and joining her husband at the side of the church.

After everyone had their chance to say goodbye, the entire hall went to the Bantu Queen, even Patron Adele. When she stepped inside, the owner, Dane, went wide-eyed, before composing himself and giving her a nod.

Later on, Pax stood at the Memorial Stone, which only displayed Maxine, forever floating above the black rock. Kali was on the bench, sitting in Janelle's lap. Music played and people chattered in the other room, but it felt a world away.

Professor Cassius appeared by her side. She acknowledged his presence by giving him room. They both craned their necks at the final picture of the fifth year.

"Does anyone else know about how the dragon salamander came to the city?" asked Pax.

"Only you and your friends, myself, and Patron Adele," said the professor.

"You didn't want Kali to be here this year either," said Pax.

He turned slightly towards her. "No, but I was proved wrong. By both your and Maxine's actions. Here we were worried about Kali's intentions, when it was a human that did the deed."

Pax wasn't going to betray that she felt some truth to his concerns. The final events in the aquarium had been revealing to everyone in different ways.

"I'm not coming back next year," said Professor Cassius. "I wanted you to be the first to know."

"What?" She turned on him. "Was this Patron Adele's idea? I'll tell her that she's wrong. That you did the best you could. It wasn't your fault."

His mouth twitched with a smile, while his eyes stayed rounded. "I appreciate the solidarity. While I am not in her best graces, it was my choice. I came back to Animalians for a break from our profession, but it seems that even here I could not escape it. And I feel like I was unsuccessful in my training sessions with you." His forehead wrinkled. "More than unsuccessful. Misguided. I was trying to make you into something you're not. You're the best of us, Pax. You and Kali both. I was wrong. We all are."

"I don't know, Professor," said Pax.

"I do. People speak by their actions, not their thoughts or intentions. At every turn, you stayed true to your convictions, even if it put yourself in harm's way."

"It's probably going to get me killed some day," said Pax.

"It might," said Professor Cassius. "But you and Kali have a special bond. I think you can rely on each other in moments of darkness, pull each other through."

"You make it sound like you expect my troubles to continue," said Pax, smirking.

"*Bovem sina pax,*" said Professor Cassius. He nodded towards Maxine's floating visage. "Just don't let your bullheadedness drag you over the edge like it did for Maxine."

"I'll try," said Pax. "Thank you, Professor. I'm sorry you won't be returning next year. I really enjoyed every bit of this year under your tutelage, even the painful parts. I'm stronger for them."

The professor put up a reluctant smile. Before he left, he turned back and said, "Hey Pax."

"Yes, Professor?"

He wrinkled his face. "*Bovem sina pax.* That's a terribly constructed nomenclature." He threw her a wink before striding from the party. It was the last time she saw Professor Cassius.

Chapter Thirty-One

The final few weeks of class were taught by Professor Ansel. They neither visited Caer Corsydd nor practiced their marks. As was the professor's specialty, they learned the skills of the battlefield medic. While no intervention would have saved Maxine's life after the dragon salamander had bitten through her shoulder, the practice gave them something to focus on in those last sessions.

After a round of sad goodbyes and promises that they would keep in touch over the summer, promises that Pax knew wouldn't be kept, as Janelle was staying in Invictus for the summer on a rotation at Golden Willow, Liam was headed to Hungary to wrangle ur-bears in the Deberecen forest, and Jae-Yong was spending the summer with Professor Didi to control his transformations, Pax left for Portland on a late-morning flight.

Pax stared out the window for the entirety of the journey while Kali slept in her own seat, barely, as she hung off the edges. Next time her companion would require two seats, which would put a strain on her meager pocketbook. At the beginning of the year, after the disaster with her parents, she thought she'd be apprehensive about returning home, but the events with the dragon salamanders, Maxine's death, and Professor Cassius' self-imposed banishment had hardened her thoughts against them. If they didn't like that she'd defended herself, then she'd move out, take a spot in Esmerelda's spare bedroom, rather than take their abuse anymore.

She wanted to fix them. Find a cure for the crag worm poison. Make them whole again. It wasn't their fault that they'd been bitten, but she didn't want to carry trauma with her forever. Maybe it was time to move on, but she wanted to give them another chance. They *were* her parents, broken and misguided as they were.

Time heals all wounds, she thought, shaking her head. *Time buries them under new scars and injuries until those first ones feel irrelevant.*

Esmerelda was away at a conference in Seoul learning the latest techniques for transporting incorporeal creatures. The zoo wanted to have a ghost exhibit—banshees, mogwais, strigois—which strayed from its usual zoologic principles, but stayed on-brand as far as being the world's most dangerous zoo.

While Pax missed her friend, she felt guilty that she was relieved to make the final journey to her home alone. Esmerelda would ask too many questions about her home life, leaving Pax to relitigate those events in her mind, and after a trying second year at Animalians, she was tired. Kali, however, did not share her exhaustion, whining softly when they boarded the bus rather than Esmerelda's old beat-up truck.

<miss zoo mom>

"Yeah, me too," said Pax, stroking the back of Kali's neck as they watched the city rumble past, Mt. Hood peeking above the buildings occasionally.

The two-story Victorian with stained glass windows, which had a magical quality when she was younger, seemed tired, especially after traversing the moors of Caer Corsydd and sleeping in a room of living moss. But it wasn't the house that had changed.

When Kali turned away from the door, content to sneak up the back way when her parents weren't watching, Pax called her back.

"You're coming with me."

<Pax>

It was a question, concern mixed with anticipation. All of Kali's messages came with smells and tastes, this one was thyme and tarragon, stronger than usual, which had a cloying effect in the back of Pax's throat.

"I'm sure. Come on, not-so little one. You're a part of this family, too."

The door creaked. She let her backpack drop noisily so she didn't startle them upon entering the kitchen. The air was stale, a hint of geraniums adding a flowery touch, but gone was Baba's green thumb, and with it, a wholesome freshness.

Her parents were frozen like startled deer in the kitchen, her father holding his newspaper—a relic of a bygone era—and her mother scrubbing a pot. Mouths opened, but no sound came out.

"Second year is over. I survived. Good to be back for the summer. I'll be working at the zoo again," she said.

Twin sets of eyes drifted to Kali, who stood in the hallway, tongue panting.

"Don't act like you haven't seen her before. She's my companion. I'm a member of Animalians after all," said Pax.

Her mother dropped a hand to her hip. "Dinner is already put away. If you wanted something, you should have told me that you were coming."

The newspaper dipped, a warning of a new salvo, but Pax went upstairs instead.

"Too tired to eat, but thanks!" she lobbed over her shoulder.

She was a little surprised that she still had a room. If she'd walked into a reading den, or storage room, there would have been little shock. The place was free of dust, which suggested that her mother had actually cleaned it when she was gone. Wonders never cease.

Kali stepped onto the bed, taking up half the space, even curled into a ball with her tail hanging over the edge.

"This isn't going to work this summer. I might see if I can drag that old mattress from the attic in here for you to sleep on," said Pax.

When Kali lifted her head and made a noise, a mix of growl and snore, Pax continued, "Don't worry, I'll clean it real good, and put some nice cushy blankets on it. Don't look at me like that. I do enjoy cuddles, but not at the expense of sleep. You're getting too big."

Her foxlike companion set her head back onto the bed. Pax pulled up a chair and stared out the window. A couple of kids went running through the backyard, which brought a smile to her lips. It'd been a lot simpler then, when she had her animal shed, and Kali, and pushed the rest of the world out of her mind.

Kali was breathing heavily, which suggested she'd fallen into a deep sleep. She didn't travel well, due to the presence of so many other minds. The quiet of the second-story room suited them both.

But as she looked at her companion, a lot of questions arose that she'd thought before but had never given serious weight. The things she'd learned about Kali and her kind—

the enmity with the dragon salamander, history from ancient Egypt, the battle in the aquarium—they reflected a new light upon her past. How did such a creature find her way to a little house on the outside of Portland? Especially into the hands of an animal obsessed little girl, after the events of her worst trauma. It seemed less and less a coincidence, but the who or why eluded her.

Those questions, while nagging, seemed insignificant compared to the burgeoning problem of Kali's growth and changes. The killing rage that the callidus was known for had been present during the battle with the dragon salamander, but had that been self-defense, or a sign of things to come?

Being in Hunters would only make those interactions more common. For all her hopes otherwise, Pax had been unable to protect the dragon salamanders from their worst instincts, forcing her to kill four of them, including the mother-twin. Would the same fate fall upon Kali?

As her eyes lay upon her sleeping companion, who curled in a black ball of fur, tail hanging over the edge, silver tip like a bright star, concerns washed away in a flood of overwhelming love. Kali twitched an eye open momentarily, before returning to slumber.

What was I thinking? Pax thought as she stared at the lights in the sky drifting towards the Portland airport. *No matter. Tomorrow is a new day, and third year feels a long way away.*

§ § §

Stay tuned for the third book
in Animalian Hall series

MARK
OF THE
PHOENIX

March 2021

Special Thanks

For this book, I had special help from a couple of friends, Stacy Jones and Fred Williams III, who provided the idea for the dragon salamanders and made sure that my animal anatomy was accurate. Thank you so much for your help! It made it extra special to weave your extensive knowledge into the story.

As usual, the rest of the team was on their game to help make sure the Hundred Halls feel real on the page. First and foremost, Rachel, my wife and First Reader, make sure the stories meet the expectations of what it means to be a Hundred Halls book. Next Tamara Blaine, my editor, ensures that each book reads smoothly, and is error free. Ravven provides the cover art which draws readers into this universe. There's also the beta readers, which for this series has been Tina Rak, Andie Alessandra Cáomhanach, Lana Turner, and Melanie Coupland. And last, but not least, are the Vanguard, who make sure no errors have snuck through the process, so thank you Phyllis Simpson, Elaine Stoker, and Jennifer Beere!

ABOUT THE AUTHOR

Thomas K. Carpenter resides near St. Louis with his wife Rachel and their two grown children. When he's not busy writing his next book, he's playing games on the computer or getting beat by his wife at cards. He keeps a regular blog at www.thomaskcarpenter.com and you can follow him on twitter @thomaskcarpente. If you want to learn when his next novel will be hitting the shelves and get free stories and occasional other goodies, please sign up for his mailing list by going to: http://tinyurl.com/thomaskcarpenter. Your email address will never be shared and you can unsubscribe at any time.

Made in the USA
Middletown, DE
17 April 2023

28981782R00158